The bronze Adonis was known from Peking to Paris, from Rome to New York, and never a more respected man lived to fight evil on the face of our planet.

Doc Savage had been trained from childhood by scientists to follow the unusual career of battling sinister elements to preserve world peace. His incredible strength and amazing scientific discoveries and weaponry are the realities of the man—the unrealities surface when you cross him.

With his five raucous and reliable aides, Doc Savage was praised by the thousands he had saved from criminals who dared to tangle with The Man of Bronze.

DOC SAVAGE'S AMAZING CREW

"Ham," Brigadier General Theodore Marley Brooks, was never without his ominous, black sword cane.

"Monk," Lieutenant Colonel Andrew Blodgett Mayfair, built low and wide, his brutish exterior concealed a great scientific mind.

"Renny," Colonel John Renwick, his favorite sport was pounding his massive fists through heavy, paneled doors.

"Long Tom," Major Thomas J. Roberts, not physically jolting, his genius was at electricity.

"Johnny," William Harper Littlejohn, the scientist and greatest living expert on geology and archaeology.

WITH THEIR LEADER, THEY SOUGHT EXCITEMENT AND PERILOUS ADVENTURE —FIGHTING ANYONE AND RISKING THE IMPOSSIBLE!

Bantam Books by Kenneth Robeson
Ask your bookseller for the books you have missed

Coming in October 1981 a double volume of
Jui San and *The Black, Black Witch*

Two Complete Adventures in One Volume

THEY DIED TWICE
and
THE SCREAMING MAN
Kenneth Robeson

THEY DIED TWICE #105
THE SCREAMING MAN #106

*A Bantam Book / published by arrangement with
The Condé Nast Publications, Inc.*

PRINTING HISTORY

They Died Twice was originally published in Doc Savage Magazine, *November 1942. Copyright 1942 by Street & Smith Publications, Inc. Copyright © renewed 1970 by The Condé Nast Publications, Inc.*

The Screaming Man was originally published in Doc Savage Magazine, *December, 1945. Copyright by Street & Smith Publications, Inc. Copyright © renewed 1973 by The Condé Nast Publications, Inc.*

Bantam edition / July 1981

Bantam Books are published by Bantam Books, Inc. Its trademark, consisting of the words "Bantam Books" and the portrayal of a bantam, is Registered in U.S. Patent and Trademark Office and in other countries. Marca Registrada. Bantam Books, Inc., 666 Fifth Avenue, New York, New York 10103.

PRINTED IN THE UNITED STATES OF AMERICA

0 9 8 7 6 5 4 3 2 1

Contents

THEY DIED TWICE

Colonel John Renwick disappeared on a Tuesday. He was gone for seven days.

That Tuesday evening, Colonel Renwick was to make an important speech. So his non-appearance on the lecture platform created surprise. As a matter of fact the speech would have meant many thousands of dollars in Renwick's pocket. The verbal outpouring was to be on "The Interdiffusion of Molybdenum by the Renwick Process," and its delivery was scheduled for the Regal Room of the Park-Ritz Hotel, where the cheapest room, even in depression times, was seven dollars a night. The Renwick process for molybdenum was actually going to cause another of those revolutions in the steel business. He had invented it himself.

Above all, Renwick was not a man to let thousands of dollars slip out of his pockets by not appearing on the lecture platform. He hated to talk in public, but he didn't hate it that badly.

"Monk" Mayfair, who was Renwick's friend, made a comment.

"A half-million-dollar stage fright," he said.

"There isn't any such thing," said "Ham" Brooks, also a friend. "Not with Renny."

"Sure," Monk agreed. "What do you suppose happened?"

"It couldn't be a woman."

"Not unless Cleopatra has come back," Monk said.

This casual crack about Cleopatra had an uncanny relativity about it that, much later, made their hair stand on end. As a matter of fact, Colonel John "Renny" Renwick was not susceptible to feminine charms. He was not proof against them, but he was not susceptible.

For seven days, no word.

Renny Renwick did not report in.

This was something particularly alarming, because it was a thing—the reporting in—that he never failed to do. All of the Savage associates did it.

Renny Renwick was a member of the group of five men who, for love of excitement and other reasons, had associated themselves with Clark Savage, Jr., better known as Doc

Savage, or the Man of Bronze, and also as an individual of mystery and legendary abilities, according to the newspapers.

Doc Savage had been trained from childhood by scientists to follow the unusual career of righting wrongs and punishing evildoers. For some time he had pursued this career with enthusiasm and success. Renny had become associated with Doc Savage. So had Ham Brooks, Monk Mayfair, and three others—Johnny Littlejohn, Long Tom Roberts, and a girl named Patricia Savage. Patricia was a cousin of Doc Savage, and not actually a member of their organization. But she liked excitement and had managed more and more to wedge herself into their group.

When the daily reports stopped coming from Renny, they launched a search. It was a thorough hunt. Doc Savage, in addition to his own group, had connections with agencies which made a business of getting information and finding people. Doc had established one of the best agencies himself, and it was extremely effective.*

No trace of Renny was found. Not the slightest.

"Shall we tell Doc about this?" Monk demanded.

Long Tom Roberts, who was the electrical wizard of their group, shook his head slowly. "I hate to do that," he said. "Doc is working on a plane locator gadget for the government, and orders are not to disturb him."

They argued about that. There was no question of the importance of the experimental work Doc was doing. Overdoing, the others were beginning to think. Doc Savage had made repeated efforts to get into active combat service, but had been refused on the ground that he was more valuable at what he was doing. "You don't stick your brains out for the enemy to shoot at," they told him in Washington. "You are one of what we would call the brains of this country. On the fighting front, you would be only one man with a gun or an

*Those who have read the adventures of Doc Savage in the past are probably familiar with this agency, which is a detective agency without having that name. Its formation was connected with the unusual treatment which Doc gives to criminals whom he catches. These crooks are sent to a secret institution in upstate New York, a place called the "College," where they undergo intricate brain operations that wipe out all memory of past, leaving, however, the normal functions of the brain intact. These "patients" are then taught useful trades and turned back into the world with a hate of crime and no memory of their own past. Because Doc has been extremely active, there are many of these "graduates," and they have spread to the corners of the earth. Doc has organized many of them into an efficient agency for getting information which he may desire. It is particularly effective because the "graduates" have been taught unswerving loyalty to the Man of Bronze, as well as to the principles of right and justice.

airplane. This way, you are fifty or a hundred thousand men, as far as effectiveness is concerned."

They left Doc alone, knowing he would drop everything if he suspected Renny was in danger. There was complete loyalty between Doc Savage and his associates.

Johnny Littlejohn, the archaeologist and geologist, made a statement.

"A subdolous durbar might deoppilate the labyrinthine aspects," he said.

They looked at him.

No one said a word for a moment.

Monk then said, "Words like them at a time like this ought to get you a kick in the ribs."

Johnny looked uncomfortable. It was a habit of his never to use a word anyone could understand whenever he could think of one they couldn't. "Sorry," he muttered.

"Did you have something on your mind beside the dictionary?" Monk asked him.

Johnny nodded. "I was wondering if anyone had noticed Renny in the company of any strangers before this happened?"

They considered this point. Long Tom Roberts, who looked as if he was going to furnish an undertaker with business next week, but who could whip wild cats, started violently.

"Hey, did anyone notice the little girl-man?" he asked.

"Girl-man?" Monk said. "What the hell?"

Johnny said, "I don't mean that the little fellow was prissy. It was just that he was small and rather fat, and had a face which reminded me of one of those little girls who play in the motion pictures. I've forgotten which one."

"How old a girl?" Monk asked.

"Oh, very young. Nine or ten years. There was something babyishly immature about the man, is what I mean."

"You saw Renny with this fellow?"

"Yes. That is, Renny remarked that the little fellow was following him around and making a nuisance of himself. Renny was working on this molybdenum thing he had perfected, and he didn't want to be bothered."

"Anybody know anything about the little fellow?"

No one did.

But then, the seven days had passed, and Renny Renwick came back.

And it was obvious something strange had happened.

Renny Renwick had lost thirty pounds. He was a big man,

4

very big—six feet four, two hundred sixty—so that loss of thirty pounds should not make him look as cadaverous as he did. Obviously, he had lost more than weight.

Just what Renny had lost was the thing that began to puzzle them.

He was scared, or dulled with horror, or stupefied from some awful discovery, or something. They began to wonder what.

First, though, he was uncommunicative. Silent. Desperately silent.

When he returned he merely walked into headquarters—the latter was situated on the eighty-sixth floor of a midtown skyscraper—and sat in a chair. Collapsed in the chair was a better word. He said, "Hello. Anything been going on?"

They stared at him in surprise and growing amazement. His face had no expression at all. It was a face normally gloomy in expression, but now it was blank. Blank, they began to decide, because he was holding it that way by great force of will.

"What happened, Renny?" Monk demanded.

"Nothing," Renny said vaguely.

A poor lie.

Later, he began to tremble. The trembling was a kind of uncontrollable thing that began in his hands and crept up to his arms, and then went all through him. He was quite pale. He looked weak and hungry.

"Where you been?" Monk asked.

"Oh, different places," Renny said, and looked sick, as if the illness was in his soul.

"Hungry?" Ham asked.

Renny shook his head vaguely. "No," he said.

"When did you eat last?"

Renny said, "Last Tues—" and did not finish.

"Last Tuesday was the day you disappeared!" Ham exploded. "Mean to say you haven't eaten since then?"

Renny stared blankly, then shook his head with care. "I didn't mean—that," he said. "I ate—regularly."

For some reason or other, this was a lie, too. It was plain that he had made up his mind to tell them no truth whatever.

They studied Renny. He did not look in the least, sitting there, like Colonel John Renny Renwick, the civil and mechanical engineer whose accomplishments were known all over the world, and whose textbooks were so advanced that they gave headaches to engineering instructors in the highest technological colleges.

He was emaciated. His eyes were sunken and there were dark hollows under them. His skin had an old cardboard quality—cardboard that had been rained upon. His clothes were disheveled, slept in, untidy.

"Look, Renny," said Monk kindly, "if you have any friends in the world, we are they. Now tell us what happened to you."

Renny sat there in complete terror.

"Nothing," he said.

Monk got the others to one side. "We won't tell Doc about this yet," he said. "But we'll keep close tab on Renny. Something has sure gone wrong with him."

That afternoon, Renny went to the Museum of Art. He started out walking, or, rather, blindly pushing his way through the crowds on the street. It struck Monk and the others, who were trailing him, that his mind was so upset that it did not occur to him to get on a bus, subway or streetcar. It was obvious from the moment he started out that he had a definite destination, which proved to be the art museum.

The Metropolitan Museum of Art is not devoted entirely to paintings, as its name might imply. It contains the art of the centuries, back through all the days of mankind, wherever man has created beauty or skill that lives.

Renny Renwick went to the section devoted to old Spanish art. He did not seem to know what he was seeking, and asked questions of a guide. He received instructions and walked on.

Monk and the others were careful not to let Renny see them. They cornered the guide. "What did that fellow want to know?" Monk asked.

"The fellow with the big fists, you mean?" asked the guide.

"Right."

"He wanted to know if we had anything on Renaticus, of the Spanish fifteenth century."

"Have you?"

"Yes. A statue of Renaticus. I told him where it was. He thanked me."

"Who," asked Monk, "is or was Renaticus?"

"Blessed if I know," said the guide. "Some big shot back about the days of Columbus, I think. I don't know much about him. Never heard of him before, in fact."

Ham Brooks said, "Come on. Let's see what Renny wants with an old Spaniard named Renaticus."

Monk thought of something and snorted. "Renaticus," he said. "And Renny. Wonder if Renaticus was an ancestor of Renny, or something?"

They overhauled Renny in time to witness a rather remarkable performance. When they first saw him in front of the statue, Renny was merely standing there, staring at it. His attitude was one of tension, with his arms down at his side and his body tilted forward slightly in a stiff manner.

They gazed at the statue of Renaticus with interest.

Renaticus, or his statue, was very large. There was a kind of iron-fisted formidability about Renaticus in statue form that indicated he must have been an individual of strong qualities in real life.

"Jeepers!" Monk gasped.

Ham had seen it, too. All of them had. The unexpected quality of the statue of Renaticus.

But there was no time for comment because Renny Renwick suddenly seized the brass stanchion which supported a velvet rope that was there to keep spectators from getting too close to the statues. Renny tore this stanchion out by its roots and used the pipe to beat the statue of Renaticus to fragments.

Renny howled as he destroyed. He bellowed in a mad rage and wielded his club with frenzied violence. He picked up fragments of the statue and hurled them against the floor and the walls. He seized half of Renaticus' head and smashed it to the floor, then jumped on the fragments.

He broke off one of the big statue's hands and beat at it with the pipe as if he was killing a snake.

Renny's screaming—part of it profanity—and the noise he was making, brought museum attendants running. They saw what probably struck them as a madman destroying museum property. They closed in.

Renny fought them off. He apparently had no animosity against the attendants, but did not want any interference until he had finished with destroying the statue. When he had smashed head, arms, legs, feet, and one shoulder off the statue, he beat his pipe against Renaticus' solid stomach until the pipe was shapeless.

Then, realization of what he was doing seemed to come to Renny. He turned and ran.

Monk said, "Long Tom, Johnny—keep track of him! Don't let these fellows get him. But keep track of him."

Monk clamped his hat on his head and made for another door.

"Where you going?" Ham demanded.

"Don't you think we had better tell Doc about this?" Monk asked.

Ham said, *That statue looked exactly like Renny.*

"That's what I mean," Monk said.

Chapter II
THE HORRIFIED MAN

Not all famous men look like great men at first glance, but in a little while, when you get to know them, the quality that makes them great always comes out. Greatness does not hide its light under a basket.

Doc Savage was stronger in this aspect than the usual celebrity, for two reasons. First, nature had given him a combination of bronze hair, bronze skin—suns had helped darken the latter—and a remarkable pair of flake-gold eyes, the gold of which seemed always in motion, as if stirred by tiny winds. Second, the scientists who had trained him from childhood had given him a body so unusual that it was instantly evident he was far above the average.

Doc Savage was working in his laboratory, but stopped and came out into the reception room to listen to the story about Renny Renwick.

"We didn't want to bother you about what might have been nothing," Monk explained. "But now it seems to be something."

Monk then told the story of Renny's seven days of vanishment, and of the statue of Renaticus.

Doc Savage listened without interruption. Doc was a physical giant, but a quiet one, and seemed never knowingly to dominate a group or a situation. Yet there was such power in him, physically and in personality, that he seemed able to command any situation without effort. His close associates knew that this, like his other abilities, was a carefully mastered achievement. Not only scientists had contributed to his development; there had been philosophers, thinkers of all kinds, even deep mental students of India and Tibet.

Doc asked, "Did you investigate this Renaticus?"

Monk said, "Ham stayed behind to do that. He should be reporting in soon."

They waited for Ham. He came in accompanied by Chem-

8

istry, his pet chimpanzee, an eccentric and unpredictable animal which he had collected in South America. Monk did not care for Chemistry, because the animal bore a distressing resemblance to Monk himself. That, Monk knew for a fact, was why Ham had collected the pet.

"Renaticus," Ham said, "was a Spaniard who lived at the time of Columbus. He was quite a fellow in Spain in that day, a sort of a noble around the court of Ferdinand and Isabella. He took a big part in the conquest of the Granada Moors, which was going on about that time. He was also a bitter enemy of Alonso de Quintanilla, who was Columbus' friend, and influenced the queen's confessor, Fray Hernando de Talavera, to report on Columbus' project to find a new route to the Indies as impractical. That's all I know about him. He was a prominent opponent of Columbus in his day."

Monk said, "But what about his fists?"

Ham shook his head. "Renaticus bore a startling resemblance to Renny. That's all I can say."

Doc Savage was silent for a while—so long that Monk glanced at him uneasily and said, "What are we going to do? You've only got to see Renny to realize that something very, very serious has happened to him."

"Renny will not talk to you about it?" Doc asked.

"He won't tell us a thing."

"Where is he now?"

"Long Tom and Johnny are trailing him. They report in now and then."

Doc said, "The next time they report tell them to seize Renny and bring him to headquarters, so that we can get to the bottom of this thing."

Long Tom Roberts and Johnny Littlejohn got their orders to fetch in Renny Renwick about an hour later. Long Tom was a short-tempered fellow, and the others were sometimes afraid of him. He was not someone on whom you perpetrated a practical joke unless you could lick him, which not many could do. Johnny Littlejohn, on the other hand, was a kind of physical freak. Monk always described him the way you describe dachshunds—two men long and half a man tall. If there was anything wrong about this description it was the thickness part. Johnny was hardly half a man thick. He was indeed thinner than it seemed any man could be and still live.

Johnny turned from the telephone and asked, "Catachetical ubiquitariness is—"

9

"Why don't you learn bug language and get it over with!" snapped Long Tom. "What do they want us to do?"

Johnny frowned. "Bring him in," he said.

Long Tom had been watching Renny's apartment window with a pair of binoculars. "It's about time," he said. "It looks to me as if he was packing a suitcase and getting ready to leave."

"What did he put in the suitcase?" Johnny asked.

"You do know small words, don't you. Well, he put in corduroy pants, laced boots, a hunting knife, some flannel shirts, a Mackinaw coat, and some heavy socks."

"Woods-country clothing."

"That's right."

They crossed the street, entered Renny's apartment building. They did not knock on the door, having a suspicion that would not get results. They hit the door together, burst it open, and went in.

Renny whirled in wild—it was hard to believe Renny could be that worried—terror. He dropped a pair of moccasins.

"Where you going?" Long Tom asked casually.

For a few seconds it did not seem that Renny was going to make an answer. Then he shrugged cautiously and said, in a manner that showed he was pitifully desperate for them to believe him, "Oh, I thought I would go out of town for a little vacation. I'm feeling a little rotten."

"I'm surprised you admit it," said Long Tom. "You look like something that had been done to the Japanese navy."

Johnny asked, "Where were you going, Renny?"

"To Lake Kakisa," Renny said.

"Where's that?"

"Oh, up north in the woods."

Long Tom said, "It's so far in the north woods that it's in the Mackenzie, which is next door to the north pole, practically speaking. What's the idea of going so far?"

Renny, white, tense, trembling, said, "I want to get away from things."

"Well, you're not," Long Tom assured him. "Doc said to bring you into headquarters, and that's what we're going to do."

Johnny yelled, "Watch out! Grab him! He's going to fight!"

Later, Johnny carefully guided Renny Renwick into the midtown headquarters of Doc Savage. "Long Tom stopped

10

downstairs to get a beefsteak for his eye," Johnny explained. "He will be up."

"You had a fight?" Monk asked.

"A tauromachian gladiatorialistic," Johnny said.

Monk examined the two of them. "It must have been every bit as big as the words," he decided.

Doc Savage addressed Renny Renwick. Doc had a voice which contained controlled power to such an extent that it was a slightly unnatural-sounding voice. "Renny, they have given me a rough idea of the way you have been acting," Doc said. "We feel that something unpleasant has happened to you, and we want to help you. Furthermore, we consider it our duty as your friends to help you, so there is not much use in your arguing about it."

Renny said nothing. He clamped his lips together.

Doc waited awhile.

"Get the truth serum," the bronze man said finally.

Renny fought them then, as much fight as there was left in him, which, considering the circumstances, and that he had been licked once within the hour, was considerable. There was ten full minutes of it, part of it getting as far as the elevator and threatening to get down to the street. Finally, they got him doped with the truth serum.

The serum was a type lately improved by Doc Savage, and while it fell far short of what the bronze man considered the ultimate perfection which would be attained for this, or similar serums, it was efficient.

Renny seemed to become sleepy and yet not asleep. When he was questioned, the answers came in a clear voice. The clarity of the voice with which the victim spoke was the main improvement in this type. Other serums made the victim so groggy that much of what was said was not intelligible.

The story came out:

There was the little fat man with the little-girl face. His name was Jones, Albert Jones.

Albert Jones was a rather harmless little squirt, Renny had thought at first. He lived in a house somewhere in the suburbs, a private home which he occupied alone.

Exactly where Albert Jones' home was located, Renny still did not know.

"He had an invention in which he wanted to interest you, Doc," Renny said.

"Why didn't he approach me, instead of you, if he wanted to interest me in it?" Doc asked.

"Albert said that he was overawed by your reputation. He was afraid to. He is a timid man, he explained."

"So he approached you about the invention?" Doc asked.

"Yes," Renny said. "He did."

"What did you do?"

"I laughed at him."

"Why?"

"The thing seemed silly."

Renny was proving to be a very good subject under the truth serum, but that was probably because, down in his heart, he had wanted to tell them what had happened. Such a subject, one with a basic motive of righteous desire, would naturally be much more responsive to the stuff.

Getting the story proved to be a matter of interminable short questions and short answers which gave a direct response to the questions, but no other information.

Albert Jones, it developed, had invented an astounding thing.

The invention of Albert Jones, stated in its simplest form, was a mechanical-electrical-chemical device, extremely complicated, which brought back the memories dormant in the human mind.

"Dormant memories," Doc interrupted. "What do you mean by that?"

"Like instincts," Renny replied.

Doc said, "The dictionary defines instinct as something implanted by nature, an outward impulse, unconscious, involuntary or unreasoning, as the result of an inherited tendency."

Renny said, "That is what he meant."

"There is not much scientific proof of anything like a dormant memory," Doc said.

"Albert Jones can prove there is."

"You were skeptical?"

"Yes."

"And he proved to your satisfaction that there was such a thing as a dormant memory?"

"Yes."

"Just what is a dormant memory?"

"Something you inherited from your ancestors."

"From your father, you mean?"

"From your ancestors. A father is an ancestor. So is a mother. Both sides of the family, Albert Jones said. But the dormant memories from the male side are the most prevalent."

Doc Savage said, "In other words, memories are passed down from generation to generation the same as instincts, but they lie back in the human mind, unknown and unnoticed?"

"Out of the reach of the consciousness," Renny said. "The consciousness has a connection with the things which it has experienced, but not with the things which it has not experienced. Things which happened to you in this life were part of your conscious experience, therefore your mind can reproduce them at demand, which is conscious memory. The memories your ancestor had a thousand years ago are not part of your present consciousness and never were, so you cannot deliberately make your brain produce them."

Doc Savage looked at Renny sharply during this rather clear—for a man under the effects of truth serum—statement about mental behavior. The thing had a logical ring, although it was not entirely in tune with the opinions of psychologists and mental students.

Monk was impressed. "He's making this sound logical."

Ham demanded, "What was this Albert Jones' invention, Renny?"

"A machine," Renny explained. "Very complicated."

"What does the machine do?"

"It stirs up the dormant memories and frightens them out into the brain, where they are like dreams, yet terribly genuine, because you seem to actually experience them."

Renny finished this statement, then shuddered violently.

Doc eyed him sharply. "Renny!"

"Yes?"

"You are out from under the influence of that truth serum, aren't you?" Doc inquired.

Renny nodded sheepishly. "To tell the truth, Doc, the first dose of the stuff only had a temporary effect. It sort of got me to talking. I could feel it wearing off, but I got to thinking that, inasmuch as I had started the story, there was no sense in not going on with it. Anyway, if I had stopped, you would only have given me more serum."

Doc Savage turned to Monk and said, "Monk, you helped in the development of this truth serum. Make a notation to do some more work on it. We have got to add a drug which will have an obvious effect on the patient for the same length of time as the truth serum, so we can tell when it is wearing off.

This way we can not be sure when the victim comes out from under the stuff and starts lying to us."

Monk said, "Yeah, that's a big fault in the stuff."

"I wasn't lying to you," Renny insisted.

Ham said, "Renny, you haven't told us what affected you so profoundly, kept you away seven days, and made you want to skip out for the North woods to forget."

"Or about Renaticus, the stone statue," Monk added.

Renny stared at them fixedly.

"I met Renaticus in the machine," he said. "He is me, in the Thirteenth Century. It is frightening to meet yourself like that and find out what you have been."

"Bad?" Ham asked.

"Bad enough," Renny said, "to just about drive me nuts."

Monk rubbed his bullet of a head and said, "This begins to sound completely goofy."

Chapter III
THE BAD RENATICUS

The little man named Mr. Albert Jones had been rather insistent, to the point of making a pest of himself at first, and, eventually, of half convincing Renny Renwick that there might be something to the dormant-memory-awakening machine after all.

"I didn't really take any stock in his thing," Renny said grimly. "I thought he was a nut."

But Mr. Albert Jones had finally prevailed on Renny to give the machine a try. "We met in a little restaurant around the corner," Renny explained, "and we had some drinks, nonalcoholic vitamin drinks which Albert Jones mixed and which he said he liked. They weren't bad. We sat there and drank them and he told me about the scientific theories of his machine. They sounded reasonable. Jones certainly knew a lot of engineering lingo."

Doc asked, "You finally went out and tried the machine."

"Yes. We rode out in a car driven by Mr. Jones' chauffeur."

"Oh, he's got money enough to hire a chauffeur?" Monk interrupted.

"He seems to have money, yes," Renny said.

14

Doc put in, "If you rode out in a car you should have noticed where this Albert Jones lives."

Renny looked uncomfortable. "To tell the truth, both of us went to sleep on the trip out there. It was late and it was a long drive."

"When you got there you didn't know where you were?"

"That's right."

"And he put you in the machine?"

"Yes."

"Can you describe it?"

"Yes," Renny said. "I can do better than that. I can draw a fairly comprehensive picture of it and label a lot of the parts, but that would take time, and I want to tell you what happened to me after I got in the gadget. Shall I go ahead with what happened to me?"

"Yes, tell us what you learned in the contraption," Doc directed.

"You lie on a table," Renny said, "and the main part of the gadget fits down over you. There is a whirring noise, and your senses get all upset."

"What do you mean by upset?"

"You smell odors, see lights and hear sounds. None of the odors, lights or sounds make sense. Then you're off. Your mind seems to sort of turn black, and then it begins to come to you. You *see* yourself in some other age."

"Then it isn't like a dream?" demanded Monk.

"Not entirely. You *feel* it the way you do in a dream, only stronger. You walk, talk and experience the whole thing, in kind of a detached way. More of a photographic way, if you get what I mean."

Doc Savage stood back and contemplated Renny thoughtfully. Outside, it was a rather biting, early-fall afternoon, with steel-colored clouds in the sky and a hint of stinging snow to come.

Doc said, "Tell me what you found in the machine, Renny."

In a voice of deepest revulsion, Renny said, "I became Renaticus, and Renaticus was *me*. It was terrible."

"What made it so bad?" Monk asked.

"This Renaticus was such a rat," Renny explained. "He turned my stomach. Then he committed such incredible crimes that it began to scare me."

"Tell us about him."

15

"Well, it was back in the days of Christopher Columbus."

"The one who discovered America?"

"Yes. It was about the time Columbus went from Cordova to Salamanca, following the court. There was a war going on at the time, and considerable tension. Columbus had built himself up with a fellow named Alonso de Quintanilla, who had some influence with the king and queen. Like the way you cultivate the favor of a politician these days if you are trying to get something a little unusual out of the government."

"Human nature hasn't changed much," Monk suggested.

Renny scowled and nodded. "It kind of discourages you."

"Go ahead."

"Columbus had this idea of finding the Indies by going around the world, and he was trying to get the king and queen, Ferdinand and Isabella, to fix him up with ships, sailors and money. The queen's right-hand man at the time was a fellow named Fray Hernando de Talavera, and Columbus tried to sell him on the idea. That's where Renaticus came in. He didn't like Columbus. He did everything he could to oppose the thing."

Monk grinned slightly. "An obstacle to progress."

Renny stared at him. "Renaticus was a beast. You have no idea how incredibly evil some of those old-timers were. This Renaticus was a practitioner of the witchcraft order known as the *Jurginas*. This was a particularly evil sect of the day, one which worshiped the devil, whom they claimed appeared to them as a monstrous buck goat, black and loathsome."

Renny frowned. "You know that little signal the kids use when they shake hands, one of them tickling the other's palm with his finger? Kids attach different meanings to the signals, but did you know the *Jurginas* originated this thing? It was their pass grip.

"The *Jurginas*," continued Renny, "made a specialty of secret poisoning of their enemies." The big-fisted engineer dropped his head and groaned. "It was awful. The most obscene, revolting, unbelievable things this Renaticus did. It sickened me. I'll never forget them."

"How did it end?" Doc Savage asked.

"When Renaticus set out deliberately to murder Columbus," Renny said. "Poor old Columbus was such a nice guy. He was a promoter, of course, and always in debt and dodging his creditors all the time."

Monk said, "I didn't know Columbus was a dead-beat."

16

"That is a matter of historical record," Doc Savage said.

Renny nodded. "Poor old Columbus at the time was so hard up that he had to make his own clothes. He wove them himself and did a fine job. He had been a weaver by trade. He liked to draw, too, and picked up spare change by drawing maps."

"What about the poisoning? Or didn't Renaticus try to poison him?"

"Yes, he tried poison. But something must have gone wrong, because this happened before Columbus set out and found America. Or found the island called Guanahani by the redskins, but called San Salvador by Columbus."

Johnny Littlejohn arose hurriedly and went into the library. The headquarters layout consisted of reception room, library and laboratory, and as Renny talked he had moved into the reception room. Johnny got a book, a historical tome, and consulted it. After he had skimmed pages awhile, he asked, "Are you a student on Columbus?"

"No, I never was," Renny said.

"Well, your historical dope on Columbus seems accurate," Johnny informed him. Johnny snapped the book shut. "I don't get this. The thing is impossible, of course."

Ham said, "Sure, it's impossible."

Monk snorted. Monk liked to disagree with Ham. He said, "They said something called radio was impossible, too."

"Nuts."

"On the face of it, this don't look any more impossible than radio to me."

Doc Savage stood at the window, thoughtful. "How did you get away?" he asked.

"From Albert Jones' house? Why, I had a fight with the little fellow, and then I was taken away."

"Why the fight?"

"I was upset. You've got to go through the thing I went through to know how I felt. There was this rat, Renaticus, who looked like me, and who was obviously an ancestor. He had a lot of evil traits. I've felt the stirrings of such things in the back of my mind at times, impulses sort of, and it was sickening to suddenly realize they were things handed down to me by an ancestor who was a twenty-four-carat devil."

Incredulously, Ham demanded, "Did this little Jones lick you?"

"Well, yes, he did. I was all weak and flustered, and he popped me over the head, tied my hands, blindfolded me, then gave me a drug to make me sleep."

"What kind of drug did he give you?"

"An ordinary one from a drugstore. He had to go out and buy it. Left me tied when he was gone. He kept me there for a week. Then he hauled me in his car this morning and dumped me out."

"Where did he dump you?"

"On a side street in Sunnyside, Long Island."

Doc Savage was thoughtful. "By the way, in the beginning of your story, you mentioned an innocent vitamin cocktail which Jones mixed, and which you drank."

Renny nodded. "You think maybe it wasn't so innocent?"

"What do you think?"

"I've been wondering." Renny knotted his enormous fists thoughtfully. "Holy cow! It looks like Jones forced me into that gadget."

Monk demanded, "Why would he do that?"

Renny shrugged. "He said he wanted to bring the thing to Doc's attention, is all I know. He seemed a little disappointed about the results he got out of me when he put me in it."

"What comment did he make about those results?" asked Doc.

"He said he didn't know I had so many crook ancestors that I would have the memory of one turned loose in my mind," Renny said. The big-fisted engineer grimaced. "He said he wished he'd picked a better strain of man for his tests."

Doc Savage made his small, trilling sound.

The trilling was a peculiarity of the bronze man in moments of mental excitement. It was a small sound, tiny and as exotic as the work of some unknown feathered creature in a tropical forest. The others stared at him. They knew it meant that something was strong in Doc's mind.

They hardly expected him to explain what it was. He had a habit of keeping his ideas and his convictions to himself. But he surprised them.

"Why did you smash the statue of Renaticus?" Doc asked.

Renny looked sheepish. "I was upset. I couldn't stand the idea of a devil like that living through history. I went up there to the museum to check on the actual existence of Renaticus, and the idea of smashing the statue just seized me overwhelmingly while I stood there."

Doc Savage nodded.

"The whole thing has a rather queer touch," he said. "It might be good if we got in touch with this Albert Jones."

"How?" demanded Renny. "I'm sure I don't know where to find him. He always found me."

"Did you say he went out and got a sedative and gave it to you?"

"Yes."

"What was the sedative?"

Renny named the drug.

Doc said, "You have to buy that on a prescription." The bronze man turned to Monk, Ham, Johnny and Long Tom. "Get hold of a retail-druggist's guide for the metropolitan New York district," he directed. "Send telegrams to each drugstore listed, giving the description of this man Jones, and the nature of the prescription, and ask if the drugstore made such a sale in the last few hours."

Doc considered and then added, "Better offer a reward for the information from the store that made the sale in which we are interested."

He turned back to Renny, asked, "Are you sure that you were hauled for at least an hour in the car?"

"Yes."

"Did you go through any metropolitan districts, do you think?"

"I don't know," Renny said. "I was too groggy."

"Send those telegrams," Doc said.

Chapter IV
PLOT, PLOT, PLOT

The man named Space was young and strong, but not much more could be said about him that was favorable. His clothing would have been good except that it was a little too carefully matched, too tuned to the man's personality, which was distinctly hard brown.

Hard and brown was a good description for him. Age, not quite thirty. Weight, a hundred and seventy-five or eighty. Eyes the hard black of bakelite. A purposeful young man, and one not too thoughtful of others. Not thoughtful at all of them, in fact, if he had to sacrifice anything himself.

He looked, as he stood on the corner, like a corner boy or

a poolroom hanger-on. He had been chain-smoking cigarettes.

Then the telegraph messenger came and looked nervously
about before he spoke.

Space said, "Why the jitters, kid? Hell, nobody knows I
hired you to do anything."

The messenger boy swallowed uncomfortably. He was a
nice clean kid, the only trouble being that five dollars was
such a lot of money.

The boy said, "I got it. A telegram from Doc Savage to the
drugstore, asking them to report if a drug had been sold to a
man of a certain description. Somebody named Albert
Jones."

"Good," said Space. "Go ahead and deliver your telegram,
kid, and forget about this."

The boy was so relieved that tears came to his eyes. He had
been afraid this man would want to take the telegram, and
the boy knew that was a serious crime. The boy trotted away
to the drugstore.

Space strode with lively excitement to his car and jumped
in. The car was the car of a man who likes easy money. A
robin blue as delicate as the sky in April and plenty of
hard-to-get chromium. A big motor and red leather and a
little bar that folded into a compartment.

Space drove to a solid house, but not an expensive house,
half a dozen blocks distant. He went inside.

"Hy'ah, chief," he said to Albert Jones.

Albert Jones, being a fat little man with a little-girl face,
prized dignity more than other men. He frowned his disapproval.

"It would be better if we kept this on a Mr. Space and Mr.
Jones footing," he said sharply.

Space stared at him. Space was clever—he did not laugh.
He was, in fact, cunning enough to look very sorry and to
apologize, "I am very sorry. It will not happen again." He
knew Albert Jones as a type, and he had nothing but contempt for the type, but showing contempt for people never got you anything, unless there was a time and a place for
it.

"You have a report?" Jones asked with pleased dignity.

"Yes. Savage has telegraphed the drugstore asking if a man
of your description bought a sleep-producing drug within the
last few hours."

Albert Jones laughed. His mirth was something like the
laugh of a little girl.

20

"Good, oh, very good!" he said. "I figured that Savage would be smart enough to spot the clue of my going out to buy the drug, but not slick enough to recognize it as a deliberately planted clue on my part."

Space nodded. For a moment his eyes were sharp, speculative. This little goof, he thought, has a brain or two in his head. Better watch him.

Jones said, "Good, very good, Space. That is all. I will not need you longer. Not today, anyway. You will return to your apartment and wait. Or you can take the afternoon off for a movie, or something."

"Sure you don't want me to help you with the rest of it?" asked Space.

"No," Jones said. "No, thank you."

"I'd be willing."

Jones became firm. Firmness in such a little effeminate-looking man was comical.

"This is a matter of great secrecy," he said. "I am sorry, Space, but I cannot accept your help."

Space stood there fighting disappointment. He clamped down on the urge to snarl out the news that he wasn't as dumb as Jones seemed to think him, and that he knew a great deal of what was going on. And that it all certainly wasn't what it seemed to be.

Which would not have been the truth, because Space did not quite know what was behind the mysterious doings of Mr. Albert Jones.

One thing sure—there was more to it than just the memory-awakening machine.

Space had reached a decision. This was evident in the way he jerked his thumb at a man named Prinz—Nickolas Prinz —who was working in a cigar store. Proprietor of the cigar store, rather.

"Lock it up," said Space, indicating the place of business. "I got something to talk to you about."

Prinz said, "Lock it up, hell. I bet nobody would even steal the stuff. You sure can't sell it to them."

They went to a milk bar. Milk bars were not very popular in that neighborhood, so the place was about empty, and a table in the back gave them plenty of privacy.

"Take it you're not getting rich," Space said.

"It don't take no genius to see that."

"You still got connections?"

"I still got the old gang together, if that's what you mean.

But hell, I can't keep 'em together much longer on what I make in that cigar store."

"Working?"

Prinz snorted. "Not in weeks. Hell, three of them even joined the army for the excitement." He cursed sourly. "Turning patriotic—can you imagine?"

Space glanced about, made sure no one was paying them any attention and that there were no mirrors which would reflect lip movements to an onlooker he hadn't noticed.

He said, "I have a dove. A lovely dove."

Prinz stared at him. Prinz had known Space in the past. "Yeah? I've heard you call them doves before. They were. You want help?"

Space leaned back. He was not afraid to talk to this man Prinz because he could dominate the fellow. He could even put him in the electric chair if necessity arose. But he did not want Prinz to get the idea he needed help. He wished to dominate Prinz and Prinz's men; he had no use for Prinz if he could not dominate him. And if he could not he would find another who would do, although probably not as good. Prinz was a murderer who had killed at least twenty men, not counting those he had killed in the one or two wars in which he had participated. Prinz had a crazy, bloodthirsty streak—like a weasel in a coop of helpless chickens. Space felt he might need such a thing.

"I'll hire you and your men," Space said sharply. "Hire you, understand?"

Prinz scowled. He took a drink of his milk. "That won't be cheap. We don't work often, but we don't work cheap."

"Ten thousand a week," said Space, knowing he was going to startle the other man, "for you and your facilities."

Prinz was satisfactorily astounded.

"Cash?" he blurted. "It'll have to be cash."

"It will be."

Prinz licked his lips. "Where'd you get dough like that? Not bootlegging. Not running guns or smuggling oil to the Japs?"

Space sneered politely and said, "You have always underestimated me, Prinz. The trouble with you is that you measure other men with yourself as a yardstick."

Prinz became cunning. "No single week's work, you understand. Not less than a month. Ten thousand a week, and another ten thousand for me, on the side, for incidental expenses. That will be fifty thousand from you."

"Fair enough." Space knew the value of impressing such

22

men as Prinz, of overawing them. "That's good. You're hired."

"I better see some money."

Space grinned thinly, brought a wallet from a pocket and fanned it open. He riffled through the bills within. They were hundreds and five-hundreds, a deck of them.

Prinz looked at the money and made the sound of a beast.

"Father Satan!" he said.

Space had his man hooked, so he relaxed. He had outsmarted Prinz, overwhelmed the man with money and hired him, before Prinz had thought to ask what he was being hired to do. Space had an idea that fifty thousand would not have been enough for Prinz if the man had thought of getting an answer to that question. But now Prinz would not back down, even for death. Space knew the strange creed of men like Prinz.

Space drank more of his milk.

"Here is the background," he said. "There is a fat little man with a girl-face named Albert Jones, who has invented a gadget."

Space described Albert Jones' so-called gadget. He gave a clear picture of the thing and what it would do, and it was much the same picture as Renny Renwick had given Doc Savage. He made Prinz understand the reasonableness of such a thing as memories from past generations locked fast in hitherto unknown storehouses of the human mind, and made the man believe that such memories might be released with the proper stimulus.

Suddenly Prinz saw the possibilities of the thing, or some of them.

"Glory road!" he gasped. "You could grab a descendant of one of those old pirates, like Blackbeard, who hid a lot of gold that was never found. You could dig the dormant memory out of the descendant's mind, and he would be able to go right to the spot where the gold was hidden."

Space grinned. "You begin to see."

Prinz breathed heavily and licked his lips. He was elated by the possibilities.

"However," Space said, "that isn't what I'm hiring you for."

"What isn't?"

"Stealing the machine. That is what you think I want, isn't it?"

23

Prinz was startled. "Sure. Isn't it?"

Space shook his head. "Not now. We'll get it. But that will be incidental. But first, we're going to cut in on Mr. Albert Jones' game, whatever it is."

A bus went by in the street outside, rattling its exhaust like a machine gun. A white-clad attendant approached them. Prinz was about to curse the man and drive him away, but Space headed him off by courteously ordering sandwiches and more milk, so that unpleasant attention would not be drawn to them.

When they were alone, Space said, "This Albert Jones has something in mind. Something big. He has hired a gang. He hired me, and he has more men like me—men who will do anything. Men who are clever. Men who are not afraid of the devil, and more than that, not afraid of Doc Savage."

Prinz jerked stiff and stared.

Space continued, "Jones kidnapped one of Doc Savage's men named Renny Renwick and put him in the machine, gave him the works, and turned him loose. When he did that it was part of his scheme. I don't know what the scheme is. But it is big. Men do not fool with this Savage for peanuts. Not men who know what Savage is. And Jones knows. Or he wouldn't have hired men like me."

Prinz continued to stare fixedly, and his lips moved and made something that had no sound, but which seemed to be merely the repetition of the name, Doc Savage.

Space continued, "Jones is going ahead with the scheme. I do not know what he is going to do next. But it is something connected with Doc Savage, a continuation of the plan that began with putting Renny Renwick in this machine."

He leaned forward impressively.

"I am going to cut in on Jones' game," he finished. "I am going to grab the ball from him and carry it over for a touchdown. I'm hiring you to help me."

Prinz stopped staring and his eyes, when they moved, were the eyes of an animal in a trap.

He said, "Why didn't you tell me Doc Savage was in it."

"I knew you weren't afraid of him," said Space, knowing that was probably the one thing that would keep Prinz from walking out.

Prinz sat there white-faced for a while.

"We'll have to kill Savage right away," he said. "We can't have him running around loose. You understand that?"

"I understand that," Space agreed.

They left their sandwiches untasted, paid the check, and got in Space's bright roadster. "We'll go out and watch Jones and his place," Space explained. "You ride out with me. You can round up your men by telephone."

Prinz nodded stiffly. "Stop by the cigar store," he said.

From the cigar store Prinz secured a small suitcase, and when they were in Space's car, rolling through the city, he opened the case to show the apparatus within. "Radio," he said proudly. "One of them transceivers. I can contact my men with it. Modern, just like the army."

Space laughed. He was genuinely pleased. He liked efficiency in such things, because he had no misunderstandings about what he was tackling. It was a big thing, and not an ordinary thing—not ordinary when men like Albert Jones and Doc Savage were involved.

Eventually, they drove past the drugstore where Albert Jones had deliberately bought the drug so that Doc Savage would learn the fact. Space did not exactly understand that. Jones wanted Savage to get on his trail, of course. But what Jones intended to do then was something Space did not understand.

Space glanced at the drugstore and saw something which gave him a chill. It was hard, very hard, for him to control himself for a moment. He did not like being so scared; however, it made him feel good that he was able to control himself so fully that Prinz did not notice the way he felt.

"We could kill him now," Space said. "But it would be a little too early in the game, don't you think?"

Prinz suddenly looked as if he wanted to jump out of the car. "Savage is around here?" he gasped.

"In that drugstore," Space said.

Chapter V
A TWISTING TRAIL

The druggist was amiable and cooperative. What was more, he had a good memory. "Yes, I know Mr. Jones," he explained. "I have known him for years—all the time he has lived in this neighborhood. A very fine man. An estimable gentleman."

"What does he do?" Doc inquired.

"Oh, he buys lots of ice cream and cigars from me," the druggist explained. "Or do you mean—what is his business?"

"Yes, what is Jones' business?"

"I don't know," the druggist admitted.

"What church does he attend?"

"I—ah—don't know."

"Is he married?"

"Well, I'm not sure."

It seemed that the druggist did not know Mr. Jones so well, after all.

"What is his address?" Doc asked.

The druggist knew that. He gave it with some relief, and effused thanks as he accepted the reward which Doc Savage paid him.

Then, when Doc was moving toward the door, the druggist called out, "Oh, wait! I thought of something else."

Doc paused. "Yes?"

"Mr. Jones has been purchasing some rather unusual chemicals through me," said the druggist. "I—ah—wasn't going to mention them, but you were so generous with the reward." He hesitated uncomfortably. "The chemical lists are unusual enough that you might be interested. Would you care to see them?"

Doc said, "I would."

"In the back room," the druggist explained, and led the way through a partition.

The back room contained the motley stuff that back rooms in drugstores usually contain. There was a young woman bending over a work table, apparently mixing something in a pestle and mortar.

"I'll show you what I have to show you," the druggist said. His voice was suddenly high and nervous.

The young woman turned slowly and picked up a cloth and then, with great quickness whisked the cloth aside and disclosed a large pistol which had the barrel sawed off.

The speech she made was long for the circumstances, and delivered all in one breath. "This is what we have to show you!—you will kindly get your hands up, because I happen to know about that bullet-proof vest you wear, and I won't shoot you there."

The druggist was white and shaking. It was plain that he had just been hired to do this.

The girl was interesting. Even to Doc Savage, who carefully thwarted his interest in such things, knowing that if he fell in love, enemies were sure to strike at him through the girl.

26

She was more than just a pretty girl. More to her than a sun-tanned skin of velvet, eyes as red-brown as the pelt of a hill fox, and clothes that were golden and in good taste. There was a racing vitality about her, a quality of speed, dash, of bounding force and lighted fuses.

She said, "Search him, Mr. Weagles."

Mr. Weagles was the druggist and he was too scared to search anyone.

She then told Doc Savage, "I'm afraid to search you myself. I've heard about you. But I don't know whether or not I am afraid to shoot you. I might not be, though."

Doc Savage made no comment. He did not look excited.

His quietness did not seem to surprise the girl.

"Back outside," she ordered. "The rear door. It will do you no good to make a noise. There is no one in the drugstore except Mr. Weagles' employees, and they know what is happening."

Doc Savage did as she ordered him. The drugstore was in a suburban section, and the rear opened into an empty lot of some size which had been planted with trees and bushes in profusion, and also surrounded by a high green hedge. Tables and chairs—for ice cream served from the drugstore—stood around. There was no one in sight.

"Mr. Jones!" the girl said sharply.

The little man with the little-girl face came out of a nearby bush. It was not hard to recognize Albert Jones.

He had told Renny that he was afraid of Doc Savage, that he was overawed by the Man of Bronze. He had not lied.

"Search him," the girl ordered.

Reluctantly, but driven by desperate determination, Jones went over Doc Savage's person and removed the more obvious objects, which consisted of a number of small metal cases. "Goodness," Jones said. "There seem to be innumerable things in his clothing. And he is wearing some kind of a vest that feels like canvas but seems to be made of steel."

The girl was impatient with Jones' nervousness. "Take him to the house," she ordered, "and we can finish the job there."

Jones nodded shakily. He seemed relieved that she took the initiative and suggested ideas. It was the girl who paid Mr. Weagles, the druggist, a sum of money for his treachery in inveigling Doc into the back room.

They walked through the bushes to a side street on which there were no houses for four blocks. They went across the lots toward a small patch of woods in which stood a house.

27

Doc asked, "Buying the drug was a clue deliberately planted to decoy me to that drugstore, I suppose?"

"Yes, it was," the young woman said.

"Whose idea?"

She nodded at the little man with the little-girl face. "Mr. Jones," she said.

Mr. Jones looked miserable.

The house was elderly but solid and made of brick. Its lawn needed mowing badly, or plowing up and reseeding. Doc was shown inside.

"My name is Rogers," the girl said. "Annice Rogers. I hope you do not mind if we finish searching you."

"Wait!" gasped the little man. He scampered away and came back soon with pale-amber liquid in a tall glass. "Drink this," he commanded.

There was no loudness or excitement, but plenty of solid firmness in Doc's voice as he said, "From this point on we can make each other a lot of trouble or get along smoothly, depending on how it is handled."

The little Jones was taken aback. "I—yes," he said. "Yes, that is probably true."

Doc said, "I want to know what this is about."

The little man seemed tongue-tied.

The girl, Annice Rogers, said, "Talk up to him, Mr. Jones. We are not committing any crime—not in our opinion, at least. So talk up to him."

Albert Jones had the facial expressions of a man squirming mentally. "I am afraid I managed this badly. I have an invention. I want your help with it. Did your friend, Mr. Renny Renwick, explain my invention to you?" he asked eagerly.

"Renny explained it," Doc said.

"Good!"

"What you did to Renny was not nice," Doc said. "He was a distraught, nervous wreck. His mental condition was so upset that, if we had not gotten hold of him he would have gone off to the Canadian Northwest. His life disrupted for months."

"He was leaving?" gasped Jones.

"Yes."

"I am so glad he didn't," Jones said nervously. "You see, my whole object in putting Mr. Renwick in the machine was to demonstrate it for your benefit."

"My benefit?"

"To draw it to your attention, I mean."

Doc asked, "Why did you want my attention?"

Jones was losing his nervousness and showing the signs of a fanatic. "The thing is wonderful!" he gasped. "Just think of its possibilities, in the right hands. All the facts of history, all the knowledge and discoveries since the beginning of mankind, all those things that have been forgotten, can be brought back to us if we get hold of the present-day descendants of the people who knew the things we want to know."

Doc Savage studied the other intently. "There are doubtless a few lost treasures for the locating, too."

"I am not interested in that," Jones said quickly. "Money does not intrigue me. It is the knowledge one could get from this thing, the infinite good one could do mankind."

Jones, in his growing excitement, stepped forward and put a hand on Doc's arm as he continued, "Think of it! Think what it would mean to Christianity, for instance, to have clear memories, memories as clear as a photographic record, of the days of Christ and His teachings. Think what that alone would mean to this troubled world today!"

His voice became shrill with agitation. "That by itself would grip the imagination of mankind today. It might even be a thing so great that it would drive from man's thoughts all this horrible cycle of wars we are having. Why, it could readily mark the beginning of a new era in humanity."

Annice Rogers was suddenly beside Doc Savage, her face eager. "You will test the thing, won't you? You see, we want you to take charge of it. Or Mr. Jones does. That is why we are doing this."

Doc Savage's metallic features remained without expression, but he was thinking, because there came into existence the tiny and exotic trilling sound which was his unconscious habit in moments of mental excitement.

And, finally, he said, "Go ahead."

"Come on!" exclaimed Jones excitedly. "No, here—drink this!" He extended his glass of amber liquid.

Doc took the glass, examined the contents and asked, "The vitamin cocktail which you gave Renny Renwick?"

Jones nodded. "Yes. It is really a mild drug, of course. A modified hypnotic, as you may be able to tell from the taste. It is intended to merely soothe you and relax your body— separate your consciousness from your body to some extent.

That is the way it works." He smiled apologetically. "As in hypnotism, my machine will not work well on a person who is tense and not relaxed."

Doc drank the liquid.

They climbed a stairway. There seemed to be an upstairs arrangement that was a great, unfurnished bare room. The stairs and walls were plain unpainted wood as they climbed.

Jones stopped dramatically before a door.

"I must warn you of something," he said.

"Yes?" Doc watched him.

"I have no control over what you will remember," Jones said.

"Then, in Renny's case, you did not deliberately make him remember Renaticus?"

"No. I have no control. I think your first memory will be the strongest one, the one which is most outstanding in your past—the past of your ancestors, that is. In the case of Mr. Renwick, it was Renaticus who tried to murder Columbus. In your case, I do not know what it will be."

"Then we understand that," Doc said.

Jones unlocked the door.

The place was a laboratory. The roof of the house was a shed-shaped affair on the south side. That entire side of the house was a huge panel of window glass.

The scientific apparatus in the place was modern, and there was a large quantity of it. In one end of the room stood an assortment of lathes, saws, grinders, a small forge, a welding outfit and other equipment for making objects out of metal and glass. Evidently, Jones manufactured most of his own stuff.

The invention itself was not immediately enlightening. It occupied the center of the room, in front of the big window, and there were curtains which could be drawn to shut it off entirely from view.

It was a great dark box of an affair. The dark box was obviously the jacket, which was made of wood, with here and there a glass-covered inspection window, or a tube which entered from another gadget, or an insulator for a wire.

Jones smiled.

"That is my first model," he said. "It is very bulky and not very efficient." He took Doc's arm. "Here is my latest model, which is much more compact."

He whisked a cloth from a smaller box which could have been a casket, except that it was much larger.

"Completely self-contained," Jones said proudly. "You

need electric current, ordinary alternating current on a light voltage, for a connection. That is all."

He opened the gadget, lifting a lid. There was a recess exposed which resembled the interior of a coffin. It had no satin lining, however. It did not look comfortable.

"You merely lie in it," Jones said. "The machine does the rest. There is no danger, I assure you."

"Now?" Doc asked.

"Now," Jones said.

Doc got in the machine.

Chapter VI
WATCHDOG

Space, the hard-brown man who was looking out for himself, kept the telephone receivers clamped to his ears. The receivers were attached to an amplifier, which was in turn attached to a series of microphones cunningly hidden in the home of Albert Jones.

Space was lying in an unused garage several blocks away, and the man named Prinz, whom he had hired, was with him.

Space cursed as he listened.

"Damned if I get it!" he snarled. "He is going right ahead and putting Savage in that thing—as he said he was going to do. It doesn't make sense."

Prinz said, "He gave Savage a logical explanation. He wants to put that machine in the hands of a man who will see that it is used right."

Space swore again.

"That's not Jones' game," he said. "I know it can't be. That Jones has gone to too much trouble."

"He could be a screwball," Prinz suggested. "Take a guy who was part-screwball to invent a thing like that, wouldn't it? Sure. A screwball is likely to do anything."

Space swore some more, made no other answer.

Prinz asked, "Who hid the microphones in Jones' house?"

Space said, "I did. I've been checking up on Jones for a week."

"And you're sure Jones is pulling something on Savage?"

"Positive."

"Where does the girl come in?"

Space muttered profanely and adjusted one of the control knobs on the amplifier.

"Something strange about her," he said.

"How you mean?"

"Her name isn't Annice Rogers, as she says."

"No?"

"Her real name is Annice Stevens, and she's the daughter of an old fellow named Secret Stevens. That's really his name."

"Which leads up to what?" Prinz asked.

"This Secret Stevens," said Space dryly, "was once a close associate of Clark Savage, Sr., who was Doc Savage's father. Now don't ask me what that means. But it means something. I'm sure of that."

Prinz lit a cigarette. He was nervous. "So Jones is putting Savage in the machine for some reason other than he just said."

"Sure," Space said. "It's as plain as the nose on your face, isn't it?"

"Why don't we just walk in and take the machine and be satisfied with that." Prinz removed from a pocket a death-dealing device of his own inventing, a package of cigarettes, each cigarette being a cleverly fashioned, spring-operated gun containing a dart coated with cyanide and other poisons. He indicated his death device proudly. "I think I could take Savage with this," he said. "Why don't we just walk in, grab him, and dispose of the contraption?"

Space was not tempted.

"There's something big behind this," he said. "Let's find out what it is."

Chapter VII
A SKELETON SO HIDEOUS

It was a sensation of dullness at first.

It was not unpleasant, nor was it particularly inviting, because there was enough consciousness for there to be awareness, and that led to doubt, and doubt engendered fear. The sensation of consciousness, or awareness, never did seem to leave.

The lights came toward the end of the dullness, and enlivened it.

They were colored lights, but in gentle shades and gentle colors. Soothing and suave, slow and peaceful, strange and interesting. They were like the lights from the colorama cameras used in insane asylums to soothe the insane.

Doc Savage had the feeling that he was relaxed, and that he could not have been anything but relaxed, completely and deliciously. It was rather pleasant.

He began to hear the voice. It was a low voice, a friendly one, but one he did not recognize, and he did not understand the words either for a while, for they seemed to come out of an infinite fog. But finally the words were understandable. The voice was telling him to bring forth a memory which he had never had before. Telling him to grope and grope and find the spot where hidden memories were locked, and to bring one of them forth.

By now Doc Savage had lost all awareness that he was in the machine which Albert Jones had invented.

The voice seemed quietly satisfied with itself, and finally it was silent, or at least Doc could no longer hear it clearly, although it might have been a background.

The memory began to come.

It was like approaching a battle.

It began gently. It was like a motion picture with sound—that is, Doc felt himself to be part of it, a living and acting presence, yet able to take no corporeal part in the thing.

A ghost must feel like that if there is any such thing as a ghost. A ghost walking among living people, seeing and hearing them, yet unable to speak or make its presence known. You try to grab one of the people before you to show him the error of his ways, and your hands pass through him, and he is not aware of your presence. That was the way it was.

Doc Savage saw his father.

He saw his father move and speak. It *was* his father. Clark Savage, Sr., was dressed as Doc had often seen him dressed. He was dressed for the jungle.

There was jungle all around. It was a tropical country.

There were *uamil* bushes all around, *ceiba* trees, *cuhoon* palms, and *chichem* trees. There were tiny parakeets and pairs of yellow-headed parrots dining off *chichem* berries.

So it was Central America.

There was a man with Clark Savage, Sr. He was a small, wide man who was thin in spite of being so wide. He was a pleasant man, with a face as square and amiable as a child's building block. He wore snake boots, laced breeches, and a

33

helmet; nothing else. An enormous machete was lying on the table.

The table was in a tent.

Doc Savage's father had just come out of the jungle.

"There is nothing," he told the small man. "Nothing at all, Stevens. I reached the Valley of the Vanished, and it is all a cock-and-bull story. There are no Mayans and no treasure."

Clark Savage, Sr., was lying.

A multitude of thoughts ran through the mind of Clark Savage, Sr.

The man in the jungle with him was Secret Stevens, and to Stevens he owed a great deal. Stevens had saved the elder Savage's life on two occasions. He had furnished money for the scientific expeditions of Clark Savage, Sr., and more than that, he had given Savage faith when it was a precious and necessary thing. Literally his life and everything that he was he owed to this little man, Stevens.

Yet he was lying to Stevens.

Clark Savage, Sr., and Stevens were here in the Central American jungle on a partnership agreement. They were looking for a fabulous hoard of gold that was rumored to be located in a lost valley deep in the Central American mountains. A lost valley, reported to be presided over by a vanished tribe of Maya. A legendary place, sacred to ancient Maya. A spot of fabulous wealth. They had come here to search for it, Savage and Stevens together, and they were to share and share alike.

Stevens had searched to the north.

Savage had hunted to the south.

They were meeting here.

Clark Savage, Sr., had found the valley, the strange Valley of the Vanished, and it was more fabulous and more amazing than any of its legends.

"I did not find it," he told Stevens. "It is not there. The legends are based on nothing. It was a wild-goose chase."

And, telling that lie, Clark Savage, Sr., thought: It is not as if I were stealing from him, because I am taking something he has never had, except in his dreams. But I have to take it. I have to have a heritage of wealth to pass on to my son, Clark Savage, Jr. The man who is already known as Doc Savage.

"That is too bad," said Secret Stevens. "It washes us up."

The elder Savage thought: I will commit this one crime. My son has to have money. I put him in the hands of scientists when he was a child, and he has been trained until

34

his abilities are beyond those of other men, and he will follow the career I have planned for him, the career of righting wrongs and punishing evildoers. He must have this gold. I will leave it to him as his heritage.

Old Secret Stevens was looking like a broken man.

"This is tough," he muttered.

Clark Savage, Sr., looked at poor old Secret Stevens and thought: This finishes him financially, of course. And his health has been wrecked by this expedition. That means he is a ruined man, financially and physically.

It was a hard thing to do to Secret Stevens. Stevens had been his friend, and more than that, his financial staff and his spiritual adviser. He was a good man, a kind man, was old Secret Stevens.

But there was incredible, fabulous wealth in that strange Valley of the Vanished.

"You are sure?" asked Stevens gloomily. "You searched everywhere?"

"I searched everywhere," lied Clark Savage, Sr. "I missed nothing."

And he thought: He will never know I am lying. I was not fool enough to bring back any samples of the gold, or anything to show that there is such a spot as the Valley of the Vanished. My native packers were not with me at the time. No one knows.

"What," asked old Secret Stevens, "do you suggest we do."

Clark Savage, Sr., shrugged carefully. "There is nothing left to do. Chalk it up to experience. Quit. Go back to civilization."

"This meant a lot to me," Stevens said.

"I know it did."

"I spent every cent I have in the world. I will not be able to make another trip like this. My health won't stand it."

I am going through with this, thought the elder Savage.

"That is too bad," he said callously.

No one will ever know of this one crime, Savage thought; it will be a skeleton buried forever in my life.

Chapter VIII
SECRET STEVENS

With an expression of anxious concern on his fat little-girl face, Albert Jones assisted Doc Savage out of the machine. "Take it easy, Mr. Savage," he warned. "The thing leaves you very dizzy and confused, I admit. The symptoms wear off quickly, but in the meantime, take it easy."

Doc Savage sank on a chair.

Albert Jones saw Doc's face.

"Oh!" Jones cried. "Oh, my! You've had an unpleasant experience!"

Doc Savage made no comment. His metallic features were like stone.

"Oh, my!" Jones gasped. "I am so sorry. Oh, I am sorry!"

The girl looked at Doc Savage with concern, then threw Jones a glance of disapproval. "What on earth is wrong with your machine, that it can't bring back pleasant things?" she asked angrily.

Jones was very concerned. He wrung his hands. "I'm so sorry, really I am. But I have no control over what the machine does. I told you that. It just unlocks the door to the secret memory boxes in the mind. Naturally, the box with the strongest memory flies open first. I can't help it. I'm so sorry."

Doc Savage said, in a thin, strained voice, "Get me some coffee. I think that will straighten me out."

"I'll make some," the girl cried, and hurried away.

Repeatedly, Albert Jones tried to talk to Savage. The bronze man made no answers. The girl brought coffee, black as octopus spit and as strong as acid. Doc drank it. He sat there awhile. He got to his feet.

"Where are you going?" Jones gasped. "Please don't leave this way! Calm yourself. I brought you here to show you the possibilities of my machine for the good of humanity, and I want you to—"

"Do you know a man named Secret Stevens?" Doc asked.

The girl, Annice, turned her face carefully away.

"Why, no," said Jones. "Stevens? Secret Stevens? No, I never heard the name." He stared at the bronze man. "Is he

36

connected in some way with the memory which you had in my machine."

"That is right," Doc said. "I have to find him."

"But—"

"I have to find Stevens," Doc said.

"But—"

"Come with me; you and the young lady," Doc Savage said quietly. "I will explain what happened while we are hunting Stevens."

"I . . . I have a car I will loan you," Jones offered.

"My own machine is parked near that drugstore," Doc Savage said grimly. "My friends will be there, too. We will speak to them so that they will not be worried."

They found Doc's aides in and around the drugstore. Monk, Ham, Long Tom, Johnny and Renny had discovered Doc's mysterious absence from the drugstore, and they had turned the place upside down. Monk had become suspicious of the druggist. The homely chemist had cornered the fellow and was frightening the story of Doc's seizure out of him.

Doc's appearance relieved them greatly.

"Return to headquarters and wait for me," Doc directed.

Big-fisted Renny Renwick looked at the bronze man's strained face. "I see you got a shock out of that machine, too, Doc."

The bronze man nodded slightly.

"Can we help you?" Renny asked.

"No, thank you."

"What is it?"

The bronze man hesitated. "A great wrong done a man," he said finally in a low voice. "Which I can right myself."

Renny saw that Doc did not wish to talk about it. He got Monk and the others in the second of their two cars which were on the scene and they departed.

Doc Savage, Annice and Albert Jones rode in Doc's car. The bronze man drove rapidly toward Manhattan. After a while he began to talk.

He told them what had happened to him in the machine. Both Annice and Jones listened intently, and both became uncomfortable. "Such a horrible thing!" Jones muttered. "About your own father! I am so sorry."

Annice sat sidewise in the seat and studied the bronze man. She seemed much impressed by him. "You never knew of this incident in Central America before?" she asked.

37

"Of course not," Doc said.

"Does this lost valley, this Valley of the Vanished, actually exist?"

The bronze man said that it did. He said so reluctantly, because the Valley of the Vanished was a secret from the world. It was known in a few quarters that he had a source of wealth that was secret, but actual existence of the place was unknown, as far as he knew, to anyone but himself and his five associates.

"What are you going to do about this?" Annice asked curiously.

"There is only one thing to do," the bronze man said grimly. "Find this Secret Stevens and make restitution."

The girl turned her face away and settled back in the seat. She looked rather strange, as if she might be disgusted with herself.

Doc Savage stopped at a police station and visited the detective bureau in order to consult the remarkably complete assortment of city directories kept on hand there. He searched for the name of Secret Stevens. Albert Jones and Annice helped him, but it was Doc himself who finally located the name of Stevens.

Stevens, Secret, 1280 Bolden Avenue, Englewood, New Jersey.

Secret Stevens did not look as old as might have been expected from his appearance in the machine-memory. There was an ageless quality in his squat, smiling figure. He recognized Doc instantly.

"Doc Savage," he said. He looked the bronze man up and down. "You look a little like your father, of course." He smiled. "A fine man, your father."

"You were very close to my father," Doc said.

"That's right."

"How does it happen that you never got in touch with me?" Doc asked.

Secret Stevens shrugged. "I had nothing to offer you," he said. "I am not a man who imposes on others. Won't you come in?"

Secret Stevens was a very poor man, Doc saw.

The shack was small, very cheap, and had the heart-rending quality that comes from cheapness and extreme cleanliness. The furniture was old and carefully patched. The house stood in a rather miserable section, shut off from the fine residences which composed a great deal of Englewood.

There was a large vegetable garden behind the house and a pen with chickens. It would be a reasonable guess that from these, Secret Stevens drew much of his livelihood.

When Stevens moved he limped slightly.

He apologized amiably for his limp. "Bullet through the knee," he explained. "Got it in Central America one time in a fight in which your father helped me."

Doc asked, "Not by chance on one of the occasions when you saved his life?"

Secret Stevens looked around sharply. "Son," he said. "I never did anything for your father for which I expected payment. An offer of payment would have made me mad. It still does. So if you've got something like that on your mind, forget it."

Doc Savage took a chair. He was uncomfortable. He said, "This is one of the hardest things I have had to do in my life."

Stevens frowned at him. "What's eating you, son?"

Doc told him, making it a complete story.

Stevens listened with obvious amazement and chuckling disbelief at the story of Albert Jones' machine for reviving dormant memories.

He became sober when he heard the part about the Valley of the Vanished—the finding of it and the withholding of the news of its existence by the elder Savage.

Doc Savage finished.

There was silence in the room for some time.

Secret Stevens wrinkled his small square face with quizzical seriousness. "Why did you come here, boy?"

"You were done a wrong," Doc said bluntly. "It is impossible for me not to do anything about it."

Secret Stevens looked at the floor. "You have had the use of that gold a great many years, I take it. In your hands it has done enough good to repay many thousandfold for any dishonesty connected with your acquiring it. Dishonesty, incidentally, for which you had no responsibility."

Doc shook his head firmly.

"There will have to be a restitution," he said.

Chapter IX
PLAN

The man named Space beat his hands against his thighs in his excitement.

"This is it!" he chortled. "This is what I've waited for all my life!"

His helper, Nickolas Prinz, was much impressed by the set of microphones which Space had previously hidden in old Secret Stevens' shack. "Say, how'd you know to plant mikes here?" he asked.

Space said, "I told you the girl, Annice, is the daughter of old Secret Stevens. As soon as I found that out I planted the mikes in old Stevens' shack."

"Oh," said Prinz admiringly. "You don't overlook many bets."

Space was trembling in excitement. "For years," he gasped, "I've heard about the enormous wealth of this Doc Savage. Now I know where it comes from! What a break for the right guy!"

Prinz, who was a practical man, said, "You lack a hell of a lot of knowing *exactly* where it came from, if you ask me."

Space said, "We'll get it! We'll get it! I've got a plan!"

"What about Albert Jones' machine?"

"We'll get that, too." Space whirled. "Get your men out here! Get them out here fast!"

"How many of them?" Prinz asked.

"How many have you got?"

"Sixteen. But if we use all of them, it will cost you more—"

"Get them all!" Space snapped. "We won't fight about expenses. You know how much money may be involved in this? Maybe a billion dollars! Maybe more!"

Prinz, lifted by the contagious excitement of the other man, unlimbered his small radio transceiver and began getting in touch with his men. "All right," he said shortly. "They're coming. What'll they do when they get here?"

"I want an airplane," Space said. "I want a big, fast ship. One that can fly to Central America."

Prinz became alarmed. "Hey, the government has a system

of checking on all planes. You can't fly anywhere without being traced."

"I want the plane traced," Space told him.

"Huh?" Prinz scowled. "Look here, what good will this do you? Suppose there is a place called the Valley of the Vanished, which is full of gold. What good is that going to do you when you don't know where it is?"

"I'll find where it is," Space said. "I tell you I've got a scheme that can't fail."

In the shack, Doc Savage had been arguing with old Secret Stevens for some time. The old fellow was surprisingly adamant about the situation. Suppose he had been wronged by Doc's father in the old days? It had been a long time ago. It was a forgotten thing. "Furthermore," old Stevens said, "that gold has been put to a lot better use than I would ever have put it."

Doc Savage looked around at the obvious evidences of poverty. "It takes a great deal of character to say that," he said.

Stevens laughed. "I'm happy here. Maybe I don't always get all I need to eat, but I'm happy enough. My days of greed and wandering the face of the earth are over."

There was a knock on the door.

Nickolas Prinz stood outside. He said, "I am sorry to bother you. I am an inspector from the county board." He walked inside without being invited.

Doc Savage, instantly alert, asked, "The county board of what?"

Prinz suddenly showed a revolver. "Board of activities," he said. "But don't be too active." He waved the gun menacingly. "Come in, guys."

His men appeared in a swarm. They scrambled in through the door. They knocked the glass out of the windows and climbed through.

Old Secret Stevens stared at them. He was a man of courage. He reached out, got a chair and threw it at Prinz. Prinz dodged the chair.

Doc Savage went down, skidded sidewise, and ended behind the large old iron stove. He took a grenade out of his clothing and tossed it. It was a smoker. It sounded like a small shotgun under water and filled the place with black, stinking smoke.

"Gas!" Doc Savage shouted, hoping that would have some

effect. It didn't. They seemed to know the difference between a plain smoke bomb and one containing gas.

There was no fire in the stove. It was suddenly still in the shack. Doc took a lid off the stove and tossed it so that it rolled through the blackness.

There were no shots. But men charged for the sound.

They were, then, not going to shoot him if they could help it.

The bronze man came out from behind the stove. He said, "Stevens, Miss Rogers, Jones, get out of here!"

"I'll stick," old Secret Stevens said dryly. "I've been in these things before."

Judging from the sound, someone then hit the old man with a fist.

Doc asked, "Do you know who they are?"

"No," Stevens said. He sounded as if he had been hit hard, probably with a fist.

Doc found a man and got him by the neck. But not before the fellow shrieked. The shriek brought aid.

After that the place was suddenly full of flashing violence. There was no shooting or knifing, but there was everything else in the way of a violent fight.

"Don't kill anyone!" Prinz kept gasping. "Don't kill Savage or Stevens."

Doc said, "Jones! Miss Rogers!"

There was no answer.

"I think they got away," yelled old Secret Stevens in the blackened, fight-filled shack. Then the old man croaked in agony. He had been hit again, with more damage this time.

A man got hold of Doc Savage. Doc tried but was not able to kick him off. Another man joined the first, then a third. Doc settled down to the grim business of getting loose.

But he was careful not to try too hard. He had decided to let them take him; he wanted to know what was behind the affair.

Wind came in through the open windows and the open door and blew the smoke away.

Prinz got up off the floor, making faces, and reached into his mouth with two fingers and brought out what seemed to be two whole teeth and part of a third. He threw these on the floor.

Prinz ran to the door and looked out. The girl, Annice, and Albert Jones, were running away. Jones was running very fast for a fat man.

Two men appeared. They could have intercepted the girl and Jones but Prinz waved them back.

Old Secret Stevens was sprawled on the floor. A man stood over him, one foot on Stevens' throat, holding a chair ready in case Stevens should move, which he did not.

Doc Savage was a center, like the seed in a cling peach, of a knot on the floor. The knot was shaggy with arms and legs, which waved.

"Hold him," Prinz pleaded. "Hold him, whatever you do!"

Prinz went looking for something that would do as a club. He found the "lifter" used to take the lids off the stove, and with this he took several judicious whacks at Doc Savage's head.

"Careful," he pleaded, as if with himself. "This guy has got to be alive so he can be seen on the plane flight to the south."

He got Doc Savage motionless on the floor.

"Don't let go of him," he warned. He looked as if he was sweating blood. "Keep hold of him. We'll get ropes and a strait jacket or something."

Prinz ran to the door and looked out. He saw no sign of Space, so he dashed outside and ran along the path.

In the distance he heard the motor of a car start. It was the machine in which Doc Savage, Jones, and the girl had arrived. It went away as fast as it could.

Space came out of the brush and confronted Prinz.

"Jones and the girl get away?" Space demanded.

"Yes. I let them escape, like you said," Prinz told him.

"You mention my name?"

"No."

"Did anybody mention my name?" Space persisted.

"No."

"That's good," Space said. "It's important. Now, here is what you do. You get Doc Savage and Secret Stevens on that plane and head south with them."

"South where?" demanded Prinz.

"Central America. The country of Hidalgo. I've heard that's where this secret source of gold of Doc Savage's comes from."

"Hidalgo," said Prinz, "ain't exactly a definite destination. That country ain't so small, and it's back in them mountains, to-hell-from-nowhere."

Space was impatient.

"You head for Hidalgo," he ordered. "Fly out to sea first, and—no, better take the inland route. Fly high, and try to keep in clouds all you can. Keep away from defense areas, and try to avoid trouble."

"I would rather take the sea route," Prinz said grimly. "At sea you meet reconnaisance bombers, and we would stand a chance of outrunning them. But we couldn't outrun army pursuit ships if they came up to investigate us."

"All right," Space snapped impatiently.

"Where do we head for in Hidalgo?"

"I'll advise you by radio," Space said, "when I find out."

"O.K."

Space said, "And I want another plane to head south with all your men, plenty of guns and ammunition. Take hand grenades, gas, and everything you would need." .

"Need for what?"

"For anything that might happen."

"O.K." Then Prinz thought of something else. "You want this flight to attract some attention, don't you? You want it to be plain that we're headed south with Doc Savage?"

"Yes."

"How do you want us to attract attention to ourselves?"

"I don't care what you do," said Space. "Land at some little out-of-the-way airport on the way south for gasoline, and wind up by shooting at the airport attendants. That will draw attention to you."

Prinz laughed unpleasantly. "Brother, you like to do things," he said, "with other people's necks."

Albert Jones and the girl who had said her name was Annice Rogers drove wildly in Doc Savage's car. The machine had a great deal of power, and it was not difficult to keep the speedometer needle around a hundred whenever the straightness of the road would allow.

Having recovered her breath, Annice asked, "What went wrong? Who were those men?"

"I don't know," said Albert Jones grimly. "But they certainly played hell with things."

Annice said, "I think they are some men who are after that gold in the Valley of the Vanished."

Albert Jones almost took a corner too fast. The car skidded off on the shoulder and threw dust and clods high in the air. He got it straightened out.

"I think you are right," Albert Jones agreed, regaining color.

"But you have no idea who they were?"

"No."

"Have you hired anyone who would double-cross you, Mr. Jones?" asked Annice.

"The only people I have hired are you and Doyle Space."

Annice tightened her fingers in her lap.

"Doyle Space—I'll bet it is him!" she said.

"Maybe."

"What are you going to do?"

Albert Jones caught sight of a building beside the road with a high flagpole and a sign announcing headquarters of the New Jersey State police.

"I am going to turn it over to the police," he said. He jammed a foot on the brake and brought the car to a stop in front of the State police station.

He and the girl exchanged glances. "What about your machine?" she asked.

"We won't mention that," Albert Jones said. They got out and went into the police station. Being in a police station, or the recent excitement, or some such factor, suddenly made fat, little-girl faced Albert Jones too excited to speak coherently.

Annice told the police, "My friend, Mr. Jones here, and Doc Savage and I were visiting my father at 1280 Bolden Avenue, in Englewood," she said. "Some men attacked and seized my father and Mr. Savage. We escaped. It was only a few seconds ago. If you hurry you may be able to catch them."

"Great grief!" exploded the officer.

There were several policemen waiting around the trooper headquarters, and these piled into patrol cars. Howling sirens made them sound like a string of cats chasing each other up the road. There was deadly efficiency in the way they piled out at 1280 Bolden Avenue, and covered the vicinity, although it proved to be much effort for nothing.

Albert Jones was still speechless. It was evident that being in the company of police officers upset him greatly.

"Got away," said the cop in charge.

Annice was suddenly near tears. "My poor dad!" she gasped. "He's not—they didn't—"

"He isn't here," said the officer. "Neither is Savage. There seems to have been a knock-down fight in the shack. They must have been overpowered and taken away."

Albert Jones gathered enough control to say, "Officer, I want you to copy down a description of the men while it is fresh in my mind."

Jones proceeded to describe Nickolas Prinz and such of the remaining assailants as he had seen. Annice, with hands knotted tightly, added some points of description which Jones had overlooked.

"You say these strangers just rushed in and seized Savage and Stevens," remarked the officer. "You have no idea why?"

Jones said firmly, "Not the slightest idea."

"All right, we'll do all we can." The police officer looked at Annice. "Do you think you'll need a doctor, miss?"

She composed herself and shook her head. "No," she said. "No, I'll bear up."

Because Albert Jones was the more agitated of the two of them, Annice, herself, drove the car away from the scene. She headed toward New York.

"I think we should tell Doc Savage's friends, so they can help us," she said. "That is what I'm going to do."

As soon as the police were out of sight, Jones began recovering.

"You shouldn't have told them Secret Stevens was your father," he said.

"Why not?" Annice demanded. "He is. Why lie about it?"

"Well, the police are likely to start questions and find out about the machine," said Jones. "I wouldn't want them to do that."

Annice frowned. "They would be a lot more suspicious if they found out I was Secret Stevens' daughter when I had said I wasn't. After all, people around Englewood know Stevens is my father."

"Not many of them, I'll bet. You have been away in schools practically all your life." He eyed her disapprovingly. "You hardly knew your father by sight when you arrived a month ago, as I recall it."

Annice was hurt by this statement. She made no answer, but drove in angry silence to the long, multiple-approach to George Washington Bridge. Jones paid the toll and they rolled out on the bridge.

"Mr. Jones," she said.

"Yes?"

"Why were you so nervous around the police?"

The little-girl-faced Jones started, then avoided her inspection. "I was nervous, wasn't I?" he admitted. "I am awfully ashamed of it."

"You acted," Annice said, "like a man with a guilty conscience. You almost acted as if this affair might not be what you have led me to believe it is."

"I have always been nervous around policemen," Jones said uncomfortably. "It is nothing more than that."

He could not keep it from sounding like a lie.

Renny Renwick, the big-fisted engineer who was one of the Doc Savage associates, admitted Annice and Albert Jones into the headquarters reception room. Renny frowned at Jones and said, "I've given the subject a lot of thought, and I don't think I like you or your invention, Jones."

"Please!" Jones gasped. "Are your friends here? Call them! Something awful has happened."

Renny eyed him, said, "Holy cow!" and called Monk, Ham, Johnny and Long Tom out of the library.

Albert Jones confronted them.

"Don't interrupt me," he said. "I seized Mr. Savage and put him in my machine, where an inherited memory was released in his mind. The memory was of Doc Savage's father having swindled his partner, Secret Stevens, out of the gold hoard in the place known as the Valley of the Vanished in Central America. Mr. Savage insisted on making restitution to Secret Stevens. We located Stevens in Englewood, New Jersey. While we were talking to him, a gang of unknown men set upon us and seized Mr. Savage and Mr. Stevens. We reported to the police, but the gang escaped with their prisoners. We came to tell you."

"Blazes!" said the homely Monk.

There came the sound of a buzzer, softly muted. Ham said, "The door," and went away.

Ham came back from the door looking astonished.

"A man who says his name is Doyle Space," Ham announced. "He wants to talk to us. Says he knows what happened to Doc and Stevens."

Chapter X
THE GUIDE

Space stood in the center of the reception room and looked at them with his hard-brown features. He was impressed by

47

the office, but not upset. The big windows were open and the cool fall wind whipped across the sills, fluttering papers under paperweights on the big inlaid desk.

"I'm responsible for this," he said flatly, "in a way."

"You make an interesting start," Ham Brooks told him. "Go ahead."

Ham Brooks was very dapper in an afternoon coat and the correct trousers. His pet, the chimpanzee named Chemistry, was crouching in one corner of the reception room. In the other corner, in no pleasant mood, was a pig. The pig had extremely long legs and ears that were like Dumbo's, fit for flying. He was Habeas Corpus, and he was Monk's pet. Ham Brooks claimed not to care for him at all. Monk had owned Habeas Corpus for a long time and he had managed to develop some remarkable qualities in the hog.

Space sucked in a deep breath. He was nervous. He let a little of it show, but not all of it. It was natural for a man to be nervous when he confronted men like these, and Space wanted to be natural.

He said, "Jones, here, hired me. He hired me to help him trap Renny Renwick, then Doc Savage, and put them in the memory-awakening machine." He turned to Jones. "That right, Jones?"

Jones admitted it was right. He seemed confused.

"I have a friend—*had* a friend," Space continued, correcting himself.

He looked from one of them to another.

"The friend's name was Prinz—Nickolas Prinz," he said. "I told him about Mr. Jones' invention."

Jones blanched. He yelled, "I told you not to breathe a word to anyone!"

Space shrugged. "I'm not perfect. The Spaces have always made mistakes. I made one of the biggest, I guess."

Suddenly the pig, Habeas Corpus, made for the chimp named Chemistry. It was done suddenly, for the shote was as fast as a fox on his feet. He hit the startled but belligerent Chemistry, bowled him over, took a couple of flying bites, and rushed onto a chair, where he followed the traditional African warthog method of reversing himself hurriedly, and going under the chair stern-first. Chemistry squalled twice and landed on top of a desk, where he crouched, glaring.

Space shrugged.

"This guy Prinz did it like that," he said. "He grabbed Doc Savage and Secret Stevens. He telephoned me, not five minuts ago, and asked me to throw in with him. Said he had

48

forced Doc Savage to show him the location of the Valley of the Vanished by threatening to kill old Stevens."

Annice gasped and clamped her hands to her cheeks. "Oh, poor dad!" she cried.

Long Tom Roberts looked at her sharply. "Is your name Stevens?"

"Annice Rogers Stevens," she said.

It occurred to no one, apparently, to question her about her previous use of the name Rogers alone. The matter of what had happened to Doc Savage and Stevens was of more importance at the moment.

Monk said, "Space—you say your name is Space? What is this friend of yours going to do with Doc and Stevens?"

"Take them to Central America to this Valley of the Vanished," Space said. "And then kill them. He'll keep them alive until he finds the place, of course, so that they can show him where it is. Then he will kill them."

Monk said, "Then the thing to do is light out on their trail."

The Hidalgo Trading Co. was a homely blimp of a warehouse on the Hudson River water front, not far from the spot where the Normandie had capsized. The warehouse had no connection with Hidalgo, the Central American republic, other than that it had occurred to someone as a name for the warehouse. There was actually no Hildalgo Trading Co., except in name.

Contents of the warehouse were a little startling unless one knew what to suspect. The submarine, for instance, was a surprising craft; it would have astonished a submarine expert, for it was an experimental craft only. Some of the boats in the place were experimental and others weren't. It was the same with the planes.

Monk Mayfair stowed his pet pig, Habeas Corpus, in the cabin of the largest plane in the place, a huge amphibian. He told Ham, "You keep that what-is-it of yours away from my hog."

"Away from your hog!" Ham was indignant. "You got a crust! Your hog started it."

"Don't try to argue with me!" Monk yelled indignantly.

The two climbed into the plane, to all appearances about to come to blows.

Annice looked anxious and Long Tom chuckled. "You'll have to get used to that," he told her. "They even fight in their sleep."

49

Albert Jones was looking uncomfortable. "You aren't planning on leaving me behind, are you?" he demanded.

"Holy cow!" Renny said. "You don't want to go along, do you?"

Space put in, "Of course he does. We all want to go along and help."

"Why?" Renny demanded.

Space looked at them grimly. "We got you in this."

Renny glanced at Monk and Long Tom and the others. They seemed undecided. "We'd better talk this over," Renny said. They drew aside, and discussed the matter. Monk was heartily in favor of letting Space, Jones and Annice—particularly Annice—come along. Ham said, "Sure, a pretty girl always sucks you in!"

Monk told him, "You better hope that music you play with your mouth qualifies you for playing a harp in the next world, you overdressed shyster. Because one of these days I'm gonna close up business on you."

It was Johnny Littlejohn, using small words, who made the suggestion that appealed to them.

"Take them along, so we can keep an eye on them," Johnny advised. "After all there is something faintly fishy about this. The girl first told Doc her name was Annice Rogers. She didn't say anything about being related to this Secret Stevens. There may be something to this we don't see."

So it was agreed.

They loaded equipment into the big plane—their fighting regalia. The array of gadgets they took along was remarkable, but loading them rapidly was no trick. The stuff was in light metal cases, marked for identification. It was always kept ready for trips such as this.

They began climbing in the plane.

Monk caught Ham's arm and held him back.

"We'll take another plane," Monk said. "That way, if something happens to this ship we'll have another one."

Renny, Long Tom and Johnny were surprised. But they decided it was a good idea. Monk and Ham, with their pets, stood in the big hangar and watched the great doors open. Soon they saw the plane move out of the hangar with motors muttering, and the massive doors closed. They listened as the big ship rushed away across the river.

"Now, master mind," Ham demanded, "what was the idea?"

"I had a brainstorm," Monk confessed.

"That's a good word for your ideas. What was it?"

"It struck me that in the excitement over Doc being grabbed we sort of overlooked Albert Jones' machine," Monk explained.

"What do you propose to do?"

"There's a landing field close to Jones' house. We'll take the other big ship, drop down there, pick up Jones' invention and take it along."

"That's robbery. Jones might not like it."

"The way he grabbed Renny and Doc was kidnaping," Monk said, "in case he wants to get playful about it."

Ham Brooks heartily approved of Monk's idea about picking up the Jones invention but he did not say so. He hated to agree with Monk about anything.

They climbed in the other ship, which was slightly smaller and faster than the one the others had taken. The tanks were kept full, so there was no delay about that. Monk worked with the complicated instrument panel, got the motors—there were two motors—kicking over. He punched a button, causing the radio-controlled hangar doors to open.

"You notice something?" Ham asked.

"Huh?"

"Jones and that girl—they didn't seem surprised by this warehouse place," Ham said. "They never even asked what it was. Sort of acted as if they already knew."

"Not many people know what this is," Monk said, which was as near as he wanted to come to agreeing with Ham.

They got out on the river and into the air.

Not quite an hour later they stood in Albert Jones' attic laboratory and eyed the apparatus which the place held. "One is as big as a box car," Monk complained, "and the other is the size of a coffin, which is big enough. I didn't think they were so bulky."

Ham said, "It is the small one Jones used. Renny told me about it while Doc was missing."

"Then we'll take the small one."

Monk rubbed his jaw. "You know something? I think I'll take a few minutes off and peek at the insides of one of these. I'd like to know how such a thing works."

The homely chemist stood back and contemplated the two devices thoughtfully.

"I'll try the big one," he decided. "It looks as if it would be easier to figure out."

51

He moved around the huge dark box, peering into the inspection ports. What he saw was complicated, but not very satisfactory. He could not get the least idea of how the gadget might work.

"Come on," Ham said impatiently. "You couldn't figure that thing out."

Monk was indignant. Since he was rated one of the world's leading industrial chemists, he figured that he had reason to be. "Listen, I have been through the best colleges in the world," he growled.

"Sure, and they all gave you black sheepskins," Ham said. "Come on."

"Keep your socks pulled up," Monk said. "I'm going to pry into the big one. It won't take a minute."

He found what seemed to be a hatch, which was sealed with wax, and bore a label that said, Do Not Open. Monk broke the seal and pried open the hatch.

Fire, violence, noise, came out of the box. The box itself flew to pieces. Since it was a very large box, one that would have held several pianos, this was quite a phenomenon.

Monk found himself getting, or trying to get, off the floor on the other side of the room. "What happened?" he gasped.

"The thing blew up," Ham said dryly. He beckoned. "Come over here and I'll show you something."

Monk, much battered and confused, followed Ham to the smaller device. Ham indicated a card which was fastened conspicuously to the end of the oversized coffin of an affair. It read:

WARNING

ANY ATTEMPT TO OPEN THIS DEVICE OR THE OTHER ONE WILL ONLY RESULT IN THE COMPLETE DESTRUCTION OF THE MECHANISM. FOR THE PROTECTION OF THE SECRET, I HAVE WIRED THE DEVICE SO IT WILL DESTROY ITSELF WHEN TAMPERED WITH.

ALBERT JONES.

It suddenly occurred to Monk that Ham had backed across the room just before the other gadget exploded. "You knew what was gonna happen to me!" Monk bellowed.

Ham laughed heartily.

As a matter of fact he had not seen the warning card until after the explosion. But it pleased him to have Monk think otherwise.

Monk shouted suddenly, whirled and rushed out of the room and down the stairs. Alarmed, Ham ran to the window.

Then he saw what had caused Monk's excitement. A passing laundry truck which they could hire to haul the smaller machine to their plane.

Ham turned back and examined the machine doubtfully. The thing was equipped with handles for carrying, indicating it was intended to be movable. But he hoped it would not explode, particularly after they got it in the plane.

He decided not to show that he was nervous. It would please Monk to think he was scared.

The machine was heavy. Monk and Ham and the laundry driver were perspiring by the time they had the thing loaded in the plane. Monk, with great contrariness, insisted on lashing the device near the front of the plane cabin. Where, Ham thought, it will blow us out through the front end if it explodes.

"That's the center of gravity and the place for it," Monk told him.

"I'll handle the radio," Ham said maliciously. "You fly."

The radio was in the far rear of the cabin, the safest spot.

Leaving a Monk who was not very happy about the whole thing, Ham took over the radio apparatus. There were two sets of equipment in the ship: the conventional one for direction-finding in the pilot's cockpit, and a very powerful outfit for long-distance communication. Ham set the crystal-controlled transmitter to the wave length used by Doc Savage and his aides.

"Any news yet?" he asked into the transmitter mike.

Johnny Littlejohn's voice said, "An evanescent semeiotic—"

"You don't need to code it," Ham said angrily.

"A slight trace of them," Johnny told him, reverting to small words. "A navy patrol plane out to sea chased a mysterious commercial plane which was flying southward. The commercial plane got away in some clouds. We think it is the plane this Prinz is using to carry Doc and Stevens to Central America."

"We had better find a plane," Ham said, "so we can be sure this Space isn't lying to us."

They flew southward. The sea was a hard, cool blue, the clouds like steel shavings in the sky. There was a little wind, enough to give them a westerly set. Ham used binoculars on the sea periodically, looking for anything that might be of interest. A naval patrol bomber dropped down toward them

53

on two different occasions, but they identified themselves by radio.

Then Johnny Littlejohn was on the distance transmitter.

"We seem to be following two planes," Johnny said. "At least, we have spotted two strange ships in radio communication with each other. They're using voice. Space says one voice belongs to this man Prinz, who grabbed Doc."

"Good," Ham said.

He went forward to tell the news to Monk, giving the boxlike machine a wide berth.

Johnny on the distance radio: "Ham . . . Ham Brooks."

"Yes."

"It's the plane that has Doc, all right. And there are two ships."

"How do you know?"

"They landed at a little airport near Titusville, Florida. They got gasoline. They refused to pay for it, and shot and wounded two people at the airport in the quarrel that followed. Then they took off."

"Any chance of Florida police or coast-guard planes overhauling them?"

"Afraid not. There a heck of a lot of poor visibility over lower Florida. Cold front just moved in."

"They seem to be heading for Hidalgo."

"Yes, they do," Johnny agreed grimly.

It was night for a long time, and then the morning sun came up with the brazen buxomness of the tropics, hot and gay. Ham Brooks had taken over the plane controls, and now he squinted his eyes in the glare. He looked around and found a small wrench, which he pitched at Monk, who was calmly asleep beside the box containing Albert Jones' machine. Monk awakened with the violence of a cat that had had its tail stepped on. Sheepishly, he got himself organized and came forward.

"How did you sleep?" Ham asked.

"Like a top," Monk assured him. "Took most of the night to stop turning and twisting. Where are we?"

"Hidalgo."

Monk was startled. He jumped to a window. "Oh," he said. "Just over the foothills."

Ham said, "Take over, will you. I want to go back and talk to the others. Too bad the radio transmitter in this plane isn't hooked up with the cockpit controls."

Monk got behind the wheel, dug out a bar of chocolate and a thermos of coffee, and began flying and eating. He looked around for familiar landmarks but saw none. The terrain below was startlingly rugged. He thought: Some day, a hundred years from now, when tourists discover this country, they will realize it is more picturesque than Switzerland.

Back at the radio, Ham said, "Johnny, you on deck this early?"

Johnny was excited.

He gave Ham a wave length in kilocycles.

"Tune in on that band," he said. "And listen! Listen to the guy with the frog voice!"

"Who'll it be?"

"Prinz."

Ham fished with the tuning dial. There was not a great deal of station interference here in the tropics, but the static was like eggs frying. Ham located the voice which he decided Johnny meant.

"Hello, Sam," it was saying. "Hello, Sam. Come in, Sam. We have located this Valley of the Vanished. I want to give you its location. Come in, Sam."

Exactly this same statement was made three times.

Then: "All right, Sam, I see your plane. Take a straight north turn and drop down carefully. We have ground signals ready." A moment later the voice said, "Go off the air, Sam. We don't want the world picking this up."

Ham switched the receiver back to Johnny's frequency.

"They're down in the Valley!" Ham exploded.

"Yes," Johnny said.

"What are you going to do?"

"Head for the Valley as fast as possible. Maybe we can knock them out, or at least get there in time to save Doc and Stevens."

Chapter XI
THE XOCHI

The two planes fought the mountains for hours.

The mountains were an incredible assortment, peculiar to Hidalgo. They had everything but height, although they were not by any means anthills. The canyons were knife slashes, and the peaks needled fangs of stone. There was dense, impenetrable jungle, and great areas of white rock blistering in the tropical heat.

The air currents were the worst. You never knew what to expect. You would be cruising across a ridge and suddenly find yourself in what could be the outpouring of a giant funnel and blown thousands of feet in the air. Or it might be the reverse, a down draft that had the awful suction of a vacuum. One of these last nearly did for Monk and Ham. Caught in the frightening downward rush of air into a canyon, Monk fought the throttles and control wheel madly. He could not get the ship climbing up again until it had hit a treetop with a roaring of loosely waving leaves.

Ham yelled, "What're you trying to do, you idiot!"

"You want to fly this thing?" Monk demanded. He had lost several shades of color.

Ham distinctly did not want to fly the ship. He fell to watching the mountains, picking out landmarks. The peaks were like stone needles and that was familiar.

Then, suddenly, there was a narrow-walled gash that seemed to sink a limitless depth into the mountain. It was of bare stone, too steep and too flintlike in hardness to support the green stain of jungle growth.

Monk yelled, "I remember that. You follow it."

Ham nodded. He was relieved. He had been half afraid that they would not be able to retrack their way to the Valley of the Vanished just from memory.

The going was smoother now, and Ham was somewhat relieved. He thought: We've done a lot of needless worrying about some aviator flying over these mountains and stumbling onto the Valley. No danger of that. Self-respecting eagles would steer shy of this place.

Johnny's plane was only a short distance ahead. Down into the monster slash of a chasm, both planes sank. Ham rolled down a cabin window, fascinated. The motor thunder was tossed from the canyon walls to his ears in jumbled waves of sound. There was a small river below. Air, cooled by the water and thus contracting and forming a down current, seemed to suck them into the cooling depths.

Later, the progress of the craft along the chasm was a procession of leaps and drops and side-whippings, as though they were riding an amusement-park jackrabbit, or a roller coaster. Ham remembered that, too. He stared ahead, holding his breath.

"The Valley!" he gasped.

A widening in the strangely devilish chasm formed the home of the lost clan of Maya, a widening that was roughly the shape of an egg, with a sloping floor that was a little too rough for the landing of a plane.

Ham's eyes went automatically to the most fascinating and spectacular object in the Valley—the pyramid. The pyramid of gold. Not actually solid gold, of course, but a stone that was incredibly rich ore.

It was there, its sides as smooth as glass from top to bottom, except only in the front where there was a flight of steps, not more than twenty feet high. Like a straight ribbon the steps rose, from base to the flat top of the pyramid, where stood the delicate temple, its flat stone roof supported by square, wondrously carved pillars. Through the open sides of the temple, Ham got a glimpse of the remarkable idol of Quetzalcoatl, who came down from the heavens and lived among the Toltes, like Christ in the Bible, then disappeared over the sea. Quetzalcoatl, who looked strangely like a white man. Quetzalcoatl, whose heart became the morning star.

Monk called sharply, "You see their planes anywhere?"

Ham frowned, moved from one side of the plane cabin to the other. There was no evidence of the other two ships.

"They had time to hide them, I guess," he said.

Monk scowled. "I don't like this. I don't think they could have hidden two big planes this quick."

"I'll find out what Johnny wants to do," Ham said.

Johnny, over the radio, was puzzled by the absence of the two planes they had been following. Renny and Long Tom and he, Johnny explained, had been ready for an immediate fight to help Doc.

"We'll land," he decided.

In circling, they swept lower over the pyramid. More of its detail was visible and they could see the water, the sizable volume of water that poured steadily down the pyramid side, coursing in a deep trough inlaid near the steps. The water came from the pyramid top by an artesian system and, flowing away from the pyramid, it fed a long, narrow lake. This body of water in turn emptied into the river that ran down the chasm which they had followed. The Valley, itself, was the source of the river, which was the River *Metale*, meaning the mortar stone used in grinding meal by the Mayans. The source, the center, the fountainhead of all that was everlasting, in the eyes of ancient Maya.

"The lake," Monk said, calling his shot.

They had landed on the lake before; they knew it could be done.

Monk set the wing flaps, did a breath-taking, nose-high forward slip, and seemed to land on the water like a duck. There was a considerable splash, and he nearly overran the narrow confines of the lake. To avoid the strong current flowing into the river at the far end, he beached the nose of the craft.

The other plane, heavier laden, made a less tumultuous landing. Long Tom, who was at the controls, beached it near the first plane.

Everyone scrambled out.

"You see any sign of those planes we are supposed to be following?" Renny demanded anxiously.

"No," Monk said.

"Holy cow!" Renny rumbled. "I wonder what went wrong."

"Where are all the natives?" Johnny demanded.

"They'll stick under cover until they see who we are," Monk told him.

The air in the valley was completely pleasant, cool without being cold, crisp without being too dry. It came to them laden with the pleasant odors of flowering plants, wonderfully fragrant.

Space burst out of the plane, leaping down to the beach sand that was as fine and white as sugar.

He stared at the pyramid, its glittering yellow wonder clearly visible over the flowering shrubs which carpeted the valley.

"That gold?" he demanded. He was very excited.

"Not pure," Monk said dryly. "We had a piece of it assayed once, and it ran about fifty thousand dollars to the ton in free gold."

Ham said, "That was before the price of gold went up, of course."

Space ogled them unbelievingly. "Then it *is* gold!"

"Yes."

"Why haven't you taken it?" Space demanded.

Monk scowled at him. "Brother, let me put you straight right now. That gold stays here. First, that's the way Doc wants it. Second, I don't think anybody could ever get that gold out of here if the Mayans didn't want them to. You see, this place is sacred to Maya, the most sacred thing they have, and there are Mayan descendants living all over Central America."

Space eyed him.

"Be tough, eh?"

"Be impossible," Monk said.

Space seemed to shrug the whole thing off. "It's cooler than° I thought," he said.

He started to go through the motions of buttoning his coat. And, suddenly, there was a revolver in his hand.

He let them look at the muzzle of the gun long enough to fully comprehend what it was.

"You can jump around all you want to," he said. "But you'll be dead."

He allowed them to think about that for a while.

He said, "I'm getting in the plane. Don't move, I used to be top man on a pistol team, in case you're wondering about that."

He backed to the larger plane. He was very careful, keeping them menaced with his weapon. They could see him finally with a receiver clamped over his ears.

"He's using the radio," Monk gritted his teeth. "Calling those friends of his!"

Johnny emitted a howl of mental anguish. "We've been gimmicked!"

"Sure we have," Monk agreed. "Those two planes didn't find the Valley. They just used their radios to make us think they had. Then we rushed here to save Doc, as we thought— and showed Space where the Valley was!"

Albert Jones, surprisingly bitter, said, "A fine bunch of protectors you turned out to be."

"You are the cutie who started this," Monk reminded him.

Ham glared at Space and said, "The blasted, treacherous, *xochi!*"

"What's an *xochi?*" Annice asked.

"A small, greenish black snake which is very poisonous in these parts," Ham told her. "It fits this Space."

"All but the color," Monk growled. "Nothing green about that guy. Did he sell us a basket of cookies!"

Space stepped out of the plane, still menacing them with his gun. Apparently he did not like the desperate expressions on their faces, because suddenly he leveled his gun at Long Tom Roberts and fired. Long Tom looked foolishly at his coat, at a missing button. Space had done a rather spectacular thing in shooting off the button.

"I told you how I could shoot," Space said. "Now, shove this plane off the beach." He bounded to the sandy shore. "Shove both planes off the beach."

Alarmed, Monk yelled, "Shove them off?"

"Yes. Quick!"

There was a strong current at this end of the lake; it would pull the ships away immediately and send them into the boiling little river and down into the canyon. They would be smashed. Ruined.

Ham said, "Space, we may need these to get out of here!"

"You won't be going out," Space said. "Shove them off!"

Suddenly, none of them were under any delusions. Space was going to shoot them down. He probably had planned to do it within the next two or three minutes, as soon as the planes were headed for destruction.

Monk, in the Mayan tongue, said, "Somebody will get shot, but we've got to gang him."

Ham, in a tight voice, said, "Say when."

Monk's homely face became composed, the mouth open a little, the eyes narrowed. Monk had learned ventriloquism, he was suddenly remembering. He had learned it as a gag, in order to make his pig seem to talk. Originally, it had been a clever gag to get the attention of pretty girls.

"Let me get my hog off the plane," he said. "Let me call him."

Space said, "Go ahead."

There was a quality in his smooth, hard-brown voice that said he was going to start shooting them in a moment.

Monk called, "Habeas!"

The pig promptly appeared in the plane door.

The pig said, seemingly, "You want me to tackle this guy."

The effect was far more astounding than seemed possible. The tension, probably, made it so. Space seemed to rise an inch off the beach and ogled the hog.

Ham and Long Tom went down, scooped up handfuls of sand. Johnny jumped at Space, which took courage. Space upped his gun and shot Johnny twice, one bullet in the arm, the other against the bullet-proof vest which Johnny wore. Ham and Long Tom threw their sand, got some of it in Space's eyes. The man tried to back-pedal.

Monk jumped. He got Space's gun arm, pulled, wrenched,

60

and nearly tore the man's arm off getting the revolver. Space screamed in pain and, still screaming, whirled and scrambled onto the plane.

Long Tom followed Space onto the plane. Space kicked madly at him. They got on a wing, both of them, slugging. They worked out toward the tip of the wing, blindly, with no purpose except to annihilate each other.

The weight of the two fighting men was enough to tip the plane, the lighter ship, and the current caught it suddenly, swinging it loose of the sand. It drifted quickly and collided with the other ship, jarring that one loose from the beach.

Desperately, Long Tom bellowed, "Don't let the planes drift out!"

The others saw the danger to the ships. They laid hold of the hulls, fought to hold the floats against the current. But the water broke away deeply from a ledge close inshore and there was little purchase for feet. The strong current dragged the planes out into the stream.

They were carried toward the narrow canyon into which the little river roared.

Monk yelled, "Jump, Long Tom! Jump!"

Long Tom did not jump. He was knocked off the plane wing by Space, who might be a devil, but who was also a fighting man. He landed in the ice-cold river with a splash.

They could see that he was stunned.

Monk, Ham, the others, raced madly down the bank. Monk said, "Join hands. That current is fast. We've got to get him."

The pig, Habeas Corpus, took a flying leap and landed in the water, then made the shore. The chimp, Chemistry, also gained the beach, hardly wetting himself.

Monk got out into the current. The water hit him like a solid, icy monster. The stone bottom was glass slick. He lost his footing, but kept hold of Renny's hand, and Renny in turn held to Ham, who gripped Albert Jones, who was anchored finally by Annice.

They got Long Tom and hauled him out. He was unconscious. When they lowered him on the beach, water ran from his mouth and nostrils.

The planes were gyrating in the current like two big, crazy leaves. Their floats hit boulders with sounds of grinding agony.

Space crawled out to a wing end and watched for a chance, then sprang into space. A moment later he scrambled out on the bank—on the opposite side of the narrow river.

61

"Where's his gun?" Monk gritted. Monk was not in sympathy with a long-established policy of Doc Savage that they should never take a human life. Annice came running with the gun which Monk had taken from Space, but had dropped. Monk grabbed it from her hand.

But Space was out of sight among boulders.

Monk groaned, watched the boulders with glaring ferocity.

The others tried vainly to save the planes. It was like trying to stop skyscrapers from toppling. The furious current hurled the ships along. Their wings bounced against stone boulders, against the rising sides of the canyon and finally began to crack up. It was a sound like tin cans being trampled.

Renny forlornly rumbled, "They won't go all the way down the canyon."

That was true. Both planes were soon lodged on the stones which fanged the river bed. But they were jammed there uselessly, the cabin of one submerged, the other out of the water, but hopelessly ruined.

They stared at the wreckage, feeling queer.

"We can rig ropes across the stream and salvage some of the equipment," Ham said grimly.

Annice went back and worked over Long Tom. After a while, Long Tom sat up. He said, "I helped a devil of a lot."

"You were very brave," Annice told him. She looked at Johnny. "You are shot, aren't you?"

Renny, startled, looking down at Johnny's fingertips and the blood leaking from them and agreed with her that he seemed to be. Ham cut open his sleeve between shoulder and elbow. The wound was ugly to look at, but probably not serious, unless there was infection.

Monk was still watching the boulders across the stream for Space, but vainly.

Renny boomed, "I can't understand where the natives are."

Monk said, "Why not call them."

Renny nodded. "Sure." Then he put back his head and yelled out in Mayan. His voice was tremendous; parrots flew out of trees at the far end of the valley. Echoes gobbled back and forth like a lion roaring, getting smaller and smaller.

Ham and Monk exchanged glances and Ham said, "I'm going to scout around and see where everybody is."

The others agreed. Ham moved away, walking cautiously and listening. He was puzzled—in fact, baffled. The lost tribe of Maya were their friends, the friends of Doc Savage.

For a long time the Mayans had been mining gold—the mining was a very simple operation, not much more than chipping the incredibly rich ore out of the vein—and taking it out of the valley, through the mountains by pack train. Eventually, and by devious route, the gold would arrive in the national bank at Blanco Grande, the capital city of Hidalgo, where it was placed to Doc Savage's credit.

In order to get a shipment of the gold out in an emergency, Doc Savage had arranged a radio receiver, current for which was supplied by a water-operated generator, here in the valley. At a certain hour on each seventh day, someone here listened in, and if Doc needed money he simply broadcast a few agreed-upon words in Mayan—and the money was on its way out of the Valley shortly.

In return, these men of ancient Maya—their customs and life differed hardly at all from the early days—demanded nothing but friendship from Doc Savage. They owed, they had always maintained, a debt of gratitude to the man of bronze. Doc had done them a great favor on two different occasions, when he had saved them from annihilation at the hands of greedy raiders.*

Monk and Renny and the others were thinking of this as they watched the spot in the luxurious jungle where Ham had disappeared.

The Mayans here in the valley were friendly. That was sure.

Yet there was nothing of friends-encountered in Ham's manner when he suddenly popped into view. He was running. His manner was wild.

"Beat it!" he gasped. "Quick! Get somewhere where we can defend ourselves!"

Monk blurted, "What on earth—"

"Run!" Ham bellowed.

The utter imperativeness in his voice put them all in motion. Johnny scrambled up, kept pace with them in spite of the bullet wound in his arm.

It was dark in the jungle. Dark, and suddenly there were figures around them. Silent, grim, fierce figures. A flood of them, pouring suddenly out of the gloom, seizing them, overpowering them.

Incredibly enough, Monk and the others realized, these

---

*The reference is to the perilous affairs of Doc's two previous visits to the Valley—first, his initial trip which occurred in "The Man of Bronze," and the second in "The Golden Peril."

silently grim figures were Mayans. They were Mayans of the ancient strain, the fellows who spoke Nahuatl, the basic tongue; they were men who had their *Shamans*, their *Chaacs* and *Mens*, the high priests whose word was their every law.

They fought a little. They might as well have saved their muscles and kept the skin on their knuckles.

"Ham!" Monk gasped. "You notice how much blue paint they're wearing."

Ham said, "Blue is the sacrificial color."

Monk, Renny—all of them who knew what the blue paint meant—lost color. It was horrifying, unbelievable. What they felt showed on their faces.

Annice Stevens stared at them."What does the blue mean?"

Ham shook his head. He didn't want to tell her that it meant death. Death, he was convinced, for themselves.

Chapter XII
BLUE NOSE

Doc Savage knew the plane was over Hidalgo, and close to the legendary Valley. He had suspected the ship was heading for the spot. Lately, the air had become incredibly rough, and several times the plane had been tossed up on its side, or over on its nose, so that he had glimpsed the nearby mountains. Mountains like those were found nowhere except in the neighborhood of the Valley of the Vanished, so that point was settled.

The bronze man had been kept handcuffed to the metal struts which formed the framework of the plane cabin. They had stripped him down to trousers, and they had ripped the pockets out of his trousers and cut the legs off above the knees so that he would not have enough cloth to do anything for which he might use cloth.

Secret Stevens was manacled nearby. They had stripped the old man also. Stevens, who was well past sixty at least, was a remarkably preserved old fellow, the age that showed in his face not being at all in evidence in the rounded velvet of his sinew-wrapped body.

Mad convulsions of the plane were making Stevens a little airsick.

"I don't think they're gonna make it," Stevens said.

Almost immediately, two men in the forward cabin screamed. Screeched out in complete horror. And the plane gave a leaping lunge.

They got a glimpse of a rock pinnacle, like a hungry gray-black monster, snapping at them, barely missing the plane.

Stevens chuckled grimly. "That's the second bad scare they've had. Third time, we may hit."

Prinz must have thought so too.

Prinz came back to them. He had handcuff keys, and the look of a man who had found a poisonous snake in his pocket. "I'll make a deal with you," he said.

Stevens said, "Deal you into hell, that's what we'll do."

"Pilot us into the Valley," Prinz offered, "and we'll turn you loose."

"Hah, hah, hah," Stevens said. "I would trust you as far as I could push one of these mountains. Exactly."

Doc Savage was thoughtful. He knew these mountains, the horrendous air currents. He had watched their pilot, and the man was not too skillful. He was convinced the flier could not get them through intact.

"Give us parachutes," Doc said suddenly. "Stevens and myself, parachutes."

Prinz scowled. "You can trust me."

Stevens snarled something that sounded like mirth without being funny.

"Parachutes," Doc said. "And a gun containing two cartridges."

Prinz stared. "Gun? Two cartridges?"

Doc said, "Insurance. We cannot shoot all of you with two cartridges. But we can guarantee our escape."

Prinz looked at him and cursed him. "What kind of a fool do you figure I am?" he snarled. He went away.

Old Stevens looked at Doc and said, "I don't like parachutes. I never used one, but I don't like them."

Doc said, "You might not like death without benefit of a coffin, either."

Later, but not much later, the plane suddenly fell off on a wing, upended and went streaking down. They could hear the pilot cursing in horror. Later, he got the ship level. But they were far down in the black maw of the canyon, with the angry white water almost under them. Death was very close.

Prinz came back to Doc again. He looked sick.

He had two parachutes and a revolver.

"All right," he said.

Doc Savage took the controls and put them into the narrow canyon, far down in the depths, where the violent air currents were at least more predictable, and where flying was smoother, or at least feasible.

The second plane followed him down. The pilot of that ship was younger, and more skilled. He managed to duplicate Doc's maneuvers and got along without too much trouble.

When Doc came out into the Valley, he turned his head to watch his passengers, studying their reaction to the pyramid of gold ore so rich that it looked like solid gold. What he saw was a little frightening.

They pounded the glass out of the plane windows in their eagerness to get a better view of the pyramid. They seemed mesmerized by it.

Doc said, "Jump, Stevens!"

"But—"

"They don't plan to let us get away. Jump!"

Stevens jumped. He moved fast. Doc followed him so quickly that his jump was almost simultaneous. Before the bronze man went out, he yelled, so that Prinz would see what was happening. The other pilot seized hold of the controls.

Out of the sliding hatch in the roof of the plane, Doc rolled clear, and bellowed, "Don't open the 'chute right away!"

Stevens probably didn't hear him, because he was dragging on the D-ring as soon as he was overboard. The chute blossomed like a white orchid. Doc, more cautious, held his yank until he got down close to the ground. A little too close, it developed, for he hit hard. He picked himself up, aching in several places, and ran to Stevens.

Stevens said, "They're worse than I thought!" Meaning the parachute.

There was a gobbling noise from the plane. Bullets made animal-running noises, loud, close by them. Stevens started to flee. Doc caught him and hauled him down, saying, "It is hard to hit a stationary man from a plane. If he runs, you can see him." He held Stevens motionless until the plane was at the far end of the valley, and banking. Then they sprinted and reached the jungle.

They watched the plane coming back. The two ships were close together. Then one pulled up, in order to leave clear air for the other one to try a landing.

Stevens said, "They can't land on the water, can they? They're ground planes?"

Doc nodded. "They're going to try to land on the beach. The wind just happens to be right for it."

The beach, as white as typing paper, was not straight, but neither did it curve enough to bother a good pilot. Its narrowness gave it treachery, but the wind was parallel with it, so there would be no cross-travel at the last moment of landing.

Both planes got down safely. First Prinz' ship, then the other.

Stevens looked at Doc's revolver. "There ain't more than two cartridges in there?" he asked longingly.

Doc broke the gun and showed him there were only two.

"We're up against something," Stevens muttered. "Two bullets, and there's fifteen of them, and us as naked as jay-birds." He eyed his abbreviated trousers disgustedly.

Doc Savage took a chance, ran out into the open, and got both parachutes. The silk and the cords, might come in handy. He lost more time folding them.

Prinz and the other men had piled out of the plane. They unloaded weapons. Six men armed themselves, then ran toward the spot where Doc and Stevens were concealed.

"They don't waste time," Stevens said.

Doc Savage said, "We had better move."

They worked back through the jungle, Doc in the lead. A moment later, they were on a trail. A well-worn trail, one that had been used for centuries, and showed it.

Surprised, Stevens said, "The way you found this trail—you know the place."

Doc made no comment. He did know this part of the Valley. But there were other parts of it where he had never gone. The Mayans had forbidden areas, spots set aside for *Tecuhtli*, the power that warmed the earth, where trespassing was taboo.

They walked the path between *sakokum* trees, in jungle where everything was *yax*, which meant fresh, green and new and good enough for use in constructing altars to the Mayan deities. Only *yax* things were used by the Mayans. There were gumbo-limbo trees where tiny parakeets loitered, and flocks of *piam-piam* birds were fluttering from tree to tree and busy with their eternal squabbling. There were *zapote* nuts on the ground, looking like baseballs with a brown cover; good eating, their flesh mealy and cool with a custard flavor. Because they had not eaten for a long time, Doc picked up some of the nuts and divided them with Stevens.

"Nice place," Stevens said, looking around. "If it wasn't for the recent arrivals."

Doc came out on a rocky upthrust and stood there where he could see the two wrecked planes. He had noticed them from the air, and they had worried him. But it was obvious from the way they lay that they had been carried into the river by the current, also that they were deserted.

He had hoped to reach the ships. But it would not be wise. Prinz had dispatched an armed squad to guard the craft, and these men, running down the beach, had almost reached the planes.

Stevens was looking around, listening and frowning.

"Isn't this place inhabited?" he asked.

"Yes."

"Well, where is everybody?"

"All around us," Doc told him.

"Huh?"

"We are being rapidly surrounded," the bronze man explained.

Stevens stared at Doc, but he did not disbelieve; already he had realized that the bronze man possessed faculties, hearing and sight among others, developed to an acuteness far beyond normal.

And a moment later, silent Mayans came out of the jungle and closed in on them. Short, solid, dark men without words and without humor.

Doc Savage stared at them. He was shocked. So shocked that he made briefly the small trilling sound that was his unconscious habit in moments of stress.

Stevens—he knew enough to be frightened—asked in a low voice, "What about this? They don't act right, do they?"

Doc Savage said, "You see the blue paint they are wearing?"

"Yes."

"The sacrificial color of death," Doc Savage said quietly.

Stevens blurted, "You mean they may knock us off?"

The bronze man said quietly, "If they put blue paint on our noses and around our eyes, and red and white on our bodies—" He fell silent, watching two natives approaching, carrying reed paint-tubes containing blue and red. When he glanced at Stevens, the man's face was very white.

He came across a stony upgrade and stood there where
he could see the two wrecked planes. He had noticed them
from the air, and they had worried him. But it was obvious
from the way they lay that they had been carried into the

Chapter XIII
SILENCE LIKE A DEVIL

Doc Savage made a speech. He made it in Mayan, being as careful as he could of the accent, and putting all the confidence possible in his voice.

He began quietly.

"I am glad to see you, and particularly you who have been my friends in the past, of whom I see several." He passed his flake gold eyes over the crowd of natives. "There is Bish, and Koltec, who fought with me once. And there is Nillo, the hunter, and Chen, whose life it was my very good fortune to save. I am indeed glad to see you, my friends. But I am sorry to have to come to you again under such circumstances as these, for again there is sorrow and unpleasantness for all of us. Certain very bad men, the men who just landed in the two white-man-birds-of-noise, have come here meaning you no good. I do not need to tell you why I am here, because you know what I have done in the past to serve you. As before, I am here to help you."

He paused to look at them, a little appalled. They were hearing him, but that seemed to be all. No word, no sound.

Doc kept his metallic features expressionless.

"I can see that all is not well," he continued. "But I wish to point out to you who is your friend. And you are my friends. A danger besets us. Those men on the lake shore are well armed with the fire sticks and the eggs that are thunder and lightning, and the clouds of fog that are death. Deal with them with care, but quickly."

There was no response when he stopped.

Now very worried, but trying not to show it, Doc said, "It is my wish to see and speak with your king, the kindly and all-benevolent Chaac."

They showed no expression, no emotion. He knew then that his words had been wasted on them, and that was strange, because these people owed him their very lives. And they were not an ungrateful people, and certainly not stupid.

One of them—Chen, whose life Doc had once saved—said, "Come" in Mayan. He said something to the two with the blue and red paint, and they retired.

Flanked solidly by the natives, Doc and Stevens were taken

69

back through the jungle. There was no sound except the multitude of treading feet, the sound they made on the hard-packed earth of the *picado* trail.

In a low voice, Stevens said, "Like talking to posts, eh? But you got some results—they didn't put that paint on us. Or is that good?"

"The paint," Doc said, "would have been a sentence to death."

Stevens swallowed. "That's nice. Where they taking us?"

Doc said he was not sure.

They came out into a clearing from which they could see the lake shore. Abruptly, as if staged for their benefit, which possibly it was, there was a commotion at the lake.

There were shots, yes. Prinz's armed squad sent to guard the planes, suddenly broke and ran. Dashed madly for cover. But two of them did not reach shelter; they went down, legs folding, convulsing on the white sand until they became still.

"Poison arrows," said Stevens, who knew the jungles. "I wonder if they use *chichem* and snake venom?"

Doc said, "They use a concentrated *chalam* concoction, or formerly did. It produces temporary paralysis."

Chalam was the tree, the sap of which was thrown into water to temporarily paralyze or stun fish. Sometimes the red berries of a certain liana was used for this purpose.

"There's something devilish about the silence of these people," Stevens complained.

They swung along through the jungle in a silence that was macabre. The natives were armed with the traditional weapons of ancient Maya, short clubs of wood which were inset with vicious-looking, razor-edged flakes of stone, like teeth in the jaw of a shark. Each man had a knife with a blade of obsidian stone.

They were men with very thick shoulders, powerfully muscled. They were not handsome by Anglo-Saxon standards, but neither were they unpleasant. There was a kind of placidity about them which even their silent grimness could not expel.

For clothing, they wore a short mantle over the shoulders, a thing made of leather, woven in a network, the ends projecting at the shoulders rather like epaulets. Their girdles were woven, dark blue, the ends forming short aprons front and rear. Their leggings were affairs similar to the shin guards worn by baseball umpires, a few of them ornamented with gold, and all of them colorful. The sandals had peculiarly high backs, a kind of gladitorial quality.

They came abruptly upon the village, which had the same solidity, the same ageless stability, which had so impressed Doc when he first saw it.

Stevens turned his head from side to side like an excited owl, staring. The architecture of everything was the Mayan of two thousand years ago, the civilization that was greater, probably, than that of ancient Egypt. There were no arches, for the arch was never used in ancient Mayan construction. And everything, every exposed foot of surface, was replete with the carvings of animals, grotesque human figures and birds. It has been said that the Mayan decorators abhorred a vacuum; there was hardly an inch that was not ornamented.

The houses were stone entirely, neat and black cut from the native obsidian rock that came from the lower end of the Valley. Inset here and there were panels of gold quartz, and Stevens ogled these, gripped by the fascination which gold always holds for civilized white men.

They came at last to the building that was the largest of them all, not a great structure by modern standards, but one which lifted slightly above the others, setting upon a foundation of masonry.

They were ushered inside. Suddenly, they were released.

A figure came toward them.

"King Chaac!" Doc exclaimed.

He was as ageless as the civilization of these lost Mayans, was their king. He was tall and solid and stooped only a little with age. His hair was snowy white and his features were as nearly perfect as Doc Savage's own. It was said that he was a direct descendant of the red-headed Quetzalcoatl, the sky god of the Maya-Aztecs who was driven from Tollan crater, and whose heart became the morning star, according to legend.

He stopped. He did not come near Doc Savage.

There was misery in his face.

"I am sorry, my son," he told Doc.

Doc Savage was astounded by the sadness on the ruler's face—and puzzled. There had been several uneasy minutes when he had wondered if the old sovereign might not be dead, and a new faction in control. But that apparently was not the case. Also, it did not seem possible that a change in administration in the Valley would make any difference in the attitude of this fragment of old Maya toward Doc Savage. He had sincerely believed there was too deep a feeling between

71

himself and these people for either of them ever to turn upon the other.

Doc asked, "Would you care to explain what happened to me—the attitude of your people? It has changed. There were very good friends of mine in the group which brought us here. They would not even speak to me."

King Chaac looked at the floor. "I am sorry," he said.

"My friends," Doc said. "Monk and Ham, Renny and Johnny, Long Tom and the others—are they safe?"

"They are all here," said the strangely miserable ruler of the Mayans.

"Safe?"

Chaac, instead of answering the question directly, made a statement that seemed at a tangent—until Doc later decided that the statement went to a very definite point, and told perhaps more than anything else that had been said.

"There have been solemnities between you and I, son, and there have been solemnities between you and my people," the ruler said. "These were solemn promises, the taking of blood oaths, the assuming of deep and everlasting obligations. All of these have been kept, you to us, and us to you, and always thus it will be. Because we of Maya keep such things sacred, even to facing *Ahpuch,* the lord of death, always and forever. So it shall be between us, as it has been, to the exact word of our promises, oaths and obligations, you to us, and we to you, for otherwise it cannot be."

The strange tone of this, the solemn manner of its uttering, the complex and subtle nature of the long statement itself, held Doc in thought for a moment.

Chaac added, "Would you care to join your friends?"

"I would be delighted," Doc said quickly.

Chaac, himself, led them through a door, and down long passages, the walls of which were wondrously carved and worked in designs of quartz so rich with gold that it was as if the stones were made of steel wool, the wool of gold instead of steel, embedded in the hard obsidian mass in the quartz.

Stevens muttered, "What was that long speech he made?"

"About our friendship and obligations," Doc said. "And how each of us would keep them forever as we had in the past."

Stevens said, "I don't like the feel of the atmosphere around here. You can feel the mood of people. The last time I felt a mood like this was in Africa a long time ago, and the cannibals ate two missionaries I was guiding."

Monk Mayfair emitted a howl of delight. His pig, Habeas, squeaked his feelings. "Doc!" Monk bellowed. "You got away from them! Where are they?"

"They got into the Valley," Doc said.

"I knew that," Monk said. "That is, Chaac, here, came and asked for Renny's help. They took Renny away with them. They were going to reach our plane, get some equipment, so they would have some way of fighting Space and Prinz with modern weapons."

"So Space was working with Prinz after all," Doc Savage said thoughtfully.

"Working with him! Space is Prinz' boss!"

Doc Savage was silent.

The room was a stone one, long, but not wide, with the flat squareness characteristic of the local architecture. There was a bench with delicious fruit, very *yax*, as fresh and fine as the priests received. There was game, and fish—freshly broiled *machaca*, which was caught with the small berry resembling grapes and called the *pixbicabam*, to which the fish rose greedily.

There was clothing for them, too, fresh and fine. Elaborate and colorful after the fashions. Headdresses of flowers and feathers which fell in graceful loops. *Maxtlis*, or broad girdles, whose ends made aprons in front and behind, and short mantles made of the woven leather. There were leggings and wrist and ankle ornaments and sandals with the strange skyscraper backs.

King Chaac had withdrawn.

And, Doc realized suddenly, the door was locked. Barred with an ominous grinding noise on the outside.

Ham Brooks nodded slowly. "That's right. Locked in."

"I have noticed something strange," Doc admitted.

"Strange is no word for it," Ham said. "They won't say a word to us. All they've said—the only time anyone has spoken—was when they came and asked Renny to help them."

A small light leaped up in Doc Savage's flake gold eyes. "When they asked Renny to help, did they first make a speech about the solemnities, the promises, the oaths, the obligations, between us? And how those promises, oaths and obligations would always be, as they always have been, kept to the exact word?"

Ham was startled.

"Yes—how did you know?" he exclaimed.

73

"And did they remind Renny of our solemn pledge to help each other out of any danger at any time?" Doc continued.

"That's exactly what they said. Of course, Renny admitted the oath. And he went to help them. The rest of us stayed here. They didn't seem to want us."

Old Secret Stevens had embraced his daughter, Annice. They were tearfully delighted to find each other safe, or at least bodily intact.

Now the girl turned thoughtfully to Doc Savage and said, "The way I understand it, for a long time these people have been sending gold out to you whenever you wanted it?"

Since the matter was no longer a secret among them, Doc nodded. "That is right."

"Then they must regard you as their friend."

Doc nodded again. He had thought so.

"Then they're behaving very strangely," she said.

Long Tom and Johnny had been making the rounds of the long room, jamming their weight against doors, boosting each other up to peer out of the high windows and noting the stone grills in place in front of them.

"We're sure locked in," Long Tom said.

Monk Mayfair looked at Doc Savage thoughtfully. "I wonder where Monja is?" he remarked.

Doc Savage looked slightly embarrassed but made no comment.

"Who is Monja?" asked Annice Stevens.

Monk looked at her, grinned and made a wonderful shape with his hands. "Oh, boy!" he said. "And I don't mean to be vulgar about it, either. You may think you have seen what can be put up in the shape of a woman, but you haven't seen anything until you've seen Monja. She is King Chaac's daughter." Then, when Doc Savage had moved to the other end of the room, out of earshot, Monk added, "She fell for Doc in a big way."

Annice looked at the bronze man. There was no lack of interest in her own gaze. But there was also thoughtful calculation. She said quietly, "This Monja hasn't forgotten him—no one could forget him. No woman. So it is just possible this Monja would come nearer helping us than anyone—if we could get hold of her."

Monk gnawed a lower lip, thinking it not a bad idea.

74

Chapter XIV
BLUE FOR DEATH

The door bar—it was of stone—made a grinding sound as
it was lifted. The door, a foot thick of solid black stone as
hard as glass, swung quietly on an ingenious pivot affair.

Renny was outside, heavily guarded.

"Doc," Renny said. "I found out you were safe. I told them
you had better help me. Will you?"

Doc Savage said, "Of course," and moved out of the room.
The door was closed behind him. Guards closed in around
them, making no sound.

Renny said, "They want me to help them overpower Space
and Prinz. I agreed, of course."

"Naturally," Doc said without emotion. "Have you found
out what is wrong here?"

"I can't make it out," Renny rumbled. "They won't talk to
me. It's queer."

They left the village, which was close against the cliff and
thickly overhung by jungle so that its presence was not
noticeable from the air. The jungle over the village, Doc
noted, was a change since he had been here last. It indicated
the Mayans were becoming apprehensive about discovery by
the outside world. Not that they could be blamed. Their
previous experience had not been good.

Renny explained, "I got to one of the planes, and removed
enough equipment to make a stab at fighting Space and
Prinz." The big-fisted engineer was thoughtfully silent for a
moment. "You know what those clowns, Monk and Ham
did?"

"What?"

"They picked up Albert Jones' memory-machine, and
didn't say anything to anyone about it. It's in one of the
planes."

Doc Savage was suddenly alert. "Damaged?" he asked.

"Doesn't seem to be. The cabin of that plane is intact.
Looks all right."

They went on. It developed that Space and Prinz and their
men had been cornered against the shore of the lake. Evidently the invaders were afraid to leave their planes, on the theory

that if the worst came to the worst, they could escape by air.

"Here is what I planned," Renny explained. "About sundown, when the sun takes its heat off the mountain tops, there is a very strong wind for a short time as the cooling air above contracts and brings the air up out of the valley. That creates a breeze along the lake."

"It was good you remembered that," Doc said.

"Oh, I was interested in air currents when we were here before," Renny explained. "What I did was this: I spread containers of that anæsthetic gas of yours around the place where Space and Prinz are holed up. When the wind starts, we'll turn the anæsthetic loose, and the wind will carry it down on them before the stuff becomes ineffective by mixing with air."

"That should work," Doc said. "But you had better add some moratory oxide—it's marked that way on the bottle—to the gas. You will find the oxide in Monk's portable chemical lab."

"That will delay the stuff?"

"Make it remain effective longer in the air."

"Good."

But the word *good* was an ill omen. There was nothing good about what happened to them now. It is said by psychologists that complete surprise is always good; at least that it cannot be entirely bad. But there was nothing even remotely favorable in this.

A man came out of the jungle. He was dressed much as the other Mayans, perhaps a little more elaborately. But the tips of his fingers—all five fingers on each hand—were stained a deep, striking vermillion. The red coloring on the fingers marked him as one of the high priests of ancient Maya, which did not mean a priest in a religious sense at all, but a practitioner of the art of preserving the culture of old Maya.

He said something to their guards which Doc did not catch.

Doc and Renny were separated.

Doc was surrounded and kept where he stood.

Renny was taken away. He was escorted down to the lake shore. Openly. Anxiety sprang up in Doc Savage like a wild animal.

"What are you doing?" he said sharply. "They will kill him?"

The Mayans heard him and understood what he said. They

looked uncomfortable, all of them, and those who had known the bronze man well on his previous visits seemed intensely distressed. But they did nothing.

Renny was turned over to Space and Prinz.

They did not shoot Renny, or harm him in any way.

They did look up in the direction of Doc Savage—they had obviously been told by the Mayans where the bronze man was being held. And one of them—Space—threw out a triumphant yell.

"We've got you licked!" he bellowed. "I asked them to deliver one of your men to show they meant business. They did it. They're on my side now."

Doc Savage was stunned.

He turned slowly to look at the Mayans. Some of them, he knew, understood English. These did not meet his eyes, and none of them seemed comfortable.

The priest with the red fingers gestured, indicating Doc Savage was to be taken back to the village.

The bronze man saw Monja as he was taken into the palace. It was accidental. She was standing behind a screen, apparently so that she could get a glimpse of the bronze man without herself being seen. A clumsy Mayan warrior upset the screen.

"You are looking more beautiful than ever," Doc Savage said genuinely. Which was far more of a Casanovan speech than he usually made to women, even ones who approached the beauty of this Mayan princess who was descended from the red-headed Quetzalcoatl.

She was more exquisite than when he had last seen her, which was remarkable, because hers was the beauty about which a man thinks, and thinking of it, exaggerates, so that often the picture in the mind is dissatisfied with the reality on a second encounter.

Tall and golden, fashioned by the gods, the exquisite fineness of her beauty was like the work of some master in gold.

She had knocked Monk speechless, the sight of her, when he first saw her. And Monk was rarely knocked speechless by beauty. He always had a word, usually several.

Now she behaved strangely.

She did not speak. Tears came to her eyes while she stood there in a kind of rigid, wordless agony.

The guards hurried Doc Savage on toward the long room that was a prison cell.

77

The bronze man walked heavily, for he knew now that something terrible was going on here. Something that was fiendish and fantastic.

Monk and Ham and Johnny and Long Tom listened in blank astonishment as Doc Savage told them what had happened. Old Secret Stevens and his daughter Annice, and Albert Jones, were impressed, but less amazed, not knowing the Mayans as did Doc and his men.

"It's unbelievable!" Ham Brooks blurted.

Albert Jones snorted. "What can you expect of savages? You fellows didn't have the pull you thought you had with them, that is all. They've sold out to a slick-talking Space and that devil, Prinz."

Monk whirled on him. "Pipe down, brother! These people don't double cross their friends."

Jones snapped, "Don't bellow at me—"

Monk lunged forward. Monk was in a bad mood. "Little man," Monk said grimly, "I've been planning to get around to you. I've got a question or two."

Jones, suddenly alarmed, tried to back away, but Monk held him. "Now, now, Mr. Mayfair," Jones protested. "You are upset by things here and—"

"I was upset before I got here," Monk told him. "I think I was most upset by a little point no one has explained. The point is this: Why did Miss Annice neglect to tell us that her last name was Stevens?"

Jones said, "Why, I don't suppose she thought to say so, or she did say so and you never heard—"

Doc Savage put in quietly, grimly, "Why quibble, Jones? She never admitted knowing her father, or where he lived, after I got out of your machine and was hunting him. She knew where he lived, knew it very well, because she had lived there herself. She pretended Stevens was a stranger. Then, when he was seized by Prinz, and the fact that he was her father was jarred out of her, she seems to have failed to explain the fact, and hoped that everybody would forget about it."

Annice had not spoken. She was standing there, her face tight with discomfort.

Doc turned to her, asked, "Care to explain?".

"Don't!" warned Jones, suddenly frightened.

"Little man, I'll tie you in a knot," Monk told Jones.

Annice swung to Secret Stevens. "Dad, what shall I do?"

78

The old man shrugged. "Tell them the truth. That's the only sensible thing to do."

The girl faced Doc Savage. She had trouble untangling her tongue from her embarrassment.

"It was a snide trick," she said. "The thing that your father did to my father was no secret to us. Dad told me about it one time, but cautioned me never to mention it to anyone, and certainly not to try to do anything about it. He did not want me going to you, Mr. Savage, because he said it was not your doing and he did not want you embarrassed."

She paused and stared uncomfortably at a window.

"Albert Jones has been a friend of dad's for a long time." She flushed. "At least, I think it was a long time. As you know, dad has been an adventurer and explorer all his life, while I grew up with relatives and in school. I haven't really known him until the last month or so. But he told me about his experience with your father, Mr. Savage. And then, a few weeks later, I learned about Mr. Jones' invention to awaken inherited memories."

She colored painfully.

"We hatched a scheme," she said. "The scheme was to convince you, Mr. Savage, that the machine was genuine, and then put *you* in it. We believed that, your father being a man of as strong character as he was, the memory of what he did to my father would be one of the memories awakened in you. We figured you would make restitution to my father—make him a rich man, in other words."

Doc asked, "Where was Jones' cut to come from?"

Jones looked indignant.

"Dad loves me," Annice confessed. "So he naturally would give me a lot of the money you gave him. I was going to turn most of that over to Mr. Jones in payment for his part in my scheme."

Old Secret Stevens said, smiling slightly, "Maybe it was a kind of shady trick, but I'm not going to apologize for my daughter, because she was doing what she thought was right. She told me about it since we arrived here in the Valley. That was the first I knew of that angle."

Monk started to say something to little Albert Jones, evidently something that would have been unpleasant, but there was an interruption, a noise of the door opening.

Mayans filed in. Two in the lead carried paint tubes, blue and red. And they were followed by other natives, large strong ones, grim with purpose.

79

They took hold of Monk. The astonished Monk stood still—until they began putting blue on his nose and around his eyes, and to stripe the rest of his body with vertical red.

Then Monk bellowed, "The sacrifice colors!" and began to fight.

Ignorance would have been bliss. Had they not known what the blue facial color and the red body stripes meant, they would have been spared at least some agony. But they knew the centuries-old significance of the colors with these people. The colors of death.

Monk, scared and fighting, was more than any normal half-dozen natives could handle. He laid his large hands, hands which could open horseshoes, on a man. He lifted the fellow.

"Ma! Ma!" the native bellowed.

Monk threw him and brought down four others.

Three Mayans began a mad effort to get the door shut. Doc lunged, picked up one of the men Monk had bowled over, and sent him skidding across the floor, to land like a log of wood in the door, blocking its closing for the moment.

Doc and Ham made for the door. They reached it, meeting a surge of Mayans from outside.

One Mayan started to use a stone-fanged club on them. He was yelled at by other Mayans, and the club yanked from his clutch.

"Take them without harm," was the order.

Monk came through the door behind Doc, said, "Harm to whom?" and hit the group of natives like a torpedo.

Long Tom and Johnny, Jones and Stevens, even Annice, joined the fight.

In English, Doc said, "We will try to get to one of the planes."

More Mayans poured into the big corridor. They fought, fantastically, with the same silence which they had maintained from the beginning. No shouts, no angry orders. They seemed reluctant to even grunt in pain.

They fought into the hall. All of them were out of the prison room now. But they were unarmed, with no weapons, and Doc without any of his gadgets.

And the Mayans were not dubs at this kind of thing. They had grown up, all of these men, playing *tlaxtli*, which was the rather fiendish game of ancient Maya. It was played with a crude rubber ball, dimpled somewhat like a huge golf ball. The goals were four-foot rings about twenty feet from the ground, engraved with intertwined serpents, usually on opposite ends of a room. Like the goals in a basketball court, somewhat. The players were allowed to strike the ball only with their hips—but there was no restriction on what or how they could strike each other. It was a fiercely strenuous game, and excellent training for rough-and-tumble.*

The prisoners were slowly beaten back, crowded together like sheep against a wall. Like fighting sheep, but nevertheless sheep.

The thing that happened then, as far as Doc Savage was concerned, was utterly unexpected.

The Mayan sovereign, Chaac, and his daughter, Monja, suddenly tried to get Doc out of the fight—rescue him.

Chapter XV
LOST CLAN

They appeared unexpectedly, Monja and Chaac, through a narrow panel set in the rear wall. Chaac, with the very violence and the impressiveness of his appearance, tried to accomplish the rescue of Doc.

"Stop this!" he shouted in Mayan. "It is my order! Cease!"

The Mayan warriors did come to a pause. Chaac sprang to Doc's side, took his arm and said in a low voice, "Come. Come with us quickly. You alone—for all of you cannot escape."

He tugged Doc toward the narrow rent of a door.

It did not work. A red-fingered priest shouted, "No, it is no king's word that commands you here!"

That touched off the fight again. But the respite had given Doc time to approach the narrow door. He fought furiously, throwing himself against the sudden flood of warriors that poured upon him.

The ruler, Chaac, went down, feet carried from under him, arms pinioned in an excellent imitation of a football scrimmage.

---

*The game of *tlaxtli*, as outlined here, is true color of ancient Maya, just as the costumes and customs of the lost clan of Maya are historically accurate, to the best of the author's knowledge—and the author has engaged in scientific exploration in the Mayan country. It is considered by some authorities that *tlaxtli*, which was to the inhabitant of the old Maya what baseball is to the inhabitant of Brooklyn, was the forerunner of the modern game of basketball.

Doc, with Monja, found himself in front of the door. The bronze man hesitated for a moment, inclined to stick, to fight it out to the end. That was, he failed to realize at the moment, a vain act, because he had no chance of winning. He was stronger than any man here, probably stronger than any three men here, but it was not three he was fighting. It was at least thirty.

"Please!" Monja gasped. "Come!"

He saw the sense of what she urged. With her, he pushed back through the door. They threw their weight against the stone slab and got it closed. It was a smooth sliding arrangement, rotating on hard stone marbles. A pin affair held it shut.

"Come," Monja said tensely.

She led the bronze man through a passage, up a flight of stairs.

Already, there was pursuit behind them.

They topped the stairs and came out on a roof. There was a shout, a yelling uproar, and men rushed across the rooftops toward them.

Monja looked suddenly defeated. "They have headed us off," she said. "We cannot escape."

Doc Savage moved to the roof edge, which was overhung by a huge jungle tree, a great spreading affair which was a part of the entwining carpet of foliage that surrounded the place.

"Here," he said.

He picked up the girl, swung her to his back. "Hang on," he said. "Cling to my neck and body. Do not hamper the movement of my arms and legs."

She looked at the trees, the gaps between them and the dizzy spaces above. She understood what the bronze man intended to do, and she was scared. But she did as he directed.

Doc made a run across the rooftop, a leap outward into space. He seemed to do easily what looked to be impossible. He landed, like a tight-rope acrobat, upright on a jungle bough. The bough sprang downward under their weight and groaned, but Doc kept his balance and ran along it. He grasped another branch with his hands, went hand over hand out along it, then higher, and once again, through space.

The Mayans stopped and stared.

"*Tizoc!*" one of them said. Which was high tribute, even for the amazing strength and agility which had gotten the bronze man and Monja away from them. *Tizoc* was the legendary eagle of Maya, the eagle which was man, a watchmen for Quetzalcoatl, who came to the Toltes after the shining snake disappeared over the sea.

Doc went on swiftly, higher and higher until they were lost in the jungle greenness and the growing dusk of evening.

The bronze man stopped in a high, remote spot, in a great ceiba tree, and placed Monja in the safety of a vast forking bough.

"Your father and you sacrificed everything for me," he said quietly, making it as a statement.

She was silent a moment. "It was no sacrifice. To you we owe everything."

Doc studied her thoughtfully "To others, you must owe much, also."

She was surprised.

"You have guessed why things are as they are?" she asked.

"Only slightly," Doc admitted. "It was my suspicion, the previous times I was here, that there was another and higher clan of Lost Maya. I was never sure, and it was never mentioned, so I made no words about it."

A flock of noisy *piam-piam* birds went past, seeking roosting-places in the dusk. In the distance, to the west, under the cliffs, there were small moving lights. Very pale lights, somewhat bluish and phosphorescent in quality. They were moving, and there were men's voices with them. Searchers, no doubt.

"You were never told of the Clan of the Very Highest," Monja informed him.

"Then there is such a clan."

She nodded. "The Clan of the Very Highest live in a valley smaller, but more impenetrable than this. It adjoins this one, and is reached by secret passages from a part of this valley which is taboo."

She was silent a moment, assembling her words.

"The Very Highest," she said, "is the custodian group of the secrets of ancient Maya. There are not many of them, but they are of highest type, higher than any in this valley. As a matter of fact, the lowest member of the Clan of the Very Highest leaves the secret valley in youth, comes into this one, and becomes ruler here."

Doc was surprised.

"Your father, then, is the lowliest member of the Clan of the Very Highest?" he asked.

"That is right."

The bronze man was puzzled. "The Very Highest have ordered this reception I received?"

"Yes."

"But didn't they know, long ago, about the bargain between the lost tribe of Maya, and myself?"

"Yes."

"Then why are they acting this way."

Monja looked at him sadly. Her face was golden in the dimming light.

"It is the gold which goes out to you that has brought terror and misery to our valley," she said. "The high priesthood, those of the Very Highest, have decided to end it."

"You mean—go back on our bargain?" Doc asked.

She shook her head.

"They are going to keep their agreement with you to the word," she said.

Doc Savage was thoughtful. "I guess they could, at that," he admitted.

"The agreement was never to keep you from the Valley, to furnish you gold when you needed it and in such quantities as you needed," Monja reminded him. "Your agreement was to help us if ever we got in trouble, never to reveal the location of the valley if you could help it, and to stop anyone who learned of it from ever coming here."

"So far, there has been no violation of that agreement," Doc said.

"That is true," she agreed.

"What are they going to do?"

"They are going to take you and your men into the inner valley, the Valley of the Very Highest, and keep you there forever. They say it was never agreed that nothing of that kind would be done to you."

Doc Savage frowned suddenly. "This agreement between myself and the Mayans all goes back to the understanding between my father and the clan," he said.

"True."

"I had the impression," Doc said, "that the agreement that we should come and go in freedom was in the bargain."

Monja looked up sharply. "You are sure?"

"Would it make any difference?"

"Yes, it would—to all of us. Because it would prove Chi-Ahpuch wrong."

"Who is Chi-Ahpuch?"

"The head of the Very Highest—the supreme leader."

84

Doc Savage was grimly silent for a while. How deeply he was thinking over the situation was evidenced when he made the small trilling noise which was his unconscious habit.

"Could we get hold of this Chi-Ahpuch?" he asked.

"Perhaps."

"Come," Doc Savage said suddenly. "We can try something."

They worked down toward the lake. Monja was puzzled, but the bronze man did not explain what he intended doing.

He asked, "What about Prinz and Space?"

"They are being tricked by Chi-Ahpuch," Monja explained.

"Tricked how?"

"They were told that they would be permitted to help the Mayans overcome you and your men. They were also told that they would then be given the gold forever."

Doc looked shocked.

"Given the gold forever," he said, "has an ominous sound. If I remember rightly, that phrase in Mayan simply means burial in the golden temple well, the old sacrificial well."

Monja nodded. "They do not know that yet. They will be told—when they can be seized and disarmed without danger."

"This Chi-Ahpuch," Doc said, "seems to be a sharp dealer."

Monja nodded.

"His name means the mouth of death, as you may notice," she explained. "But he is a just man, although hard. The honor of old Maya, and its integrity forever, are his life."

Doc made no comment on that. It was probably true. The Mayans here had a high conception of honor, after their own philosophy.

The darkness gathered, became black and pleasant. The soft light from moon and stars made a kind of silvery reflected glow that was gentle in the canyon, and a brighter platinum ahead of them, on the lake.

"You are going to your plane," Monja said suddenly.

"Yes."

"There is a guard. One man."

Doc said, "We will take care of him not without too much trouble."

"I will show you where he is," Monja said.

The guard, a stocky man with a flint-studded club and an absent-minded way of standing watch, probably did not know, until he revived later, what happened to him. Doc came out of the darkness suddenly and was upon him. He got him down and worked on the man's neck nerve centers, bringing a kind of paralysis which would last for hours, an art which Doc had spent much time mastering.

"Drag him aside, where he will not be found for a while," Doc told Monja.

The bronze man, himself, worked out to the wrecked plane which contained the machine invented by Albert Jones.

It was his first hope to remove the machine from the plane. But that proved impossible. The thing was too heavy, too bulky, for one man to handle under the conditions.

Doc directed the girl, "Keep a watch. It will take some time. A long time, perhaps, depending on how complicated this thing is."

She said quietly, "I will be very watchful."

It was long past midnight before Doc Savage left the plane, joined Monja and said, "Everything is set. Now if we can get this high priest, Chi-Ahpuch."

"You are sure this plan will work?" Monja asked anxiously.

"It is worth trying."

She nodded. They moved away into the darkness, toward the taboo section of the valley.

They made the trip without incident, except once, when they were forced to conceal themselves from a party of searching Mayan warriors carrying lanterns. The lanterns were astounding, although not entirely unknown outside the valley. They were made of *Locuyo,* the gigantic fireflies, an inch long, from which light emanated from two lamps or wells back of the eyes. They had a hard, greenish-black carapace, and furnished a rather inadequate illumination.

Monja stopped close to the cliff.

"There is a passage, well concealed," she said.

"A guard?"

"There has never been. The Mayans obey their laws."

She located the passage mouth, a simple affair, and stepped inside. Here also, lanterns of *Locuyo* furnished the illumination. They walked rapidly, side by side.

Monja was trembling. "This is sacrilege for me," she said, in a low, emotion-twisted voice.

Doc Savage had known that, and he was very uncomfortable. The sacrifice this girl was making was more, probably, than he or his men had been able to give to the clan of Maya altogether in the past. There did not seem to be any words to fit the situation.

They came out of the passage abruptly, into full moonlight that, through some freak in the slope of the cliffs in this new valley, penetrated with a brightness not found in the other valley.

Monja gasped, clutched the bronze man's arm and pointed.

"Chi-Ahpuch!" she whispered. "What luck! Walking alone!"

This very small valley seemed entirely a garden, and the high-man of this ancient clan of Maya seemed to be taking a night constitutional which indicated, considering that the hour was long past midnight, that his conscience was not easy.

He was a tall, thin man and his age seemed an indefinable thing because painstaking living had preserved him so well. His hair was very white, which meant nothing about his age, because many of the Mayans became white-haired early in life.

He was a strong man by Mayan standards, but not strong enough to put up much of a fight when Doc Savage came upon him from behind.

"What are you going to do with him?" Monja asked, very frightened.

"Introduce him to Albert Jones' memory machine," Doc Savage said.

Chapter XVI
MEMORY, THE FRIEND

Introducing Chi-Ahpuch to the memory machine was conducted in a friendly and matter-of-fact way.

First, it developed that Doc Savage had seen Chi-Ahpuch before, in the other valley, when the high priest was passing himself off as a simple Mayan. Not being complete strangers was a help.

In a far corner of the larger valley, away from interruptions, Doc began with a speech.

In the quiet, reserved fashion of conversation which the Mayans liked to affect, even when the excitement was intense, Doc told the story of Renny Renwick and Columbus. Chi-

Ahpuch had heard of Columbus. In fact, the high priests of the lost clan of Maya were somewhat in touch, mentally at least, with the outside world. They knew of its historical development, even its current troubles.

Doc tried to sense the feelings of Chi-Ahpuch as he went along. He succeeded to some extent; at least he knew that the story of the memory machine took hold of the other man and interested him intensely.

Completing the recital of Renny's troubles with the memory the machine had evoked, Doc Savage launched into his own troubles, telling them exactly as they had happened. He told about his seizure, told of what he had found in the machine—of the treachery of his father against old Secret Stevens.

Chi-Ahpuch was much impressed. Enough, so that he put a hand on Doc Savage's arm. "It was very terrible, to learn a thing like that about your father," he said sympathetically.

Terrible was no word for it, Doc admitted soberly.

"I did not know your father well," Chi-Ahpuch said. "His dealings here were made with my father, who was the highest of the priests before me."

For a moment, Doc Savage made his tiny trilling. He could not help it.

This was it! It was everything! His guess had been good. He had surmised that Chi-Ahpuch was too young a man to have dealt with Doc's father. And he was.

Doc hurriedly worked around to the matter at hand.

"It is my belief, humbly presented to you now, that the agreement between my father and your father concerning myself, was to the effect that I should be permitted to enter and leave the Valley, always unmolested, together with such of my friends as I deemed trustworthy," Doc told the high priest.

Chi-Ahpuch was gentle, but firm.

"The word-records of the transaction say differently," he pointed out. "We were very careful to check on that, when we were looking for a method of rescinding our bargain with you."

Doc nodded.

"We have a way of making sure," he said, "about which one of us is right."

"How?"

"The memory machine of which I have told you."

It took some selling to get Chi-Ahpuch to agree to try out the machine. But he finally consented.

88

Renny Renwick would have been amazed to watch Doc put Chi-Ahpuch through the machine.

What would have amazed Renny more was that Doc duplicated the exact system which had been used on both of them.

First, there was the hypnotic. The vitamin-cocktail, Albert Jones had called it.

It was nothing more or less than a drug which dulled and soothed the mind and weakened its strong reaction to consciousness so that the subject was susceptible to suggestion.

Doc next used another drug, stronger. It was a drug which was particularly kept out of the hands of the public, because while under its influence, a person was literally hypnotized and could be made to believe anything he saw or heard.

Doc put Chi-Ahpuch in the coffin-like box.

He did this carefully, first locating and disconnecting the system of wires and contacts which would set off the explosive designed to destroy the device if it was tampered with.

Albert Jones had arranged the explosive so that no one would be likely to learn that the device was all—every bit of it—a clever fake.

Lying in the box, Chi-Ahpuch was to all intents a hypnotized man. He breathed heavily. His eyes were wide open.

Doc talked to him. It was a very unpleasant job of talking for the bronze man, because much of what he said was possibly lies.

He told Chi-Ahpuch to see certain things—just as a hypnotist tells his victim to see or hear certain things. A hypnotist with a good subject can make the victim turn into, the victim believes, a dog, which will get down on the floor and bark and otherwise imitate a dog. Doc's system with Chi-Ahpuch was similar.

The machine had certain finer touches, however.

The movie, for instance. A 16-millimeter projector, handling short lengths of film silently. Doc had converted the projector over so that it would function from the plane's radio battery.

The film was the one which Jones had used on him in New York but Doc had edited it to take out Secret Stevens.

The part of the film which Doc used dealt with his father. It was a genuine picture, taken during one of the elder Savage's trips of exploration into Central America. No doubt it was a trip with Secret Stevens, since Jones must have gotten the negative from Stevens.

Part of the film had been faked, using a double, disguised

as Doc's father—something a victim under the influence of the strong hypnotic would fail to recognize.

Doc had edited out everything but the individual pictures of his father.

As he showed these to Chi-Ahpuch, he spoke slowly, distinctly, repeating an imaginary conversation between the elder Savage and Chi-Ahpuch's own father.

High point of the conversation was the agreement that young Doc Savage was to come and go from the Valley at will, with his friends.

After he had put that across, Doc let the gadget taper off, and waited for Chi-Ahpuch to come out from under the effects of the drug.

Monja was astounded.

"The machine is not genuine!" she exclaimed.

"Not in the least."

"But what is its purpose?"

"The one it served," Doc explained. "To trick me into telling Secret Stevens the location of the Valley of the Vanished."

Monja was puzzled. "You say it served its purpose—yet it was not you who gave them the location of the Valley?"

Doc nodded.

"Secret Stevens and Albert Jones worked out the scheme," Doc explained. "But Space and Prinz cut in on them, and things did not turn out exactly as they had hoped. Space and Prinz were slick enough to trick my friends into showing them the location of the Valley."

Chi-Ahpuch came out from under the effects of the hypnotic. He was very impressed. As impressed, no doubt, as Renny Renwick had been, when he awakened thinking he had looked at the memory of his devilish—but imaginary—ancestor who had tried to murder Columbus.

He sat there for a while.

"We have done you a great wrong," he said finally. "It must be righted."

Chapter XVII
DEATH WARNING

In the Inner Valley, in a pleasant glade, a campfire burned. Space and Prinz squatted near the campfire, too excited to sleep. Their men were awake also, for they had all been drinking *balche,* the Mayan drink compound of bark and honey fermented in water, and they were slightly intoxicated. Mayan warriors came and went quietly, for Space and Prinz and their men were under guard—to keep Doc Savage from them, they had been told. The Mayan warriors wore anklets of *cucuji,* the lantern bug, to light their path and to identify themselves to each other.

Doc Savage walked boldly into the firelight.

Space and Prinz nearly turned handsprings in their astonishment.

"Help!" Space bellowed. "Here's Savage! Quick!"

Doc said quietly, "The natives brought me here, so they know where I am. They brought me here to tell you something."

The pair stared at him, too amazed to move.

Doc said, "I have been asked to tell you that you are prisoners. Your cache of ammunition and weapons has been taken. All the arms you have are those which you have on you, and most of those have been unloaded by the Mayan warriors—in cases where your men became intoxicated on *balche."*

"You're crazy!" Space blurted.

Doc told them about the decision of the Very Highest in the Inner Valley, the decision which Chi-Ahpuch had reversed. The telling did not take long.

Stunned, Space demanded, "What will happen to us?"

"You will be kept here."

"How long?"

"Forever."

"The hell we will!" Space snarled.

"Be careful," Doc warned hastily. "Only a few of you have weapons. You can not get out of the Valley."

"We can fly out."

"Not at night," the bronze man said. "The air currents are even more treacherous at night. You would not get above the Valley wall."

Space swore wordlessly, dove a hand into his clothing, and brought out a gun. Doc Savage had half-expected that. He moved backward, got behind a tree and kept going.

Space's gun made a rip-slam roaring in the night and brought thunderous echoes whooping down from the cliff walls.

Instantly, there was a bedlam of shouting around them. Mayan warriors yelling in the darkness. Yelling warnings to the white men not to resist. Some of them shouted in English, but it had no meaning to Space and Prinz and the others. The only thing that had meaning to them, probably, was the gold, and the prospect of losing it. They were gripped with a cornered madness, feeling their lives were in danger.

"The hole into the big valley," Space yelled. "Head for it."

Doc Savage, clear of danger himself, began shouting for the Mayans not to resist, not to risk their lives needlessly.

But an instant later, he was shocked into silence.

Two figures dashed into the glow of the campfire.

Albert Jones and Secret Stevens. They joined Space and Prinz. They were welcomed. Obviously, Jones and Stevens had already come to some kind of an agreement with Space.

The bronze man thought of pretty Annice Stevens and was sickened.

Space and Prinz, Jones and Stevens, and their men, fought their way out of the smaller valley into the larger, down the larger to the lake, and finally to the planes.

The plane motors roared and threw thumping echoes against the walls of the larger valley. Their exhaust stacks spilled streams of sparks, and the ships swirled out on the beach surface. There was some shooting from the plane windows, but it was needless shooting. The Mayans had stopped their pursuit.

Both planes shot across the sand side by side, a dangerous thing to do. The motors got full gun; the craft lifted. The beach was very narrow, but they got off together. They banked out slightly over the lake, for the smoother air there. Then they climbed.

They were lost suddenly in the shadows against the cliff. But they banked in time, and came back, climbing. There were a few shots from them, triumphant, directed at nothing. Shots that were undoubtedly the promise of a bloodthirsty return at a later date.

Twice, the ships circled. Then they tried to mount over the cliff edge. Right at the lip, the terrific air currents caught them. A boiling maelstrom of night air that was like the eddy behind a stick dragged fast through the water. The ships rolled and pitched and went out of control.

The sound of their crashing was weird, gruesome in the night. A long-drawn noise as if a monster had swallowed both ships and was digesting them in a mechanical insides. There was no fire, just a long grinding and rending as the ships twisted and fell down the face of the great cliff, striking and grinding, dropping and smashing, until they lost recognizability.

In the silence that followed, a few dislodged boulders bounded down the cliff face.

The parrots in the Valley quarreled for a while, and were silent.

Chapter XVIII
DONKEY SAM

The morning sun came up with a glory that was breathless wonder to the Mayans, for their heritage was the sun. This morning in particular they stood at the *temalacatl*, the sacrificial stone, giving thanks for deliverance from their troubles.

There was, as further business this morning, the drafting of a speech of apology to Doc Savage, the Man of Bronze, for what had happened, and an invitation to continue as he had in the past to receive what he wished from the lost people of Maya. Chi-Ahpuch had arranged the matter. Chi-Ahpuch was clever enough to know that the previous treatment of Doc Savage had not been a popular matter, and he was more or less sincere himself, in wishing to right the wrong.

As part of the ceremonies at the *temalacatl*, King Chaac and Monja were forgiven, and commended as well, for their course of action. That, too, was a concession to popular favor by Chi-Ahpuch, possibly. But a smart move.

Monk took the occasion to get Doc Savage aside, alone.

"I got that memory machine," Monk whispered. "Renny and Ham and I got it, and consigned it to the deepest part of the lake. Nobody'll know it was a fake now."

Doc Savage thought that was good for more reasons than one, and said so.

Monk glanced around, making sure that Annice Stevens was not in sight.

"That girl is taking it hard," he said. "They found old Secret Stevens' body with Prinz and Space and the others. All of them were killed instantly when the planes crashed."

Doc asked sharply, "It was arranged that she should not know the truth about her father?"

"Sure."

"How?"

"Oh, we told her he was seized by Space as a hostage," Monk explained. "Told her Jones was seized for the same reason. But Doc, I don't get it. How come she did not know about her father being in cahoots with Jones?"

"That's easy," Doc explained. "When she came from boarding school, Jones said it would be much better for Secret Stevens to keep in the background and let her contact me. They thought I wouldn't be suspicious."

"Yeah, but what about the memory machine? She knew that was a phony."

"I guess she did," said Doc. "But Secret Stevens had filled her up with that story about my father cheating him and told her that the machine was the only way to get me to right the wrong. Of course, the whole story was a lie. My father never cheated Stevens because he found the Valley of the Vanished on a trip by himself, years after he and Stevens broke up. Stevens found out somehow about the Valley and concocted this whole plan. Then he brought Albert Jones into it and Jones, who was afraid of us, hired Space, who, in turn brought Prinz and his gang into it."

Monk shook his head. "I wouldn't have believed it of Secret Stevens. He was such a nice old man."

Doc said dryly, "You can't tell by looks. But anyway, we mustn't let Annice know he was a crook. Do the Mayans know that they are not to tell her anything?"

"Yeah," Monk said. "Monja arranged that."

Doc looked at the homely chemist sharply. "Monja?"

Monk shrugged. "She thinks you might be in love with Annice Stevens."

Astounded, Doc blurted, "What gave her such an impossible idea?"

Monk chuckled. "I guess because you don't give her a tumble. She can't see that any natural-born man could fail to fall for her, unless there was a good reason. She doesn't see any reason here except Annice."

Doc got hot under the collar.

Monk eyed Doc Savage. "What do you think we had better do about this Monja and Annice situation?" he asked slyly.

Doc, carefully pretending not to hear the remark, said, "We had better get back to New York at once."

Monk laughed. "I've found it pays to run from 'em, too," he said.

THE SCREAMING MAN

I

It was, unfortunately, not humility, nor anything remotely related to modesty, which caused Annie Flinders to call herself Annie Flinders. Her true and full name was Miss Angelica Carstair-Flinders, Rhinemoor Manor, Rhinecliff-on-the-Hudson, Duchess County, N.Y., and modesty had little to do with the change. There were not two spoonfuls of modesty in Annie Flinders, even measuring her on one of her sweet days.

Annie's sweet days, always few, had lately become as scarce as diamonds for sale at ten cents in ten-cent stores. Unhappy, if we put it conservatively, was Annie Flinders. She had brought this sadness on herself—by wangling the credentials and transportation necessary to become a lady Economic Planning Representative in the Pacific Area.

Now the truth was that Annie was no more fitted to be an Economic Planning Representative in the Pacific Area than she was to be a ditch-digger. She was rigged for it about the way a butterfly is equipped to shovel coal. Annie was artistic. Annie was, exactly speaking, an *artiste*. An *artiste*, says Webster, is a performer whose work shows unusual æsthetic qualities. That was Annie, and certainly she could never really have, in her heart, given a damn whether the United Household Appliance Company could sell more of its superduper refrigerators in the Philippines, or whether it should stick to pots and pans and whisk-brooms—which was partially what an Economic Planning Representative in the Pacific Area was supposed to find out.

Actually, Annie's Uncle Jessup, her money-making uncle, was president of United Household Appliance, and Annie had hit him up for a job that would take her somewhere where there was, or lately had been, a war. She didn't at the moment have the Pacific in mind, although she had been agreeable when it was mentioned, overlooking the proportions of the Pacific Ocean, and the fact that the war had not exactly stood still. The Pacific? Oh, goody! Marines, sailors, soldiers, excitement

In due course of time, Annie found that the Philippines, as a war theater, had become well-fizzled. This would have delighted a true Economic Planning Representative, but for Annie, it was hell.

Annie had even shortened her name from Miss Angelica Carstair-Flinders to plain Annie Flinders to make people think she was vigorous and two-fisted and entitled to get around and see a war. She could have saved this psychological touch. The war, the Philippine part of it, was a strangled duck.

This was very discouraging, because Annie had been trying since Pearl Harbor to see a war. On December 8, the day after Pearl Harbor, she joined the Red Cross. She was assigned to Iceland. She got out of Iceland finally, joined the WAACs, and was assigned a desk job in St. Joseph, Missouri. It had taken her the intervening two years to persuade them the war was near enough over that they could afford to discharge her from the WAAC.

All of this is by way of explaining that Annie Flinders was in the Philippines, was an *artiste,* was a thwarted excitement-lover, and hence the sort of a person who would become quite excited when she saw Clark Savage, Jr., who was also known as Doc Savage.

Also Annie was a delicious-looking package herself. Marines whistled loudly when she passed. Sometimes they stood on their hands.

When Annie Flinders first saw Doc Savage—technically, it was the second time she'd seen him—she grabbed the arm of the Lieutenant, j.g., who was escorting her, and spoke with unsubdued excitement:

"Am I," said Annie, "dreaming? Or is that Clark Savage? I'm dreaming, aren't I? Luck can't have caught up with me this late in life."

The Lieutenant, j.g., looked at the hand she had clamped on his arm, and considered grabbing the hand's owner right then and there. The j.g. had been under the impression he was in love with a carrot-haired girl in Gillette, Wyoming, until that afternoon, when he'd met Annie.

"Forget Clark Gable," he said, sounding a little as if he were panting.

"Not Gable. Savage. Clark Savage." Annie sounded a bit short of normal breath herself.

"Good," said the j.g.

"Surely," said Annie, "I'm not mistaken."

"Hey."

"It *is* Doc Savage," said Annie.

97

"Hey!" said the j.g.

Annie went into a conference with herself, saying, "I am sure it must be. I saw him once before, in New York, when a friend of mine who was a surgeon took me to hear him lecture. Mr. Savage gave a wonderful lecture. I didn't understand practically one single word of what he was talking about. But it must have been super, because all the famous surgeons sat there with their mouths open."

"Hey, hey, hey!" said the j.g. urgently.

"I wonder," pondered Annie, "what Doc Savage is doing in the Philippine Islands?"

"Remember me, lady?" the j.g. asked. "I'm the guy you picked up at the canteen two hours ago."

"What? Oh, of course, Bill."

The Lieutenant became somewhat bitter. "My name's Arthur."

"Oh, of course. So nice to have met you, Arthur." Annie extended a hand, adding vaguely, "By all means do that, Arthur."

"Do what?" growled Arthur.

"Whatever we were talking about," said Annie, still more vaguely. "By all means. Goodbye, Bill."

This completed the acquaintanceship of Annie and the Lieutenant, junior grade, who at once entered a convenient bar to obtain, as he expressed it, several hookers of bourbon for a fellow who had just come unhooked.

Annie had already taken up the business of observing Doc Savage. In a serious way, and carefully.

For twenty-four hours thereafter, Annie Flinders kept close tab on Doc Savage. She followed Doc Savage to Alamosa, where he visited a war-prisoner camp containing Japs. She shadowed him to Los Antiniso, where Doc Savage visited a war-prisoner camp containing Nazis. And to Calmeda, where he visited one containing both Japs and Nazis.

It was not very satisfactory because Annie was unable to find out what Doc Savage was talking to the war prisoners about.

She tried. She tried to vamp a Staff Sergeant named Coons into telling her what Doc Savage wanted with the prisoners.

The Staff Sergeant had her thrown in jail.

It was not a comfortable jail, and Annie was made to realize that her first weeks at the WAAC training center in Des Moines hadn't been nearly as tough as she had thought.

She occupied the calaboose forty-eight hours, long enough

for a Colonel somebody to cable the F.B.I., the police chief of Rhinecliff-on-the-Hudson, Uncle Jessup, and somebody in Washington, and even then the Colonel was not entirely reassured.

"Young lady, I am going to turn you loose," said the Colonel finally. "Providing you will make me a promise."

"Why," demanded Annie, "was I tossed in your bastille?"

"That," replied the Colonel, "brings us to the promise. To wit, you are to say nothing to anyone, and are to put nothing in writing in any form, hinting or indicating in any way that you have seen Doc Savage or have any idea what he is doing."

"But I don't know what he is doing. That's what I want to know."

"How did you like our jail?"

"Ugh!"

"Then say nothing and write nothing."

"I promise to say nothing and write nothing," Annie promised, showing the Colonel she didn't have her fingers crossed.

"Good day," said the Colonel.

"Goodbye, I hope," said Annie.

"Oh, I almost forgot," called the Colonel. "I have here a cablegram which came for you an hour or so ago."

The cable message was from Annie's employer, her Uncle Jessup, and it contained four words: *You're fired. Come home.*

Freed of the tentacles of military law, Annie Flinders sped at once to the Hotel Northern, which had been destroyed by the Japs and already rebuilt by the industrious Filipinos, and where, in the course of her shadowing, she had learned Doc Savage was staying.

She was delighted to discover Doc Savage in the dining room, having fried chicken Mindoro style.

"This," said Annie to herself, "is proving to be even better than I expected."

Conceivably this remark, with the pleased enthusiasm the young lady put into it, would have interested a psychiatrist. Because Annie was not the victim of any sort of bobby-sox feeling toward Doc Savage, who was manly enough to have inspired it. Passion was consuming Annie, but passion of a different sort.

The psychiatrist, if there had been one, and if he had diagnosed correctly, would have said that Annie Flinders was the victim of a frustration which gradually became deeply seated in the bones of a lot of American citizens who didn't get to take a shot at a Nazi or a Jap. This yen to take a whack at the rats, meeting the obstacle of not being able to, did some unpleasant complexing to lots of people. It made perfect strangers take pokes at each other in bars, made teen-agers run wild, and did lots of other things which were blamed on bad tempers, carelessness and moral decline. Annie's complex was very strongly developed. She'd spent the war trying to get into the war, the frustration was all corked up inside her, and the cork just had to blow. Excitement would pull the cork. Ergo, she had to have some excitement.

She got it when she went to her room. She had, during her trailing activity, transferred her residence to the hotel for convenience.

There was a young man waiting in the hall outside her door. He was leaning against the wall. He had small eyes, a scar on his chin, and a strangely large knot which his hand and something else made in his coat pocket.

"Hello, Annie," he said.

Annie examined him. "I don't believe I know you."

"Good," said the young man, unveiling the mystery of what made his hand in his pocket so large. It was a gun. "Let us step inside, baby, and converse," he added.

Annie thought of several things, all of them different ways of yelling for help. She was scared.

"Open up," ordered the young man.

"I—I haven't got a key!"

"Then I'll use mine, tutz." He employed a key with which he was provided, flung open the door, assured Annie she wouldn't make a lovely corpse, and followed her inside, closing the door.

"W-what—"

"I'll make all the words necessary," said the unpleasant young man. "Listen carefully, baby. Because if you don't hear me the first time, and abide thereby, you'll be nice and dead damned quick. There is a steamship named the *Empress Margaret* which is sailing for San Francisco tomorrow morning, which is about eighteen hours from now, giving you plenty of time to be aboard. You will find the *Empress Margaret* quite comfortable, since it is a former luxury trans-Pacific liner converted to war use, but not converted as much as you'd think. I think you will find it suitable. Much preferable, I will add, to a cold, cold grave here in the Philippines."

"You're ordering me to leave on a boat!" Annie gasped.

"I told you to listen," said the young man. "I will now give you rough ideas of what will transpire if you don't."

With horrifying suddenness, he cocked his gun and jammed it against Annie's temple. While she waited, eyes closed in terror, for her brains to be blown out, he hit her on the jaw. The blow wasn't light. Things were black as road tar for a moment. When Annie's head cleared, she was on the floor, a hard braided noose of some sort was around her neck, and she was unable to obtain air. She was being strangled. The strangling continued until more blackness, shot with red flashes, came.

The thug permitted her to resume breathing.

"Just samples, tutz," he explained. "Too bad I cannot demonstrate what would then happen to your body, but I do not have with me any deep, slimy pools of swamp mud, nor any sharks hungry for pretty human flesh, nor even any dark alleys all ready and waiting for a female corpse. However, I trust that your imagination can supply these missing ingredients."

"It can," Annie admitted tremulously.

"We have then," said the young man, "only one more thing to discuss."

Annie didn't feel like asking questions. She waited.

"You keep your trap shut about this!" said the young man ominously. "Get me?"

"I—I—y-yes." Annie had great difficulty with words.

"Goodbye, I hope," said the young man.

He made his departure.

II

Doc Savage was lingering with pleasure over the empty dish which had contained his chicken Mindoro when he observed a feminine vision enter the dining room. He was not, however, possessed of any yen to meet her. Quite the contrary. He wished nothing whatever of the sort, because he was already equipped with troubles.

None of this showed in his manner or on his person. Doc Savage was a very large young man who was, fortunately, developed in a symmetrical fashion which made him seem not so startlingly like a giant. He had deeply bronzed skin, hair a little darker shade of bronze, and flake gold eyes which were so unusual that people were always staring at them, and getting funny hypnotized feelings. Although he made genuine efforts to seem a commonplace individual, strangers always ogled him, and sensed that Savage was a physical marvel, a mental wizard, and very important. Which he frequently doubted he was.

The lovely young woman came directly to his table, seated herself, and informed him that he was an unsanitary rodent.

"You're a dirty rat," she said.

Doc Savage said nothing, in quite a startled way.

Annie Flinders added, "Having your Sergeant throw me in jail and your Colonel bulldoze me was bad enough."

This statement led Doc Savage to reflect that he might know who she was.

"But you needn't," Annie continued angrily, "have sent a thug to scare the skirts off me!"

"I beg pardon," Doc remarked politely.

"I should think you would!"

"I mean—I don't believe I know your name," Doc explained carefully.

"Annie Flinders."

"I see," Doc said, and he did. For he had recalled that Colonel Madden of Army Intelligence had advised him that a mysterious young woman had been caught asking suspicious questions, and had been instantly incarcerated pending investigation. Annie Flinders was the name this female had given.

Annie was surveying him with the expression she probably reserved for snakes.

"I should think you'd be ashamed," she said.

"I? Of what?"

"A man with your gallant, romantic reputation, behaving the way you have!" explained Annie bitterly. "You're a fraud, that's what. You're a rat."

"Thank you," Doc Savage said pleasantly.

"I'm not complimenting you, so why thank me?" demanded Annie.

"The speaking of truth should always be complimented," said Doc.

Annie frowned. "Who's complimenting who, anyway?"

"I don't know. Do you?"

Annie examined him wrathfully.

"Listen, wise-guy, you're trying to dance out of this with dizzy words," she said. "Well, you won't get away with it. You're going to listen to what I think of you. I think what you did to me was dirty. You didn't need to"—she indicated her temple where the young thug had jammed his gun muzzle—"have a loaded gun presented to my head! Nor have me hit on the jaw." She exhibited the bruise on her chin. "Nor have me choked half to death with a garrote cord." She displayed the grim mark on her neck.

Doc Savage, examining the charms of the chin and neck she had indicated, was momentarily stricken into forgetfulness. Then he jumped violently.

"I didn't have any of those things done to you!" he exploded.

Disbelieving, Annie eyed him for a moment, then stated, "Besides a rat, now you're a liar."

By lifting a finger at a hovering waiter, and asking for the check, Doc Savage obtained some time in which he assembled his thoughts, not too successfully. The young lady had been gun-scared, choked, then biffed, and this was not in the program.

"You," Doc said when the waiter went away with his ten-dollar bill, "were found on investigation to be a foolish but presumably harmless young woman with a wealthy Uncle Jessup. It was then decided to release you upon your promise to forgive and forget, and your Uncle Jessup was further persuaded to fire you and order you home in the hope that you would have gumption enough to obey."

"I wondered who got Uncle Jessup to fire me!" Annie said ominously. "That's another black mark after your name."

"There," Doc said, "is where I stopped."

"Oh, no you didn't!"

"But I did!"

"What," asked Annie grimly, "about the hard-as-nails young pug-ugly with the gun, fist and throat-string?"

Doc Savage plunged into serious thought, endeavoring however to keep the full scope of his seriousness from showing in his expression.

"I wonder if that could have been something Colonel Madden could have tossed in on his own hook," he remarked presently.

"You're not kidding me for a minute," Annie said.

"I think I'd better make a telephone call."

Colonel Madden, when his ear was eventually obtained over the repaired telephone system of the city of Manila, spoke with positive certainty. The pug-ugly was not his.

Annie wasn't quite convinced.

"You probably had it fixed with the Colonel to whitewash you with innocence," she said.

Doc said thoughtfully, "The Colonel wants to arrest you again and throw you in jail where you will be safe and out of our way."

"You can't scare me, you rat!" Annie eyed him with alarm. "You mean I've *really* been threatened? Oh, great grief!"

"Where," Doc asked, "did this thug do his impressing of you?"

"Here at the hotel. My room."

Doc seized her arm and started for the elevator, then thought of another thing, and stopped to ask, "When did it happen?"

"Just a few minutes ago," Annie explained.

"First, we'll look around and see if you notice the fellow," Doc said. "He may have lingered in the neighborhood, but it's doubtful."

While they were visiting the public rooms of the hotel, Doc Savage decided that he liked the way Annie walked, but didn't care for her calmness. She wasn't entirely calm by a long shot, but neither was she as terrified as he knew she was justified in being. He was, as a matter of fact, surprised that she was still breathing. He told her so. "I'm surprised that you're still alive," he said.

Annie sniffed. "I half-way think you're still trying to scare me," she said.

"Do you see any sign of the pug?"

"No. You must have told him not to hang around."

"He knew that without being told," Doc said grimly. "Let's have a look at the exact spot where he accosted you."

They went upstairs, and Annie experienced a shiver when she looked at the places where the hard young man had stood. She pointed out the different places, and said, "Here is where he choked me on the floor." The spot where she had been throttled was significant to Annie, but Doc Savage didn't seem interested.

"You say he had a key?" he asked.

"Yes."

Doc examined the door lock, and remarked, "Probably nothing in that. The lock has numbers on it, and a good locksmith can make a key to fit it from the numbers if he has them. It's a system the hotels sometimes use so they won't have too much trouble when guests carry off keys."

104

"There isn't a clue, really," Annie said.

Doc was contemplating marks on the rug, noticing that there was one fairly clear masculine footprint. It might belong to a bellhop, however.

"I'm surprised," added Annie, "that you believe there really was a pug."

"Oh, our reports on you indicated that veracity was one of your rather scattered good qualities," Doc told her. "So I believe you, temporarily."

"They're not as scattered as you think." Annie was a trifle injured. "Why do you think it happened?"

Doc noted that the baggage in the room, while expensive, was in good taste and not too bountiful. It had been his experience that personable young women usually traveled with five times as much baggage as they needed.

"It happened because you stuck your nose in where it didn't belong," he explained.

"I mean," Annie explained, "why did the pug toss in his two bits worth? I had already been jailed and bamboozled."

"Evidently he, or his boss, had a low opinion of our bamboozling ability."

A maid appeared in the hall with a broom. Doc went out and spoke with her a while, learning that she had observed a young man in the hall about fifteen minutes ago. The fellow answered the description of Annie's pug. The maid thought she would know him if she saw him again, but she hadn't seen him before.

"Annie," Doc said, "I think you'd better take their advice."

"You mean leave?"

"Yes. Sail on that ship. What was its name?"

"The *Empress Margaret*."

"That is a nice ship, a liner. You will be comfortable aboard."

Annie examined him with marked suspicion. "You are giving me the same advice that Jack the Ripper gave me. That's funny."

"Not funny. Sensible." Doc moved to the door. "You had better think it over."

"I'll think it over," Annie promised. "Say, where are you going?"

"I'm leaving you," Doc explained. "Things to do."

Annie got in his way. "Hold on here, bub. I want to know what is happening." She put a hand on his arm and urged,

"Come on, tell me. After all, I've been the whipping post for enough projects around here that I think I've earned some information."

Doc shook his head. "Sorry."

"Why not?"

"Sorry, nothing doing."

Annie did some things with her fingers on his arm and turned loose her special man-cracking smile. "Oh, come on, please," she urged.

Doc straightened out his toes with some difficulty, counted his pulse by fives for a moment, and shook his head firmly.

"Too secret. Too hush-hush," he said. "Well, goodbye now."

"You're still a rat," Annie said.

Downstairs in the lobby, Doc Savage approached a young man in a sailor suit. The young man was long and amiable looking and gave the appearance of being about ten years younger than he was and a great deal more innocent.

"Seen anything, Carter?" Doc asked.

Carter rolled a roguish eye. "I saw you pass through here with the gorgeous sunset, the flowers that bloom in the spring, on your arm."

"That was Miss Annie Flinders."

"She should change that name," Carter said emphatically. "It doesn't rhyme."

"I want you to keep an eye on Miss Flinders," Doc said.

"That will not be too hard to do."

"And protect her."

"Excellent!" said Carter enthusiastically.

"From a distance," Doc added.

Carter winced.

"Oh, hell now, does there have to be a catch in it?" he asked. "I do my best protecting at short range. In fact, I'm known as Short-range Carter, the nonpareil, the fellow who—"

"Keep an open eye and mind," Doc advised. "Or you may be Carter, the fellow they ordered a tombstone for."

Carter sobered. Doc Savage described the young man to whom Annie had referred as the thug, and advised Carter to keep a lookout for that one particularly.

"Do I glom on to him if I see him?" Carter asked.

"If he doesn't glom you first, you do," Doc said, nodding.

III

Doc Savage visited Colonel Madden. The latter sat in his office with his feet on his desk, drinking a malted milk to wash down a dose of milk of magnesia. He explained, "This thing is ruining my digestion."

"I think," Doc told him, "that we have just gotten a whiff of tiger."

Colonel Madden yanked his feet off the desk violently and yelled, "The hell you say! What's happened?"

Doc outlined Annie's experience with the grim young man who had put a gun to her ear, banged her jaw and given her a sample of garroting. By that time the Colonel's jaw was thrust out like an angry bulldozer and he growled, "Where was that mutt of a sailor, Carter, when this was going on?"

"Mothering me, as his orders said he was to do," Doc explained.

"Well, he should have had his eyes open!"

Doc nodded. "That goes for us, too."

"What," asked the Colonel sourly, "do you suppose that bird jumped the girl for?"

Doc had been thinking about this. He wasn't sure he could put a finger on the reason. There were several possibilities. "May not have wanted her around where she would get hurt," he ventured.

Colonel Madden gave him a bitter look. "You're kidding."

"I guess so."

"If we're up against what we think we are, they wouldn't give a damn who got hurt, or how badly. They wouldn't, specifically, give a damn if ten million people got hurt. This they have demonstrated, I might add."

"Provided," Doc reminded, "we're up against what we suspect we are."

Colonel Madden nodded. "You can surely think of better reasons why the girl was threatened."

Doc said he could. "But I wish I knew for sure whether they are better," he added. "The girl may not be as innocent as she has panned out so far. I wish I knew."

"What are some of the other reasons for her being molested?"

"They might have felt that if she resumed following me

around, it would cause me to become shadow-minded, with the result that I might accidentally collar one of their own men who was trailing me."

The Colonel jumped violently. "Godamighty! Are they following you?"

"I haven't noticed anyone, so they are smooth about it, if they are."

Blowing out his breath heavily, the Colonel said, "You gave me a scare."

"I got one myself, when she told me about the pug." Doc leaned back in his chair, hands resting on the chair arm-rests, his eyes half closed. He was not, however, relaxing. He was experiencing an attack of the nastiest kind of premonition, of danger.

"I wish," Doc added gloomily, "that we could find some trace of Johnny Littlejohn."

Colonel Madden nodded, but was silent; Doc Savage was also silent; they were both thinking about Johnny Littlejohn, and worrying.

William Harper Littlejohn, the archaeologist and geologist, was a very tall and bony young man, addicted to the use of the most startling big words, who was one of Doc Savage's closest friends. Johnny and Doc had frequently worked together, although on a basis of friendship rather than a business arrangement.

Some time previously, about six months ago, Johnny Littlejohn had undertaken something which Doc Savage didn't quite understand, because he didn't have the details. He thought Johnny had been rather secretive about it, which wasn't like Johnny.

Johnny's venture had surely been important, because it had entailed his entering Japan. The Japanese homeland territory, which was being pasted by B29's, was about as healthy for an American as a hornet's nest. How the devil Johnny had gotten into Japan, and how he had kept from being discovered and shot forthwith, Doc couldn't imagine. Disguise, probably. Johnny was an infinitely capable fellow, and being one of the best archaeologists extant, he knew a lot about races and customs and languages. That would help. Anyway, Johnny had made it into Japan and out and to the Philippines —they thought.

Two weeks ago, here in Manila, Colonel Madden had received a telephone call. From Johnny Littlejohn. Not a long-distance call. A local one. Johnny was in Manila. Johnny wanted Doc Savage in Manila, and in a hurry. Would Colonel Madden see that Doc got this summons at once? There was absolutely no doubt about it being Johnny's voice.

Doc Savage had come to the Philippines without asking questions. He knew Johnny, and if Johnny said it was important, it was.

Johnny Littlejohn thereupon disappeared .

The arrangement made verbally over the telephone with Colonel Madden was that Johnny was to meet Doc at the Hotel Northern at a certain day and hour. He hadn't kept the date. He hadn't appeared later.

When his alarm became enough to move him to do so, Colonel Madden told Doc Savage what the Colonel and the United States Army Intelligence suspected—only suspected, mind—had caused Johnny Littlejohn to take the appreciable risk of entering Japan.

The Colonel further imparted something Doc hadn't known—that the U.S. Army had cooperated to the extent of taking Johnny into Japan by bomber and parachute. Hush-hush, of course.

Sitting there listening to Colonel Madden tell, with plain Anglo-Saxon words, what Johnny thought he had discovered, had been shocking to Doc. Not surprising entirely. He had toyed with the suspicion himself in the past, when allowing his thoughts to get a bit wild and hair-raising. But to hear the Colonel put it in plain American words—that was terrifying.

After the Colonel stated the facts, they didn't discuss it much. In fact they did not discuss it afterward at all, not directly. They moved about the subject warily, as if it was something that was taboo, unmentionable, forbidden, poisonous.

Doc Savage had decided why they were so reticent about it. The reason was simple.

They were afraid to discuss it, for fear it might be true.

Doc Savage jerked his thoughts back to the present. He stood up.

"I just wanted to be sure you didn't send the pug to scare the girl," he said.

"Well, he was not my man," the Colonel said.

"I'll be leaving, then."

Colonel Madden shuddered. "I wish that silly girl were back in God's country, or at least in California. You say Carter's taking care of her? Did you warn him to be careful?"

Doc repeated what he had told Carter, omitted Carter's rather sassy reception of the advice, and added, "I'm going to take over the job of guarding her myself."

The Colonel scowled at him. "If you're neglecting this other thing to chase a skirt, I may personally cut your throat."

Doc looked at the Colonel unpleasantly, for the Colonel sounded very much as if he meant what he had said.

"I'll run this to suit myself," Doc advised.

Still wearing the scowl, the Colonel stated, "You had better be the hotshot they say you are!"

"Good afternoon!" Doc put on his hat.

"Goodbye," said the Colonel darkly.

Doc Savage returned to the Hotel Northern with a dissatisfied feeling about the interview. Being a civilian, the Army's iron-fisted methods often rather jolted him. He was slightly sensitive about the Army, probably, because they'd made him go through the war without putting on a uniform. He had been labelled as essential at what he was doing, which he was. But the trouble with wars was that they gave you all kinds of complexes. A man wasn't satisfied out of the Army; when he got in the Army, he frequently wasn't pleased either. It was disconcerting.

Annie Flinders answered her telephone with marked caution when he called her room. She said, "Mrs. Josephus Williams speaking."

"If your husband isn't around, how about dining with me?" Doc suggested, deciding that she also had something in her mouth to change her voice.

"I'm afraid to go out," Annie said. "And I don't like you anyway."

Doc explained that he had just checked with certain powers, and that they, like himself, were by no manner or means responsible for the pug-ugly. "I want to ask you questions," he added.

"All right," Annie said eagerly, "but if anything happens to me, you'll be responsible."

"Okay."

"Be down in fifteen minutes."

Doc hung up and approached Carter, who was dapper and languid in his sailor suit. "Why aren't you upstairs, posted outside the young lady's door like the watchdog you're supposed to be," Doc demanded.

110

Carter grinned. "The management doesn't allow sailors to stand aimlessly in the halls of this hostelry."

"Who told you that?"

"The assistant manager who kicked me out of the hall."

"You probably had an amorous look on your face," Doc suggested.

"I probably had. Say, how would it be if I really did this job up brown by striking up an acquaintance with the babe and taking her out to dinner."

"No good."

"You've already done it, eh?" Carter frowned. "That's fine. If shooting starts, don't expect any protection from me."

Doc made a mental note to ask Colonel Madden to assign another man to this watchdog job. He didn't believe Carter was actually taking it seriously.

"You stick around," Doc ordered sharply. "Keep us in sight and be ready to lend a hand."

Carter shrugged. "Okay. But I'll have to put on a disguise of some kind."

"Don't be silly!"

"Silly nothing—half the guests in this hotel are beginning to give me sidelong looks. I've been standing around here wearing this face too long."

"You sound like a detective book!"

"I'm going to change my looks anyway," Carter said. He sauntered off.

Doc bought a newspaper, found a comfortable chair and looked over the lobby for suspicious persons while pretending to read. I'm getting jumpy, he thought.

Presently Annie came toward him, a silver dream in the thing she wore. She didn't look like a young lady who had lately spent twenty-four hours in jail. Except that she didn't speak to him very lovingly.

"Why'd you want to buy me dinner?" she demanded.

"You're lovely as two bushels of orchids," Doc assured her.

"Come on, bulletproof, give me the truth," Annie requested.

"I'm fascinated by you."

"I'll try to cure that," Annie said.

He took her to the Avion, which had good food and plenty of M.P. and S.P. around in case trouble should rear its ugly head. The Avion hadn't had an orchestra the last time he was

111

there, which was yesterday, but tonight it had one. Presently he had to confess, "I can't dance."

"For Heaven's sake," Annie said.

Doc made some suggestions about the food. Annie was contrary, and didn't order anything he had suggested.

She asked, "Why were you visiting prisoner-of-war camps?"

He examined the orchestra and asked, "When was that?"

"You were pretty slinky about it, too," she added. "I noticed that you didn't draw attention to yourself, and that you spoke to quite a number of Japs and Nazis. You spoke privately, and to some of them you spoke quite a while."

He held silence.

"It struck me," added Annie, "that you were conducting a very secret investigation. Tell me, what were—and are—you investigating?"

He shook his head.

She persisted, "Why the great interest in prisoners-of-war?"

He shook his head again and remarked, "The fish is a wonderful creature. It has no nose to stick in other people's business."

Annie leered at him. "Come on. I'll teach you to dance."

He said no, thanks, and put down his napkin. His eye lingered on a table near the door, and passed on. He said, "Excuse me a moment." He stood up.

He had just become positive that they had been followed to the Avion. He had noticed a man seat himself behind a phony palm tree, at a table. If the man had not sneaked in there, his suspicions might not have crystallized.

"Stay right here," he said. "I've got to see a man about a palm tree."

By the time he was halfway to the palm tree, though, he wished he had kept his seat, and hadn't been so impulsive. This boilermaker way of doing things was apt to be noisy and undignified. However he kept going. He knew the lad behind the palm must have seen him.

Then the fat man got in his way. They hit with a hard bump. The fat man said, "Oops!"

Doc eyed the fat man with suspicion, finding the man to be enormous and rounded, almost as if he was made of baseballs, footballs, a sack of wool and a round Dutch cheese.

Over the rounded hillocks of the fat man, Doc saw the palm tree skulker arise and make for the door.

For no really sound reason, Doc concluded the fat man had bumped into him deliberately.

He put his face near the fat man's and said, "Brother, you're making an error. This way, you won't last!"

The fat man had small, creamed, new potatoes for eyes. He said, "Beg pardon?"

"Sit down," Doc said. "And don't try to leave here!"

He passed around the mountain.

"I don't get it!" the fat man said.

Doc continued, rapidly. He passed into a hallway, which was rather dark; from this corridor branched another, somewhat more gloomy, down which he saw the palm tree man traveling on tiptoes. Doc ran lightly and collared the fellow.

Jamming a knuckle in the man's back to represent a gun's nose, Doc said, "Get your hands up and behave!"

"Whoosh!" the palm tree man gasped. "What the hell!"

"Yes, you tell me," Doc invited grimly.

"Creepers! Don't you know me?"

"Eh?"

"Boy, I'm good," the palm tree man said. "I'm better than I thought."

"Eh?"

"I'm Carter," the palm tree man explained. "Boy, you didn't think I was going to fool around when I put on a disguise, did you?"

IV

Doc Savage tasted a number of emotions, all of them savoring of damned fool. He released the palm tree man, who began to laugh. "Boy, I sucked you in, didn't I?"

"You should have gotten out in the light where I could get a good look at you," Doc said unpleasantly.

"I'm not that confident. Still, I must be pretty good to have fooled you."

Doc thought Carter was. He was awfully good. He had even made his voice guttural.

He ordered, "Continue to keep your eyes open."

"How about joining you and the dish?"

"No."

"I don't see why not."

"I don't care what you see," Doc informed him. "Did you notice a fat man who got in my way a minute ago?"

"I noticed you stumble over a diner. What makes you think

he got in your way? From the wild look in your eye as you came across the dining room, I thought you were going to start jumping over tables."

"Never mind," Doc said bitterly.

He went back to the dining room. The extent of the relief he felt at seeing Annie safe gave him quite a surprise.

In a moment, a dirigible was barring his path. "Mister," said the fat man, "I didn't like the way you spoke to me a moment ago."

"That's nice," Doc said, scowling. "What do you generally get for bumping into people?"

"You ran over me," the fat man said.

"Okay. What are you going to do about it?" Doc asked, aware that his manners were becoming unusually bad.

"Invite you to have a drink," the fat man said. "What do you think of that?"

Doc was surprised. "No, thanks. But I'm sorry I collided with you. I was upset."

The fat man nodded in Annie's direction. "I understand. I can see she's an upsetter."

"Do you know Annie?"

"Ah, no," said the mountain. "But I'd love to meet her."

"I'm not that mad at you," Doc told him, and went on.

Annie waved her cigarette peevishly when Doc was seating himself. "You behave like a crazy man."

"It was that fellow behind the palm tree," Doc explained.

"What about him?"

He told Annie what about him. He explained that Carter was looking out for her welfare. He realized he was bragging, trying to impress Annie with what good care he was taking of her.

"Oh, he was the loitering sailor!" Annie said, wide-eyed.

"What sailor?"

"The one I saw skulking in the hall outside my room," Annie explained. "I called the hotel management, and they removed him."

Doc recalled that Carter had mentioned something about the assistant manager of the hotel throwing him out, and admitted, "That must have been Carter."

"Why are you so jumpy?" Annie asked.

"Because I think I've got reasons to be."

"Am I in danger?"

"Let's eat," Doc said, on the theory that while food was going in, questions wouldn't be coming out.

114

The floor show, which the place hadn't had yesterday either, was noisy and rather bad. Everyone seemed to enjoy it like everything, and afterward the lights were kept low and the orchestra went into wriggly music, and Doc was surprised to hear a voice addressing Annie. "Wouldst thou dance this one with me, O angel?" the voice asked.

Doc scowled at the young man who had hidden behind the palm.

"Scram," Doc said.

Obviously because she thought it would irritate Doc, Annie sprang into the young man's arms, and they twirled away.

It had all happened very suddenly, and the light wasn't any too good anyway. Doc was somewhat confused. However the confusion departed him suddenly, blown out through his eyeballs, almost literally, by the horrible discovery that the palm tree man *was not Carter!*

The guy had said he was Carter, but he wasn't Carter. He had got away with being Carter because he had kept out of places where there was enough light to read a newspaper. Doc understood perfectly how he had made the mistake. He had made it because he had been pretty dumb, hence easily outsmarted.

No wonder the fellow had dashed from behind the palm tree when he saw Doc start for him. He'd thought the jig was up.

They must think I'm a pushover, Doc thought.

He pretended great nonchalance and surveyed the situation. The fat man was moving toward the door, and there was another man with him, a tall lean young man with shell-rimmed glasses—one hardly ever saw shell-rimmed spectacles on men any more, possibly because so many Japs wore them that the fashion had become unpopular. The young man had an erudite air, an air which often meant the owner was a sap. At any rate, the blimp and his studious-looking stooge were departing.

The situation of Annie was more alarming. The young man was engaged in dancing the breath out of her, not an easy task, and was skilfully maneuvering for a veranda on which there was a potted plant jungle that might hold anything.

Doc gauged Annie's stamina, and decided it would be another couple of minutes before the phony had her out of breath. Doc rose, headed for the place marked Men, turned right, and astonished a waiter by jumping through a window. He landed on a lawn, and moved fast, his objective the veranda.

115

A man stepped into view on the lawn. He whistled.

Doc took to a bush wildly, thinking he was discovered, although it soon proved he wasn't.

The Avion was not like New York dinner spots, because there was an ample lawn, well-furred with shrubbery, surrounding it. A sweeping driveway passed the entrance, and the car had been parked on this drive with other cars.

The car, a yellow touring model as gay looking as a Broadway blonde, lurched over the low curbing and approached the veranda. The driver put his head out.

"Well, get started," he said.

"Any time now," said the man who had whistled.

They both begin watching the veranda.

It was just possible, Doc reflected, that he had made a mistake coming outdoors. He hadn't expected this formidable a force outside—his darker suspicions indicated there were two or more men concealed on the veranda itself.

He decided to mark the car for future handling, so he quit the shelter of his bush with infinite care, crossed silently to the shadows behind the gaudy touring car, and crouched there. He dropped a hand inside his coat, and brought out a flat plastic case somewhat larger, but not much larger, than a five-cigar capacity cigar case.

There was a switch on the case. Desperately unable to remember whether the switch would make a noise, he spent a grim five seconds with thumb poised. But there was no noise. He wished, next, that he was sure the gadget was working. Science, particularly the science of electricity, was wonderful. But only when it worked.

He placed the case against the car. It stuck there when he took his hand away. There was a good permanent magnet in it, but that was about the only simple thing inside the case.

Colonel Madden would be surprised to know what use was being made of the thing. The case was one of Colonel Madden's ideas.

"Psssssst!" said one of the men.

A head appeared from the thicket of potted plants on the veranda. "What is it?"

"How much longer?"

The question remained unanswered; the reply was an explicit statement of where the quizzer could go.

Doc waited and watched. He became nervous. It seemed to him that too much time had passed. He hoped Annie hadn't

116

become suspicious, thus forcing them to knock her brains out there on the dance floor.

Splendor flashed among the potted vegetation. Annie. Doc heaved a sigh and set himself to cope with what seemed to be a very dark immediate future.

He should have, he reflected later, expected the worst from the way the thing got started. Annie didn't do her part. Annie didn't stay dumb, and worse, didn't play dumb.

Without warning, she picked up a potted plant and slammed her escort over the head.

She should have screamed for help then, but she didn't. She whirled to go back into the Avion—her escort was still in the act of falling senseless—and she saw one of the men whom Doc had suspected was planted on the balcony.

Annie still didn't scream, although it wouldn't have been a bad idea. She endeavored to handle things herself, by wheeling, giving an unladylike leap to the railing, and preparing to spring down on the lawn.

Doc now moved. He decided to take the nearest man, and made for him.

He ran into something. He knew, vaguely, what it was, but he didn't fully get this until some time later. There was a crashing report on—and in—his head, a kind of crunching crash which made him think his skull must be breaking. It was really something breaking. A flower pot, which had been heaved on his head from the balcony.

He caved down. He thought he ran for a while on his knees, and never was sure about that. He had decided to neglect Annie, being in no condition to do her good. He believed he might get into the bushes and away. A gun said *bang! bang! bang!* with ugly effect. He made the bushes.

A man jumped out of the shrubs on the balcony and gave Annie a shove. She fell off the railing. A man was below to receive her in his arms, and another man handy to rap her over the head.

They heaved her in the gay touring car.

A man on the balcony spoke in distress.

"She knocked Eli cold," he said.

"Toss him down to us," he was directed.

They fired some shots into the Avion to discourage attention, then hauled Eli to the rail, dropped him over, followed themselves, and became busy climbing into the car.

Each one, when he was in the car, settled down to making

117

an earnest business of pumping bullets into the bush behind which Doc Savage had disappeared, and into any other bushes to which he might have moved. The neighborhood sounded like another Iwo Jima.

During a lull, Doc began bellowing.

"Annie!" he yelled. "Don't tell them anything! Don't tell them our plans!"

He hoped that would keep Annie alive. Being kept alive for questioning, even the kind of questioning she was likely to get, was better than being dead.

Bullets flew thickly for a while. Then someone suggested that they get out and examine Doc's corpse. This suggestion was vetoed in favor of immediate departure.

The car left in haste.

Doc Savage crawled from behind the luxuriously thick-bottomed palm tree which had sheltered him. He saw no advantage in remaining in the vicinity, so he didn't.

V

The Hotel Northern appeared peaceful when Doc arrived. However, now that the fireworks had started, he felt the enemy could be almost anywhere, and so he went in via a window. The hallways were still, except that there was a noisy party in one of the rooms, and he had just become quite positive that nothing was wrong here when he discovered the lock had been broken out of the door to his room.

The lock-smashing was crude. Someone apparently had tossed himself against the door until the lock gave way. Doc stood very still and listened.

Presently he was sure that it was hard, deep breathing he could hear in the room. Not Annie, either. Not breathing like that.

The sensible thing to do was call a houseful of policemen. He was, however, angry enough to be reckless.

He spoke loudly, so that anyone who was in the room could hear.

"The hotel is full of policemen," he said. "Now you can back out of there with your hands up, or we can start tossing in tear gas and bullets. Take your choice."

"For God's sake!" said Carter's voice, nearly hysterical with relief. "It's about time you got here."

Doc did not go in immediately. He waited. He finally said, "Come on out, Carter!"

"Hell!" Carter said. He was having difficulties, the sounds indicated. But he appeared in the door. He was a wreck.

"My arm's broken!" he croaked. Then, when he observed that Doc was more interested in what might possibly be in the room than in his problems, he swore violently, said, "Hell, there's no dragon in here."

"Lie down on the bed," Doc told him, "and let me work on that arm."

Carter scowled at him. "Get a doctor."

"I'm a doctor."

"Oh, that's right," Carter said. "I must be beginning to feel you are around for ornamental purposes only." He stretched out on the bed, showing his teeth with pain, and added, "If you hurt me, I'm going to get up and kick your head off."

"What happened to you?" Doc asked.

"I got ketched," said Carter bitterly.

"When?"

"While I was putting on that disguise I told you about. I was in my car, parked about two blocks from here. I had some makeup stuff, and had just done what I thought was a pretty good job altering my looks—"

"Not," Doc said, "as good a job as I thought—for a while—that you'd done."

"Eh?"

"Why did they turn you loose?"

"They didn't. I fought my way free, against overwhelming odds, I might add. You know what they were going to do? Give me a little accident. They planned to hold me on the pavement and run over my skull a few times with an automobile. Man, when I got away, did I run!"

"They follow you?"

"No farther than I could help. I ran up and down half the alleys in town."

"Why," Doc asked, "didn't you call the police?"

Carter scowled at him. "This isn't a police matter, and you know it isn't."

Doc seized a pillow and suddenly jammed it down over Carter's face. He sat on the pillow to hold it in place, forced one of Carter's arms down with one knee, used both hands to work on Carter's other arm; the man made mewing sounds under the muffling pillow. Then he released Carter.

"It was only out of joint," he explained.

Carter, suddenly wet with cold sweat, began cursing him,

119

swearing for perhaps two minutes without pausing, repeating himself only infrequently. Then he apologized.

"It had to hurt," Doc told him. "So there was no point in warning you."

"You're telling me!" Carter said bitterly. He moved the arm slightly and made a face.

"What did you find out from them?" Doc asked.

"Nothing."

"How many were there?"

"I saw four."

Doc described some of the group who had staged the affair at the Avion. "Familiar?"

"Two of them were in the gang that got me," Carter decided.

Doc added a description, as an afterthought, of the fat man and his studious-looking companion, then eyed Carter expectantly. But Carter shook his head. "They weren't included in the ones I saw."

Doc pondered. "We had better get hold of Colonel Madden."

"What do you think I came up here for?" Carter demanded, nodding at the telephone. "I tried to get hold of him on the phone. No dice."

"Where is he?"

"I gather that his physician sent him home, and gave positive orders that he was not to be disturbed for anything. Which means this thing finally got to him. Incipient nervous breakdown."

Doc Savage was not surprised. There had been plenty of signs that the thing was getting Colonel Madden on the ragged edge.

"How long will Madden be out of the picture?"

"Forty-eight hours anyway, the way I get it," Carter said gloomily. "That's a tough break for us, too."

"Who is going to take his place?"

"I'm supposed to," Carter said. He rubbed the back of a hand across his mouth slowly. "And that's what I meant by it being a tough break. I'm not a very big boy tonight."

Doc glanced at Carter approvingly. He decided Carter wasn't as frothy as he had seemed at times; either that, or the recent bad scare had blown the bubbles off Carter.

"You get hurt anywhere other than the arm?" Doc asked.

"Not that I've noticed yet."

"Then you can still function?"

"In my one-cylinder fashion."

Doc explained about the gadget he had attached to the loudly colored automobile. "That thing was a radio transmitter. It puts out an intermittent dash on a very short wave, a dash every second or so, something like one of those electric fencers the farmers use. All we need now is a radio receiver and a directional loop, and some good luck."

He dug into a small metal case about the size of a suitcase and came up with a portable radio—a special job, not a broadcast receiver—and a directional loop.

Carter was puzzled. "What," he demanded, "is the plaything for? You say you attached something to an automobile. What automobile and why?" He frowned and demanded, "And while we're covering everything, what happened to the lovely Annie?"

"Annie and I," Doc explained, "parted company at the Avion restaurant." While he was rigging the radio direction finder, he elaborated the details of the parting.

Carter gave him a stupefied stare.

"It was my fault they got her," he muttered, a near-illness in his voice.

"Take it easy. You weren't even there, so it wasn't your fault," Doc said. He would have liked to add that he had a better opinion of Carter than he'd had at any time previously, but he couldn't think of a way of phrasing it without letting Carter know he hadn't been considered very highly a bit earlier. Carter's concern was genuine, as was his feeling of guilt.

Carter hauled himself off the bed and pointed at the radio. "Does that gimmick work? What are we waiting on?"

Doc put on a headset and adjusted the frequency and volume on the receiver. He moved the loop carefully, finding the signal null.

"It's working," he said.

He placed the apparatus on a table, pulled up a chair and sat down. "There's not much, really, that can be done for your arm," he explained. "It's going to hurt you for a few days."

Carter was dumfounded. "Hell, are you going to just sit here?"

Doc explained about radio direction-finders. You couldn't tell, first pop-out-of-the-box, whether the transmitting station you had spotted was in front of the loop or behind it, but if the receiver was moved an effective distance and a second bearing taken, the point where the two bearing lines crossed

121

would be the location of the sending station. "But we're up against the fact that the transmitter is attached to an automobile which may be moving, and that could get us snarled up. So I'm going to wait a few minutes and take a second shot. If the bearing then is different, the car is moving."

Carter nodded gloomily. "I wish you wouldn't sound so calm about it. You worry me."

"Have you a street map of the city?"

"Sure."

"Spread it out. We'll mark the first bearing on it."

They did this. Then Doc took another bearing with the loop. They drew this line on the city map, and Carter pointed excitedly. "It's different. Their car is still moving. What have we gotta do, sit until they stop?"

Doc Savage examined the bearing lines thoughtfully.

"I think," he said, "that we can now start boiling our kettle."

Carter kept a hand pressed to his injured arm, and pain and confusion gave his face a loose-lipped expression of idiocy. He watched Doc pick up the telephone and ask for a number.

"What," he demanded, "do you think you're doing?"

"Kindling a fire. To boil a kettle, a fire is necessary."

"You mean there's something we can do?"

"We can close in on them."

Carter jumped violently. "Oh, my God! You can't use dynamite to repair a watch! This thing is so terrific that even the Army and Navy hasn't dared let its bright boys in the Intelligence know what is really going on. And grabbing the minnows isn't going to get all the fish out of the puddle. It may drive the main devil under cover, where we'll never find him."

Doc addressed the telephone mouthpiece. "Monk?" he asked.

The receiver squawked at him. It sounded impatient.

Doc said, "Get your direction finder and get me a bearing on a transmitter on number two frequency. I'll hold the wire. Is Ham there? . . . Fine. Put him on and I'll talk to him while you're getting the radio fixed."

Carter was registering astonishment.

"Who the devil are you talking to?"

"Friends of mine."

"This thing was supposed to be secret as hell! You weren't

122

supposed to tell anybody anything! You're going to get into trouble."

Doc Savage gestured at him impatiently.

"Be still," he said. He addressed the telephone. "Ham? . . . All right, listen. They took their first bite at our bait tonight. I'm going to tell you what happened, and you can tell Monk. My activity finally got them stirred up. I don't know what it was, whether it was visiting the prison camps and asking the questions I asked, or whether it was the interest I showed in that girl, Annie Flinders, or whether it was something else. But tonight they made an open move. They grabbed Carter, the agent Colonel Madden assigned, and ran a double for him in on me—clever job that was, too—at a restaurant called the Avion. I'm not sure whether they planned to grab the girl, and nothing else, or grab the girl and use her as a bait to draw me into a trap. At any rate, they got the girl, took a few shots at me, and left. But I planted a radio gadget on their car. Monk's getting a bearing on it now."

There was an interruption at the other end of the wire.

Presently Ham Brooks said, "Monk says the radio bearing is one hundred and ninety-five degrees."

"Good. They're in the neighborhood of the waterfront. You and Monk jump in your car and get right down there. Keep the short-wave outfit in the car turned on and I'll contact you."

Ham asked a question.

In response, Doc ran off a quick description of the men who had seized Annie.

"There are two other fellows," Doc added, "who may be in it, or who may not." He gave a quick word picture of the fat man and his studious-looking companion. "Keep your eye open for those two. And get going. I'll probably join-up with you in half an hour."

He hung up and turned to Carter.

"Feel like coming along?"

"I don't feel like it. But you couldn't keep me away," Carter said suspiciously.

Carter was doubly suspicious when Doc turned into an empty lot which had been cleared of bombing rubble, and entered a touring car.

"I didn't know you had this car. You've been holding out on us."

"Get in," Doc said. "I haven't been holding out. What gave

123

you the idea I was supposed to tell you fellows every move I made?"

"I thought you were."

"You thought wrong. I was called here because a friend of mine, Johnny Littlejohn, asked for me. You and Colonel Madden were supposed to be helping me, not the reverse."

Carter pondered this while Doc got the car moving. The streets through which they passed were dark, for the lighting system had not been fully restored. But there was quite a bit of night life about. Manila, since its liberation from the Japs, had been active the clock around, for some of the reconstruction was proceeding through a full twenty-four hours every day.

"You should have told Colonel Madden you had two friends here with you."

Doc spoke bluntly. "The trouble with you and Colonel Madden is that you've been making no headway, and are looking around for somebody to blame for it. It's not my fault you are confused."

Carter scowled. "That's plain talk."

Doc made no comment.

Presently Carter demanded, "This Monk and Ham you just talked to on the telephone, they're two of your assistants, aren't they?"

"That's right."

"Monk is Lieutenant Colonel Andrew Blodgett Mayfair, the chemist? And Ham is Brigadier General Theodore Marley Brooks, the attorney?"

"That's right."

"What," demanded Carter, "are they doing here?"

"Helping me."

"When did they come?"

"The same day I came."

Carter said, "I don't think they did. We checked the other passengers on your plane that day, and they weren't aboard."

"They were on a different plane," Doc said briefly. Then he glanced sidewise at Carter and said, "You and Madden seem to have spent more time investigating me than attending to business."

Rage darkened Carter's face.

"We weren't taking any chances with something this big!" he snapped.

"Are you," Doc demanded, "coming along to keep a suspicious watch on me, or to give some honest help?"

Carter controlled a mixture of wrath and embarrassment. "If you want to know why I'm here, it's because I think that girl is in danger!" he snapped.

"That's a good enough reason for me," Doc said in a tone that invited friendliness.

VI

Doc swung the car to the curb in a side street two blocks from the waterfront in the El Puerto section. A short, very wide man approached with a shambling gait. He thrust an astonishingly homely face into the car and complained, "That shyster lawyer pulled a fast one on me."

Doc didn't seem surprised. "Where is Ham now?"

"We got here right on the trail of that loud-looking car you tied the radio on to," the homely man explained. "Ham jumped out and followed the occupants. He told me to wait here and tell you what had happened, and he got away before I could do anything about it."

Carter demanded suspiciously, "Who pulled a fast one?"

"Ham Brooks. He handed me the job of waiting, while he grabbed the action. Say, who are you?"

Doc Savage performed an introduction.

"This is Carter, Colonel Madden's assistant. Carter, this is Monk Mayfair, one of my associates."

Carter didn't offer to shake hands.

Doc added, "I don't believe Carter fully trusts us, Monk."

"And why," asked Monk ominously, "doesn't he trust us?"

"Ask him," Doc said.

After a brief embarrassed silence, Carter muttered, "I guess you fellows are okay. It's just that this whole damned business is so terrific it's got me not knowing which way to turn."

Doc got out of the car. "Monk, where is their machine?"

The gay-colored automobile which Monk pointed out was standing in the street which was near the steamship piers, most of which had been repaired of the war damage.

"That the one?"

Doc nodded. "Where did they go?"

"Toward the piers."

"Did they have a girl with them?"

125

"I think so. They were carrying a figure wrapped in a blanket."

"Ham followed them?"

"Yes."

"How is he going to report back to us?"

"In person. That's the only way he can. He didn't take a radio along, he dashed off in such a hurry."

Doc was not pleased.

"I do not think we can afford to wait around," he said.

They withdrew into shadows where they would not be observed, and Doc studied the vicinity. This was the busiest section of the waterfront. Before the war, Manila had been an active port; now the activity had redoubled several times. The large government docks which had been the city's pride, lay across the thoroughfare. Some of these had been reconstructed, but the majority of them were still war casualties.

More than one large ship was lying at the docks, and Doc frowned at the vessels, recalling that Annie had told him she had been warned to take a liner back to San Francisco. The *Empress Margaret* was the name of this vessel. He wondered if this was one of the vessels in the neighborhood, and why would the gang put Annie on the ship by force?

Why was Annie such a center of interest, anyway? Was there something phony about Annie?

Monk jolted into his thoughts with: "Here comes Ham!"

Ham Brooks said excitedly, "They took the girl aboard a ship."

He was a man of about average height, but with a very thin midsection, wide and lean shoulders, and his face, handsome in a predatory way, was made striking by a large, mobile orator's mouth.

"What ship?" Doc demanded.

"The *Empress Margaret*."

Carter exclaimed, "The hell they did!"

"Who is this chap?" asked Ham, affecting the Harvard accent which he employed on strangers of whom he didn't, at first glance, entirely approve.

"Carter," Doc said.

"Oh, the lad who balled things up tonight," Ham said.

Carter became indignantly silent.

"Ham, how did they get the girl aboard?" Doc wished to know.

"They had it rigged, and rigged slick, too," Ham explained. "You know those rope baskets they swing cargo aboard with?

126

They just tossed her in one of those, on top of some cargo, and she was swung aboard as slick as you please."

"Didn't anyone see them?"

"Sure. But those who saw it were getting paid not to see it."

"That's a pretty serious charge," Doc warned.

"It's the way it happened."

Doc was thoughtful. "In that case, we had better be careful who sees us. No telling who has been bought—oh, oh." He was staring at the loud-colored car. "There's a man getting in their car." Then he added, a moment later, "It's one of the fellows who staged the fireworks at the restaurant."

Suddenly Monk made a grab at Carter, who had started forward. "Where *you* going?"

"To arrest that fellow." Carter jerked at Monk's hand. "Take your hand off me."

"What about it, Doc? Shall I let him go?"

"Hang on to him."

"You fools! He'll get away!" Carter said gratingly.

Doc was grim, but determined. "Let him. Better all the small fry get away than lose the big thing we're after." He turned to Ham. "Ham, you trail that fellow. Use the car you and Monk were using."

Ham departed, running silently. They watched the bright-colored car, heard the motor start, and saw it move away from the curbing. It carried only the one man. It moved away, and a moment later Ham appeared, driving after the machine.

"There's been too much doodling around," Carter complained bitterly. "Whenever we can put our hands on a bird, I say grab him!"

Doc made no comment. He was listening to a measured cadence of many tramping feet which had come gradually out of the night. The sound got louder.

A column of men appeared, marching four abreast, keeping in the street. As the column passed under a street light, they could distinguish the identifying PW on many of the men.

"Jap war prisoners," Monk remarked. "They're heading for the *Empress Margaret*. I guess the liner is taking a gob of them to prison camps in the States."

Doc watched the war prisoners pass on to the dock to which the liner was tied. His expression was narrow-eyed, and not happy.

"Someone is coming," Doc warned.

It was Ham Brooks, somewhat out of breath.

"That guy was just ditching the car," he explained. "He drove it in an empty building and left it. He's going aboard the *Margaret*."

"Let's get on his trail," Doc said. "He may lead us to what we want."

Their quarry—he was the man who had stepped out on the Avion lawn and whistled to bring the getaway car at the beginning of the excitement at the restaurant—strolled on to the busy dock. The dock was not small nor quiet, and the man attracted little attention in the noise and bustle of getting an ocean liner ready for sailing. Presently he drew near a group of workmen who were loading crude rubber in the form of baled sheets of straw-colored crepe rubber.

Casually, the man stepped forward, took a grip and a handhold on a cargo net, and was lifted and swung aboard the liner.

"That's how they sent the girl aboard," Ham explained.

Doc retreated.

"Come on, fellows. They're keeping a sharp lookout, undoubtedly, and we're asking for trouble if we stand around making ourselves conspicuous."

The main gangplank, passenger section, seemed to be the best spot to go aboard. It was busiest. But it was certain to be watched if anything was being watched.

"Carter, have you got your Army credentials?"

"The rats took them when they grabbed me."

"We'll try mine—"

"If we walk up that gangplank, they'll spot us," Carter objected.

"—to see about getting us aboard without being seen," Doc finished.

Doc visited the dock office, consulting with the Army officer in charge, and with the Navy officer and the Merchant Marine man.

As a result, four stretchers were presently borne aboard the *Empress Margaret* with no fuss and feathers. Quite a few stretchers occupied by wounded soldiers had gone aboard anyway. The litters were borne to an unoccupied cabin, the blankets were removed from Doc, Monk, Ham and Carter, and they arose.

"I wouldn't have thought of this," Carter confessed.

The medical corpsmen who had carried the stretchers took their departure.

Doc consulted his watch.

"We have about four hours before the ship sails," he remarked. "Considering the size of the vessel, that isn't much time."

Monk took a cautious look into the corridor. "How are we going to do this?"

"They may not know you and Ham by sight, so you two park yourselves where you can watch who comes and goes. Monk, you take the gangplank. Ham, you get your eye on the cargo loading. They may leave by the same route."

"If they haven't left already," Ham said gloomily. "Come on, you missing link," he added to Monk.

Carter ran a finger around his collar, which seemed to have become uncomfortably tight. "What about us?"

"We'll wander," Doc said, "and keep our eyes open."

Carter nodded. He followed Doc out into the corridor, and they headed toward the midship area where the passengers were milling. "For a guy who is reported to get the results you do, your methods seem pretty commonplace to me."

"If you have any better ideas, I'll gladly use them," Doc told him.

"This is too risky. If I had my idea—ouch! What's the idea?"

He had been silenced by Doc's hand on his arm, hard enough to hurt.

"That fat man and his friend!" Doc exclaimed. "Quick! Duck for that door—no. No, they've seen us."

The fat man, now wearing a full dress suit and a purple ribbon across his chest in the grand style, had observed them. His white shirt bosom looked large enough to be a boat sail as he cruised toward them. He had his hand out.

"Well, well, it's my blind friend from the restaurant. Are you a passenger, too?"

"No, we came down to see that some friends got off before the boat sailed," Doc told him.

The fat man, Doc reflected, sounded resoundingly hearty without at the same time seeming at all sincerely glad to see him. That might mean the fellow was acting.

"I'm Basset," the fat man explained. "Full name's Van Zandt Basset. I'm Dutch. Oil business in Borneo before the war, and a refugee since. I'm going to America to see what prospects I can find in the oil business."

"Smith," Doc said dryly, taking the fat hand and shaking it. He indicated Carter and said, "This is Mr. Stalin."

129

Van Zandt Basset shook Carter's hand. "First name isn't Joe, I hope. Glad to meet you, Stalin."

Doc was watching Basset and if the man knew he was being kidded about the names, he gave no sign of it.

Basset turned back to Doc.

"Funny thing happened at the Avion tonight. Or were you there to see it?"

"You mean my bumping into you?" Doc asked innocently.

"Gosh, hadn't you heard? There was an uproar outside the restaurant, a lot of shooting and yelling and, I heard, a young woman kidnapped."

Doc was thinking of how the fat man and his companion had risen and left the restaurant a few moments before the excitement began.

"You don't say!"

"Then you didn't see it! You missed something. I got in on the tail end of it myself. Jack and I were just leaving—Jack Thomas, the friend who was with me—when the shooting began. Naturally, we've seen enough war to know about ducking when bullets fly, so we ducked. But it must have been interesting."

"Yes, I imagine it was interesting."

"By the way, how about having that drink with me now?"

"Sorry," Doc said pleasantly. "Wish I could. But I've got to scout around for those friends of mine."

"If you find them, join me in the bar, eh?"

"Be glad to," Doc said. "Sorry I bumped into you in the restaurant."

"Oh, forget it. I have."

The only convenient route of escape was out on deck, and Doc took it, with Carter at his heels. They walked rapidly and did not stop until they stood at a deserted section of rail.

"I don't like the looks of that guy," Carter said. "He struck me as a phony."

"For once," Doc agreed, "you might be right."

"Whatcha mean—for once?"

"You don't seem to like anyone."

Carter snorted.

Doc stared absently at the darkened city, trying to decide whether the fat man should be filed under the heading of menace. The coincidence of his turning up aboard the *Empress Margaret* was startling. He continued to stare and ponder.

Manila at night looked much better than it did by day, for only a fraction of the war damage had been repaired; whole sections of the city, particularly the old area where the Japs had made their final stand, were still a shambles. It was terrible. But the darkness made it look all right. A little weird in places, where the toothy ruins stuck up, but not bad. He got an empty feeling, the way he did when he looked at war ruins, and remembered that he'd been kept out of it by the brass hats.

"I like that Annie," Carter said.

Doc released a long breath. "All right. Let's go on hunting."

They walked the decks, the corridors, the salons. The first-class salon, the second-class salon, the dining rooms, all the lounges. They even looked in at the swimming pool, now empty, and they found nothing interesting.

There was a difference, Doc thought, in the liner. It wasn't changed much from peacetime, but things were different. There were the uniforms. The wounded. And, in the third class section, the prisoners of war. A lot of war prisoners. Nazis as well as Japs.

"Creepy," Carter said. "Kind of creepy. You begin to feel like anything could happen on this tub, sort of. I wish we could find one of those guys."

It was creepy, Doc reflected. Creepy. Strangeness and trouble. There must be, he thought, a thousand people aboard, and probably that meant a thousand different stories of terror and disrupted lives, of hopes lost, of disappointments, dangers. War was an upsetting thing, and the agony of it got into your heart quickly.

Doc moved sidewise one pace, stepped heavily on one of Carter's toes, then when Carter yelped in pain and grabbed at him, he shoved Carter violently and the man went down out of the path of fire and lead that began coming out of a steamer robe being carried past by a squat man who was going past, pretending to be a deck steward.

The short man was nervous and made a mistake, endeavoring to stop in the middle of his attack and shake the robe off his gun to get better action. That gave time for Doc to reach him, diving, and get his hands on the robe. Doc jerked. The squat man jerked also. Doc got robe and gun, and the short man took flight, his feet rasping the deck in frantic haste.

Carter, on hands and knees, suddenly rolled over on one shoulder. His injured arm had given way.

131

Doc shook the robe, hoping the gun would fall out. It didn't.

Trying to get up, Carter said, "Thanks." He didn't sound particularly excited.

Doc raced after the squat man. The latter, short-legged, was made for sprinting and quick turns. Doc began having trouble making the turns the quarry made. He could hear Carter pounding behind him. He fumbled in the blanket, hoping to obtain the gun; he could feel it, but couldn't get it free. They traveled fast. People stared at them. There was some excitement, but it was behind them, after they had gone, and did them no good. The squat man, Doc reflected, seemed to know exactly where he was going. That was what made him so hard to catch.

VII

They were deep in the ship now. They had gone down many steps, traversed endless passages, doubled and twisted, until Doc was not exactly certain where they were. But in a part of the ship devoted to cargo and stores, probably the bow section. They plunged into a low place malodorous from bilge and ill ventilation. The small man was not more than twenty feet ahead, but he got through a door, slammed it. The bolt on the other side made a loud whacking sound as it was thrown.

Three things happened to Doc in vicious succession.

Number one was in his head. The squat man hadn't slammed doors until he got to this one. That was blasted strange, he suddenly realized, and not good.

Second, the lights went out.

The third was a conglomeration of action, a hard fist in his middle, an arm around his neck, and a squeaky-voiced promise, "I'll tear your head off!"

The fist had driven the air out of Doc's lungs, so he couldn't make any sound that was coherent. He tried to. Also, he sought to avoid his assailant, but failed. In exasperation, he began hammering back with his fists, at the same time trying to organize a speech.

Another fight broke out behind him in the darkness. This one involved Carter; he could hear Carter's wail of pain as his damaged arm suffered.

"By Jove!" said Carter's attacker in astonishment. "This sounds like Carter!"

Doc's assailant yelled, "Who you got, Ham?"

"That bird Carter, I think."

"I'm not surprised. I didn't trust that cookie anyway."

Doc Savage got his breath and made some words. He said, "Monk, I ought to beat your brains out. Let go of me, you idiot!"

Astonishment paralyzed Monk for a moment.

"Doc?"

"Who do you think? Turn me loose."

Monk muttered, "Blazes I thought something was wrong, because I was about to get knocked loose from my wits."

Ham yelled, "What's going on?"

"The guy I got was Doc."

"For God's sake. What has gone wrong?"

Doc demanded, "Who turned off the lights?"

"Ham did." Monk lifted his voice. "Ham, turn on the light."

When light blazed into the hold, Carter immediately got to his feet, looked around, picked up a small box from a cargo pile, and hurled it at Ham Brooks in a rage.

"Stop that!" Doc ordered.

Carter looked around for something else he could throw one-handed, but located nothing. His arm had been hurt and he was furious. He told Ham several things which came to his mind.

Doc tried the door through which the squat man had gone, and found it barred, and barred solidly. It was a steel door.

"Monk, how did you fellows get here?" Doc demanded.

"We spotted a guy on deck. He was to meet a pal here."

"How do you know?"

"Heard him say so."

"Just how," Doc asked, "did you pick up that information?"

"Nothing to it. We saw this bird, and we were about to grab him, when he called down a passage to someone to meet him in Hold Five in ten minutes. This is Hold Five. We figured why grab one bird when we could grab two, so we came down here and waited."

"What about the man you had spotted."

"To tell the truth," Monk confessed, "he gave us the slip. How the devil he did it, we don't know. But he lost us."

"Did he know you had seen him?"

"No."

"Would you," Doc asked grimly, "like to make a bet on that?"

Monk didn't answer immediately. He became alarmed, and anxiety caused his voice to go up in register. "What do you mean? You think we were foxed?"

"If we weren't, some awfully prominent signs are going to turn out to be wrong."

Ham and Carter approached. Carter, worried now, had forgotten his anger with Ham. "You mean they decoyed us down here and lost us?"

"Worse than that," Doc said, and ran toward the bulkhead door by which they had entered. The door, he had discovered, was closed. He didn't recall closing it.

The door was locked.

"Carter, did you close this door?"

"Me? No. Of course not." Fright suddenly made Carter's eyes round.

"We're in a mess, I think," Doc said quietly.

"You mean they've locked us in?"

"That's part of it, yes."

"Part—" Carter didn't finish. He moistened his lips instead.

Doc was examining the hold. It was low-ceilinged, but the floorspace was quite large. It didn't cover the entire beam of the ship, however, the beam being about eighty feet. The cargo, boxed and baled native stuff, mostly crude rubber and tin, did not nearly fill the hold. Doc searched for ventilating grills, knowing they must be located somewhere.

"Grab something and start work on those doors."

Carter said, "The doors are heavy steel. It'll take a cutting torch to—"

Monk told him, "What's to keep somebody from hearing us and letting us out? Is everyone on the ship deaf? Let's get out of here."

Ham was opening cargo boxes. "Here's some good hammers." He had found bars of tin.

They began beating on the bulkheads. There was a hatch overhead, but out of reach unless cargo was stacked. Doc was eyeing it. He suspected it would be battened on the outside.

Results were surprisingly quick.

From outside, beyond the bow bulkhead, a voice yelled, "Ahoy! What's going on in there?"

"Ahoy yourself We're trapped in here. Unfasten the door

134

and let us out!" Monk, when he lifted his voice, could make a deafening amount of noise.

"Take it easy. Let's have a look," advised the voice outside.

They crowded close to the bow bulkhead door. There was a clanking sound, some hammering. The door remained closed.

"You there?"

"Yes."

"This damned thing is locked," the voice said. "We'll have to get a hacksaw."

"Make it quick, will you," Monk yelled.

"Keep your shirt on. It will take at least five minutes."

"Well, step on it," Monk urged.

The owner of the voice outside said that he would. He had tried to sound cheerful, which was difficult, and now he withdrew a few yards, joining two other men.

"I think I sucked them in," he said.

He was the squat man who had served as decoy.

"I don't think they knew who I was," he added.

"If it keeps them quiet five minutes, fine," one of the others said. "Give me a hand. This thing is heavy." He bent down and began to wrestle a metal cylinder.

In shape, thickness, but not in length, the cylinder resembled those in which welders buy their oxygen and bottled-gas users the gas for their stoves. This one was not quite three feet long, and evidently designed for one man to handle with a back pack. But without the pack harness, it was awkward.

"Sh-h-h-h. Don't let them hear us."

Their objective was in a secluded spot, where they had used an electric drill to put a seven-eighths-inch hole through the steel bulkhead into the compartment where Doc, Monk, Ham and Carter were cornered.

"Where's the hose?"

"Here. Want me to screw it on?"

"Go ahead. Hans, you get the other end fastened in that hole."

Hans was a short, fierce-looking blond-headed man who carried himself with the straight-backed air of one who had stood at attention too much. The hose was about seven feet long, and he had a fastener-coupling which he attempted to screw into the hole they had bored. It broke off.

135

"Ach! Gott!" he gasped.

"Now what?"

"Das ist zu arg! The fitting broke off. Now I have no way of attach the fitting to the hole."

The squat man spoke excellent Japanese, although he was obviously not Japanese. *"Kore de wa idenai!"* He continued in English, and described the man Hans as the illegitimate offspring of a dog raised on worms. He sounded sincere. "You can just stand there and hold that thing in the hole."

Hans' face lost color until it was almost as pale as his very blond hair. *"Nein!"*

"Oh, yes! We haven't got time to rig up another connector."

Hans swallowed his mental sickness as much he could, and got busy, jerkily at first, then with frantic haste, forcing the hose into the hole in the bulkhead, then making a padding around it with his handkerchief. By the time he had finished that, his shirt was wet through with perspiration that terror had brought. He licked his lips nervously. "Ready."

The squat man wheeled, walked back a few yards, and said, "All right. Short the ventilating circuit."

Far down the passage, another man lifted an arm to indicate he understood, then climbed on a box and thrust a pair of pliers into an open connection box. There was a play of sparks for a moment.

The short man listened to the rushing sound of the ventilating system; when this could no longer be heard, his tension relaxed.

"Turn the gas into the hold," he said. "There won't be enough gravity circulation of air to carry it out."

"How much do you want to give them?"

"All of it."

The gassing took about five minutes, and they were interrupted at the halfway mark. There was a startled voice somewhere nearby; it asked a question. There was a blow, a falling noise. The squat man ran to the noise. The others, except for the marble-faced Hans who was holding the hose for dear life, deployed behind him. They all had guns.

They reached one of their number, who was standing spraddle-legged over a fallen man.

"Who is he?"

"One of the crew, I guess."

"How hard did you hit him?"

"Hard enough."

The stocky man examined the one on the floor. His outblown breath made his lips flutter. "Skull crushed. Dead as a mackerel."

The man who had done the killing looked alarmed. "What was I to do? He comes up to me and wants to know what the hell happened to the ventilating fans? I guess he was the electrician."

"You could," said the short man unpleasantly, "have been satisfied with knocking him unconscious."

"That's all I intended to do."

The small man snorted. "Well, it was a damned poor thing to do. So now you can take the body and get rid of it."

The man blanched. "What—what'll I do with it?"

"Get rid of it, I said," the small man said in a conversational tone that seemed, either because of its calmness or what the other knew about the nature of the voice's owner, to reduce the second man to shaking terror.

The fellow picked up the body, not without some difficulty, and went away with it.

One of the others said, "I hope the fool doesn't get caught carrying the body around."

"He'd better not."

In a few minutes the killer returned, looking pleased with himself.

"What did you do with it?"

"Put it at the foot of a companionway, where it'd look as if he lost his balance and fell."

"Good enough."

They went back to Hans. The short man examined the gas container, listened with an ear close to its ugly zinc-chromated iron surface. He turned the shut-off valve.

"Jerk the hose out of the hole and stuff that rag in it," he told Hans. Hans didn't move, didn't turn his head. His face was slick with sweat and his lips were parted, twisted, colorless. "Take the hose out, Hans." The squat man moved forward. "What the hell's wrong with you?" He jerked the hose out himself and stuffed Hans' handkerchief into the aperture. Then he punched Hans. "Come on, snap out of it."

Hans put his head back, lowered his hands to his sides, and dropped.

"Fainted," the short man said, and flew into a rage during which he kicked Hans in the ribs, and again referred to Hans' dog ancestry, ending by adding a bitter apology to all dogs. "Pick the fool up and carry him," he ordered.

Their progress to the deck—they went all the way up to the better-class A deck—was menaced only once, when a well-meaning steward asked them if he could be of service. They said no, thanks, that their friend had imbibed a bit freely in celebrating the sailing.

"By the way, when do we sail?"

"About half an hour, sir," the steward said, and went his way.

Their cabin—Suite C, A Deck—showed signs of shabbiness, and extra bunks had been added for use during the time when the vessel had served as a troop transport. The man who admitted them was about fifty, rather hard-faced. He examined them intently before he let them in, but after that he said and did nothing. He was obviously efficient at his business, whatever it was.

The other man, for there were only the two, was probably older than he looked. He looked about seventeen, and effeminate. His voice was high-pitched and moulded in gentle tones. He looked sissified. But there was no tendency to regard him with disrespect, or take him lightly.

He regarded them pleasantly, then observed, "I think you gentlemen need a drink."

There were no refusals.

The squat man said, "Everything went satisfactorily, Mr. Wilberforce."

Mr. Wilberforce was pouring the drinks with effeminate care.

"All four of them?"

"Yes. All four."

Mr. Wilberforce lifted his glass. "To four souls, may they reside in Heaven." He touched his lips to the glass, added, "I imagine they are destined for Heaven without our bon-voyages, but it makes a nice toast."

They had put Hans on the floor. A man was beside Hans, tilting his head back, pouring bourbon whiskey into Hans' mouth which he had opened veterinary fashion by jamming a thumb into the jaw joint. Hans coughed, spraying whiskey like a geyser. The man slapped him in a rage.

Seeing Mr. Wilberforce eyeing Hans, the squat fan ex-explained, "Hans passed out. Maybe he got a whiff of the gas. He had to hold the hose in the hole."

"He didn't get a whiff of the gas," Mr. Wilberforce said positively. "He wouldn't be coughing now if he did."

"We ran the whole cylinder into the hold."

"It should be enough."

"We got the ventilation system shut off all right. Some guy come down to investigate that. Sean cracked his skull, then put him at the foot of a companionway where they would think he fell."

"Sure he's dead?"

"His skull was like gravel in a sack when I felt it."

Mr. Wilberfore winced and exclaimed, "Please!" He consumed the rest of his drink hastily.

"What," asked the small man, "about the girl?"

Mr. Wilberforce shrugged. "I imagine she can be disposed of now. She has served her purpose, which was a device to attract Doc Savage."

The squat man registered surprise. "I thought she was supposed to be an agent of the Screaming Man."

"Oh, we've decided that isn't likely," Mr. Wilberforce said. Smiling slightly, he added, "You sound rather dramatic when you refer to him as the Screaming Man."

The short man licked his lips. "That's as good a name as any for him."

"True enough, until we learn who he is."

"Any sign of him aboard?"

"I don't know. If the girl isn't working for him, and apparently she isn't, there hasn't been a trace of him, no."

"Good." The squat man was genuinely relieved. "If he's not aboard, I'll feel a lot better."

"So," said Mr. Wilberforce, "will we all."

One of the others said, "For my part, I'll take this Screaming Man, as you're calling him, three times a day in preference to Doc Savage. I'll take him for breakfast, lunch and dinner, if you'll keep Savage away from me."

"Savage," said the squat man positively, "is a dead duck."

"He'd better be," said Mr. Wilberforce quietly.

"I'll stake my neck on it."

"You probably have already." Mr. Wilberforce put down his glass as if putting aside the matters they had been discussing. "I imagine you gentlemen had better go on deck and circulate, passing the word that Savage is no longer a factor."

"Who," asked the short man, "will tell Jonas Sown?"

Mr. Wilberforce underwent a change, the sort of a change which explained why none of the men, although they were

139

obviously hard-souled fellows, had regarded his effeminacy with any ridicule. Mr. Wilberforce became completely frightening to look at.

"The name of Jonas Sown," he said, "is not to be mentioned hereafter. Not at any time. Do you understand me?"

VIII

The *Empress Margaret* dropped her springlines at the scheduled hour for sailing, and with an amount of whistle tooting and shouting of farewells that almost reached pre-war volume, the vessel was nursed out by the tugs and pointed to sea. It was now daylight and those passengers who remained on deck could suddenly get the full benefit of Manila's demolished condition as a result of the war. It was sobering.

Among those who weren't on deck to see anything were the war prisoners being shipped to the States. These were kept below decks; their schedule called for exercise intervals on one section of the deck at specified times. They would naturally be under guard.

There were three hundred and forty-six Japanese war prisoners who had been taken in many different actions in the Pacific. Practically all of them claimed to be Koreans instead of Japanese, but this was a standard lie which Jap prisoners usually told, and to be regarded dubiously. They were an oddly assorted lot, emotionally, which was not unusual for Japanese prisoners. The dopey ones, still corked up on Jap propaganda, were in the majority. There were a few, possibly the genuine Koreans, who were not sullen.

The Nazi war prisoners numbered a hundred and eleven, mostly sailors who had been bagged when a submarine was taken. They had the typical Nazi attitude, the superman air that was quite insulting and, considering their status, rather funny. They didn't think it was humorous. They didn't seem to think anything was humorous.

The skipper of the *Empress Margaret*, Captain Joel Stromberg, of Annapolis, Maryland, made a brief tour of the prisoner quarters with Major Sam Stevens, of Kansas City, Missouri, the Army officer in charge of the prisoner contingent.

"I don't like the idea of war prisoners on my ship," Captain Stromberg explained. "But there's nothing I can do about that, so I'd like to see what precautions are being taken to avoid trouble."

Major Stevens said he didn't blame the skipper.

They made an inspection of the prisoner quarters. The Japanese were segregated from the Nazis, although they were in the same section of the vessel. The quarters were clean and comfortable. Better, Captain Stromberg was thinking, than the prisoners deserved. When a Nazi oberleutenant confronted him haughtily, and demanded better quarters, the skipper did a poor job of controlling his rage. The Nazi officer was insulting. Major Stevens, to avoid trouble, got Captain Stromberg out on deck.

"What the hell are we doing with these Nazi prisoners?" the Captain demanded.

"Those fellows were helping the Japs."

"They must be crazy!"

"They are," agreed Major Stevens. "The way all the Nazis are crazy."

The *Empress Margaret* passed safely through the mine fields and lined out on the regular steamship lane run for San Francisco. Captain Stromberg finished his routine bridge check, and remarked with considerable pleasure on what a relief it was to finally make the Frisco run without the handicaps of being a fast ship in a convoy limited to the pace of the slowest vessel. "If it wasn't for the damned war prisoners, it would be almost like a peacetime run," he declared. "Let's have a drink."

Over gin and bitters, which they both liked, the Captain and the Major became philosophical. Now that the war was on its way to becoming a bad memory, it was good to discuss humanity and what made it get into such messes, the skipper remarked. He made a speech on the subject.

"The thing that has always struck fear into me," he said, "was the dramatic abruptness with which the identical way of thinking pervaded Germany, Italy and Japan. True, a few years were occupied in Germans becoming Nazis and the Japanese becoming whatever you'd say they became. But I still say it was sudden. And I say it was almost a machine-made thing, that sameness of thinking, like something that was deliberately created."

Major Stevens said that he was reminded of something he had heard about mass hynotism, and the psychology of mobs.

He said he believed it was a fact beyond argument that mob spirit was contagious, that it was a disease which bystanders could hardly help catching. Had any man ever witnessed a spectacular parade without feeling a strong impulse to jump in and march? There was a close resemblance between this psychology and the psychology of suggestion which was the basis of hypnotism. In fact, hypnotism *was* suggestion, and it seemed to him fairly obvious that Hitler's power had been founded on such fundamentals of hypnosis as, for example, the continued repetition of one fact. A hypnotist, of course, usually began the inducing of the hypnotic state by repeating over and over that the subject was going into a sound sleep.

Captain Stromberg shook his head dubiously.

"I am not going to try to insist there is no such thing as hypnotism, or even mass hypnotism, although I understand there is considerable doubt about the feasibility of the latter. But I do doubt its application to whole nations. Psychology, yes. But psychology is not a hypnotic force that will warp people as completely as the Axis was warped."

"But you were just saying," the Major reminded, "that the attitude of the Japanese and German people was something deliberately created."

"Exactly."

"How else could it be done, if not by psychology or hypnotism?"

"I wouldn't know. Whoever did it would have to be a master psychologist." The Captain scowled at his drink. "And perhaps more than that. The fellow might have discovered some mechanical means of doing it."

"Some sort of gadget, you mean?"

"Perhaps. It might not be as far-fetched as it sounds. As a matter of fact, it seems to me that our scientists have devoted an unfair—better say unwise—majority of their time and skill to the solving of such mysteries as how many electrons in an atom, and not enough to figuring out what makes a man mad."

"That's too simple. An insult makes a man angry."

"It's not so simple, not when you start asking *why*. What is the actual process in the human body or nervous system, electrical or bio-chemical or whatever it is? I tell you, the great discoveries of the future will be in the fields of psychology."

The Major grinned slightly. "You think some guy may have been ahead of his time? Some guy with a warped mind?"

Captain Stromberg snorted.

"Don't regard it too facetiously. It seems to me—" There was a knock on the cabin door. The Captain, as a matter of old-maidish precaution, ditched his drink under the bunk before he said, "Come in."

The sailor who entered had his hat in hand. "Sir, the Mate wishes to report the finding of a body in one of the forward holds."

"Who was it?"

"One of the electricians, sir. Kinnick was his name."

"A murder?"

"Why, no, sir. Nothing was said about it being murder. He fell, crushing his skull."

"The way you said body made me think it was murder." Captain Stromberg got up suddenly. "I'm going to take a look, anyway. Has the body been moved?"

"No, sir."

"Want to go along, Stevens?"

The Major did. "That talk we were having got me to feeling creepy," he confessed.

Captain Stromberg nodded gloomily and said the Major's creeps bore out what he had said about a feeling of sinister omen pervading the world, and, right at the moment, the ship.

The liner's doctor, a rotund saturnine man named Powell, was finishing an examination of the body. "Death from a crushed skull, if you want it without the technical wording."

"Induced by a fall down these steps," someone added.

"I didn't say that" Powell snapped. "I said a crushed skull."

Captain Stromberg frowned. "You don't think he fell down the steps?"

"I didn't say that either. Maybe he fell down the steps, but it looks to me as if he would have made some marks on the steps if he had, and would have had more bruises than he has."

The Captain and the Major gave consideration to this.

"What do you think, Major?"

"I'm no detective," Major Stevens said. "However, that companionway is steep, and a man falling would reasonably be expected to collect bruises, although whether a bruise would show up if he was killed instantly is something the doctor—"

There was another interruption. Another sailor, an excited

143

one, who reported, "Something is wrong on deck! The passengers are fainting!"

Near a ventilator on the upper deck, three bodies were stretched. They were alone, the passengers and crew having retreated from the spot.

Dr. Powell became cautious.

"Stay back, everyone."

He approached the figures with care from upwind, sniffing the air dubiously. Suddenly, when he was near the ventilator, he turned and ran.

"Gas," he said. "It's coming out of that ventilator."

Captain Stromberg growled, "Will it be safe to hold our breath, and go get those people who were overcome."

"Better be sure to hold your breath," the doctor warned.

The victims were duly dragged to safety by Captain Stromberg, a piece of heroism which did not go unnoticed by the passengers.

"They're not dead," the doctor reported after an examination. "Get them to the hospital, and I think they'll be all right."

Major Stevens scowled at the ventilator. "Captain, is there poison gas in your cargo?"

"No, of course not."

"There might be, mightn't there?"

"Not a chance. I would have been notified of any such cargo. They don't ship that stuff around in boxes like ordinary freight."

"Where does that ventilator come from?"

"Hold Four. Come on."

They went below, and there was some delay while gas masks were brought. The masks were a part of the ship fire fighting equipment, but many soldiers aboard also had masks, and there was some argument about which masks to use. Finally they put on the military ones.

The bulkhead door was unbarred and yanked open. The spectators, those who didn't have gas masks, took to their heels.

Captain Stromberg entered the hold. Major Stevens trailed him. Their search, which was thorough, took about fifteen minutes, and they emerged mystified.

"The gas came from there, Major. But I'm damned if I can imagine what the source was."

Major Stevens took off his mask and mopped his face. It had been hot in the hold.

"Well, we didn't find any bodies," he remarked. "So I guess no one was in there."

IX

The first hint that something was wrong among the war prisoners came that afternoon during the exercise period for the Japanese. It was a brief thing, happening in the space of a few moments, catching the guards by surprise. The exercise pen for the prisoners was the small area of open deck between the forecastle and cabin superstructures. The prisoners were turned loose here among the ventilators, hatches, capstans and cargo booms, and guards with Tommy guns were posted on the forecastle and on the companionway leading up to the part of the superstructure below the bridge.

It was not an attack on the guards. In fact, at no time were the guards menaced.

Captain Stromberg, who happened to be looking down from the bridge at the time, described it with one word. Fear. It was the first time, he remarked later, that he had ever been able to *see* fear.

The prisoners seemed particularly sullen, or what Captain Stromberg took to be sullenness—he was not the only one who made this error of judgment—as they milled about in the well-deck area. There was almost no conversation among them, and no display of emotion, no laughter, no gags, no fraternizing of groups. The Captain observed this, but he took it to be just the nature of Japs when they were licked. He hadn't had much previous experience with Jap prisoners, nor even with the Orient, for most of his life had been spent on the Atlantic passenger runs. Surly devils, he was thinking.

And then one of the prisoners, a rounded roly-poly Jap, shrieked.

"*Baka iu-na!*" he screeched. Apparently he addressed this at one or more men near him.

Then the round-faced Nip whirled, sprinted for the rail, made a mighty leap and shot over the rail and down toward the sea water swirling past. He howled again before he hit the sea, this time only a yell of terror.

Captain Stromberg turned his head. "Reverse engines. Pass the order to prepare a boat for lowering."

Calmly, the Captain turned his gaze back to the section of

145

deck where the prisoners were exercising, and his eyes flew wide with wonder. Because he was witnessing terror, a strange and completely utter terror, seizing a body of men. The degree of fear so nearly approached madness that he imagined for a moment that some kind of a break was being staged. So did one of the Army guards. He fired his Tommy gun briefly.

"Attention! Get back in line, you rats!" The guard's gun blasted warningly again, and he remembered the Japanese words for attention. *"Ki wo tsuke!"* he roared, not doing a very good job with the pronunciation.

The warning shots, his shouting, and the yelling of the other guards, seemed to have no effect. But they presently realized it was fear they were witnessing, not mutiny.

Captain Stromberg thrust his head over the bridge rail. "What's wrong with them?"

A guard lifted an amazed face. "Blessed if I know, sir."

"They're afraid."

"There's nothing to be afraid of, is there?"

"Not that I know of, sir."

Now one of the Japanese managed to open the door to the companion which led to their quarters below decks. Like dirty water spilling out of a hole in a bucket, the Japs went through the door. The guards dived after them, guns ready. Responding to what had evidently been a quick alarm, more armed guards appeared, and these went below deck.

The liner had lost headway.

"Have a boat lowered, Mister, and pick up that Jap who jumped." Captain Stromberg turned and descended to learn what was happening down in the prisoner quarters.

Major Stevens overtook Captain Stromberg on the well deck. "What happened, Captain?" The skipper shrugged, said, "You've got me. The Japs all seemed to have a fit at once, but what caused it I don't know. They were scared, it seemed to me. Funny thing." They clattered down companionway steps toward the war prisoner quarters, listening anxiously for sounds of fighting, but hearing none. Major Stevens apologized, "Sorry something went wrong, Captain."

"Who can predict what a Jap will do?"

"I know, but damn the luck, keeping them in line is my responsibility, and I'm sorry something came up to bother you."

A figure suddenly confronted them, a gun muzzle was presented threateningly.

146

"Oh!" The gun was lowered. "Sorry, sir."

They had been stopped by a guard who was somewhat nervous.

"What are those Japs trying to pull?"

"We can't imagine, sir. They aren't trying to fight, or escape, apparently."

Captain Stromberg strode on, remarking to the Major that what had happened on deck was the damndest thing he had ever seen. He had never seen anything the equal of it. Never.

"If there wasn't god-awful terror in every man's heart, I never want to see it," he said.

They encountered more guards. The Major spoke to them, and they replied, saying the Japs had merely fled to their quarters, where they waited in terror. "Some of them actually crawled under the bunks, and others covered their heads with the blankets, I swear it's a fact," the guard said. "It sounds funny when you tell it, but it wasn't so funny to watch. It sort of turned your stomach."

Turning the stomach, Captain Stromberg thought, was a good way to describe it. He realized now that he was a little sick, and didn't understand why.

He went back to the bridge. The liner was lying with all way off, rolling slightly, and starboard amidships they had lowered a boat. The Captain went to the end of the bridge. The boat was some distance away, but he could tell what was happening. They had reached the Jap, were trying to get him into the dory. The Jap seemed to be unconscious, or dead; at any rate he was limp when they hauled him aboard.

Major Stevens appeared on the bridge. Apparently plunged in startled wonder, he stood frowning at the distant small boat, and was wordless for quite a while.

Finally he spoke. "There's something scary about the way those Japs are acting."

The Captain lit his pipe. He rarely smoked on duty. "What do you make of it?"

"I don't know." The Major shook his head. "I sure don't know, but it gives me the creeps."

The Japanese who had jumped was named Kusumura, first name Hans. They learned this by checking his identification tag with the prisoner list, but this was all because he had followed the general behavior of Jap prisoners in refusing to say anything at all about himself. They found out nothing at the moment by questioning, because he was unconscious.

147

"Knocked out by the fall into the sea," the ship's physician decided. "But he'll come out of it eventually. Thing to do is leave him alone."

Captain Stromberg asked a question.

"Kinnick, that electrician who was found dead—did you find anything queer there, Dr. Powell?"

"Nothing more than I found right away."

"You think the fall killed him?"

"I think a crushed skull killed him," Doctor Powell said, picking up his bag. "What got into those Japs, anyway?"

"They seemed to go nuts all at once."

"They went nuts as a nation several years ago. But this was a peculiar whingding they threw, from what I hear. I wish I could have seen it."

They left a Corporal posted at the door of the cabin they were using as a hospital for the Jap. Major Stevens ordered, "Just keep him in here, and see that he doesn't do away with himself. We want to question him later."

"Yes, sir." The Corporal saluted, then pulled a chair to the center of the cabin when the officers had gone and seated himself. He had not seen the mass seizure which had affected the Japs, and he was not particularly interested. He had seen all of the Japs he cared for from Tarawa and points north. He frowned impersonally at the round Jap on the bed, dismissed the fellow from his thoughts, and began thinking about home.

It was hot, the door gaped open, and presently he heard voices. Three men. They were outside in the corridor.

"Well, here's the cabin," said one of the voices. "Be seeing you later."

"All right. As soon as I take a look at this Jap."

Presently a slender man put his head in the cabin, waved at the guard, glanced at the Jap, and withdrew saying, "Doesn't look as if he's awake yet."

"I'm supposed to examine him anyway."

A giant of a man wearing civilian clothes stepped into the cabin, calling over his shoulder, "In the main lounge, eh? Be about ten minutes." He turned to the guard, asked, "Captain Stromberg or Major Stevens tell you I was to examine this Nip?"

"No, sir," said the guard.

The big man looked tired. "I imagine it's okay if I go ahead anyway, eh? I won't need to move him, and you can keep an eye on me."

The guard nodded.

The big man hauled a sheet off the Jap's torso, held the wrist a while testing for pulse, then rolled the eyelids back from the eyes.

"He's still knocked out," the guard said.

The large man's response was to slap the Jap violently, then seize the Nip's left hand and double the thumb in an extremely painful judo trick which all small boys know.

"*Urusai!*" The word came from the Jap in a painful hiss.

"You speak English?"

The guard straightened. "Hell, he was conscious!" He stood up and came to look down at the Nip. "Them birds can't act like people. They got to be a polecat sneak with everything they do."

"Do you speak English?" the big man repeated.

"Yes," the Jap admitted.

"What's your name?"

"Hans Kusumura."

"How come the Hans?"

The Japanese didn't speak.

"*Sprechen Sie Deutsch?*" the large man inquired.

"*Ja.*"

The guard grinned. "He's quite a linguist. Speaks Japanese, English and German."

Hans Kusumura rolled his eyes slightly, examining the cabin. "Where am I?"

"Back on the boat you jumped off of," the guard told him.

The big man advised the guard, "I'll do the questioning if you don't mind."

"Yes, sir." The guard, slightly offended, returned to his chair.

The big man contemplated the Japanese intently for a while, noting the smaller signs of emotion which Kusumura, who came of a race that had for generations considered it essential to learn to hide the feelings, could not keep from showing themselves.

"You," the giant said suddenly, "know who I am."

"*Chigai nai.*"

"Speak English."

"Certainly. Yes, I know you."

"Did you know I was aboard?"

"No."

"What do you know about that business in Hold Four?"

"Of Hold Four? Nothing."

"It was pretty slick. It almost got us."

149

"I know not of what you speak," Kusumura hissed painfully, but positively.

The big man drew up a chair, the only other one in the cabin, seated himself and became comfortable. "I just happened to see what happened on the exercise deck a while ago, and it was quite interesting. I think it would be even more interesting if you told me what was behind it. Why not tell me the story? Some of it I would know, or already have guessed. But there is naturally a lot that would be new."

Kusumura showed his teeth quickly, more in fear than in unpleasantness. "And what would then happen to me?"

The big man shrugged. "Nothing more, quite possibly, than already will."

The Jap hissed painfully. He was silent. Then, as if the silence brought him terrifying thoughts, he fled to speech. "There is no more room for thought inside me. I have used all that room. There is no door in the terror through which I can pass safely, and so I must take the other door. I am going to kill myself. I tried by leaping overboard. It was not successful. I will try again."

The Corporal, who had fought Japs for a year, told the Jap unpleasantly, "I'll loan you my knife for your throat, bub."

Kusumura looked at him levelly. "Very well."

The guard, his bluff called, scowled. "Don't be funny!"

"Very well. I will find a way. Death is not like great wealth of honor or the respect of other human beings. Death is something any man may easily take for himself."

"This guy," the guard said, "is a philosopher."

"He's serious, too," the big man agreed. He turned to the Japanese. "Where is Johnny Littlejohn?"

"Eh?"

"Where is Littlejohn? Is he aboard?"

Kusumura thought about the question seriously. "He is aboard, I think."

"Where?"

"That I do not know."

The bronzed giant was silent, silent because he felt all of a sudden that if he made any sound, it would be a hysterical giggle of relief. He leaned back, forcing calmness. He breathed inward deeply, because happiness felt in his chest as if it would explode if he wasn't careful.

"So Johnny's aboard," he said. "That means he's alive. But you don't know exactly where he is."

Kusumura closed his eyes. "I have brought you great

150

pleasure. And that, I find, makes me glad. Is it not strange that I should be glad to please you?"

"You're a funny guy," the big man said.

"Perhaps," said Kusumura, "I am, for this one short moment, the great person that almost every man secretly thinks he is. Possibly, for a moment now, I am great. I think it is true. I think I am. It must be, for in this moment I find myself wishing that my country, my native Japan, could have had a citizen, just one, such as yourself. Or Germany. Or Italy. I think that, had this been the case, things would not have been as they now are."

The Corporal scratched his head.

"This brownie's nuts," he said.

The big man was contemplating the round-faced Japanese. The big man's bronzed features were intense, the fire of interest was in his flake gold eyes, and some of the pleasure that he felt at learning Johnny Littlejohn was alive—he believed it was the truth, that Johnny was living—crowded into his voice and gave it a facetious quality he didn't intend when he spoke.

"That was a fine speech you made," he told Kusumura. "But it would be more convincing if you would tell me something I can use . . . For instance, you might tell me about Jonas Sown."

Kusumura jerked visibly. It was as if the name had stuck a thorn into him. And his lips moved, but he didn't make sound. What he said with his lips was, "No one is to mention that name." But he said it in Japanese.

The big man, in English, said, "So no one is to mention Jonas Sown's name."

Kusumura straightened out stiffly on the bed and didn't say anything.

"Hans, could you tell me much about Jonas Sown if you wished?"

"No," Kusumura's voice was queer. "No, not much. Nothing is known of him. Only those of us who were—who did his most confidential work—only such as much as knew his name, and those who did found it out by accident, one way or another. We were not supposed to know that Jonas Sown existed, or that anyone of the sort, anyone that incredible and horrible of personality and purpose, existed. Some of my—of my—I shall call them associates—have never believed. But I am not as gullible."

"Is Jonas Sown aboard?"

Kusumura rolled his eyes. "I do not, and I swear this by my ancestors, know that he is aboard."

"But you're fairly sure he is, because of what happened to you and the other Japanese a while ago."

This statement seemed to put a second thorn into the Jap's soul. His eyes grew startled, then thoughtful.

"You know more than they think you know, do you not?"

"I couldn't answer that. I can't imagine how much they think I have found out, or how much Johnny Littlejohn found out."

"Their opinion of you is not high."

"That's fine."

"They are fools. You are a clever antagonist."

"Let's hope so."

Kusumura closed his eyes, and this time he kept them shut. "I am going to kill myself."

"Hari-kari, eh?"

"No. That is a death of honor. I feel no honor. It is simply that I am ashamed, and can face my own thoughts no longer. I think you understand me when I say that I, and the others who thought as I did, and helped with the doing of it as I did, are guilty of eclipsing the Japanese Empire. Our guilt is the greatest guilt possible, far greater than a death of honor can redeem. No, I shall die as a coward dies."

"That's a fool move."

"Nevertheless, I have decided."

The big man changed the subject abruptly. "What about the girl?"

"The American girl?"

"Is there more than one?"

"No. I merely heard there was an American girl who became involved in Manila."

"That's the one. Is she aboard?"

"I suppose so."

"Alive?"

"Perhaps so. But possibly not. I heard very little of her, only that she was suspected of working with the Screaming Man—"

"Who?"

"Your friend, Littlejohn. They call him that. The Screaming Man."

"Why did they give him that name?"

"Littlejohn is a man of many words, none small."

The big man looked pleased. "That is Johnny, all right. No

small words when he can think of big ones. I don't get the screaming angle, but we'll let that slide. You think they may kill the girl?"

"Why not?"

"Can you help me find her? Give me some information?"

"No."

"Would you, if you could?"

"I might."

"This about all you're going to tell me?"

"Yes."

The large bronze man turned to the guard. "I guess that is about all we can do with him. He didn't do badly for a Jap."

The guard was confused. The questioning, all of which he had taken in with open-mouthed interest, had been nothing like what he had expected. It had touched on so much about which he knew nothing that he was thoroughly puzzled.

He said, "That's the first time I ever heard one of those brownies really spill himself. He talked plenty, didn't he?"

"Not enough to really help, I'm afraid." The big man moved to the door. "Well, thanks. You've been very accommodating, and I don't think you will regret it, in the end."

He went out.

The Corporal scratched his head. He had liked the big man, had been impressed by the easy pleasant way the fellow had gone about getting information. He had spoken the truth when he had said that he had never seen a Japanese prisoner talk so freely, and he believed it was the big man's competent and confident manner which had caused the Nip to talk.

"Quite a guy," the Corporal remarked to the Jap. "I wonder who he is?"

Kusumura kept his eyes closed. The Corporal saw that Kusumura's lips were moving slowly, forming words without sound. Alarmed, the Corporal stepped to the side of the bed and demanded, "What's the matter, Tojo? You unhappy?"

"Not at all unhappy," Kusumura said without opening his eyes. "I am praying a prayer, a Christian prayer. Once long ago I attended the University of Southern California, and at that time I attended Christian Church services frequently out of curiosity. I imagine my prayer will be technically correct, although more than that I cannot guarantee."

The Corporal blinked.

"You're the nuttiest Jap I ever saw," he declared.

"You wish to know who that man was?" Kusumura asked.

"Yeah. I asked you, didn't I?"

Kusumura moved his tongue over his lips and said rather softly, "He is a very remarkable man whose name is Doc Savage."

The Corporal rubbed his jaw. The name meant nothing to him. None of it meant anything to him, except that he was puzzled.

Shortly Captain Stromberg and Major Stevens arrived. They looked at Kusumura, and Captain Stromberg remarked, "So he's conscious now. Has he had anything to say, Corporal?"

"A lot."

"You mean you've talked to him?" Major Stevens demanded.

"No, sir. But he talked a lot to that fellow you sent to question him."

The skipper of the *Empress Margaret* started, then scowled; he and the Major exchanged sharply startled glances.

"You say somebody questioned this Nip?" the Major barked.

"Yes, sir."

"Who in the hell," yelled the Major, "was it?"

"Somebody named Doc Savage, sir." The Corporal was apprehensive.

Captain Stromberg and Major Stevens stared at each other again, and finally the Major muttered something under his breath that Stromberg didn't catch. "What did you say?" Stromberg asked. The Major explained, "What I said, I think, was, 'God almighty!'"

"Ditto," the Captain said.

X

Doc Savage passed Ham Brooks aft of the amidships passenger elevator, and he made a slight beckoning gesture with a thumb. Ham, who was in a chair in an alcove pretending to read a newspaper, but actually keeping an eye open for anything worth noticing, arose and joined Doc.

"Haven't seen any of them," he reported.

"You want to be careful," Doc warned. "There are so many of them aboard that there are bound to be some we haven't seen, and don't know by sight. One of those might put a bullet or a knife into you before you knew it."

Ham said he was being careful. "Was that Jap one of them?"

"The Jap was an unusual customer. He had been one of them, but it had turned his stomach, and he decided the thing for him to do was commit suicide and get away from it all."

Ham shuddered. "It must be pretty bad to sicken a Jap."

"It *is* pretty bad," Doc said grimly.

They entered a cabin which they had taken over by the simple expedient of moving in—they hadn't met the rightful occupants who were, judging from the suitcases in the cabin, two men. The rightful occupants had not shown up.

Monk Mayfair and Carter were waiting in the cabin, signs of strain on their faces. They were relieved when Doc and Ham came in. Monk said, "Staying parked in here is running me nuts, and getting me more scared by the minute to boot. When are we going to see some action?"

Doc shook his head warningly.

"We've got to keep them from finding us if we expect to live through this," Doc said. "I'm quite sure they know by now that our bodies weren't found in Number Four hold, which tipped them off the gas didn't get us."

"I'll bet," Monk said, "they wonder why the gas didn't function."

Carter snorted. "It won't take them long to find out there was a case of Jap gas masks in the cargo in that hold." He scowled, and added, "We should have hid that box of masks under the other cargo, then they would have really been flabbergasted. I should have thought of that."

"You did all right," Monk told Carter. "You knew enough about Army supply markings to realize that case had gas masks in it. If it hadn't been for that, we would have been in a devil of a mess."

Carter grinned slightly. "I don't deserve any credit. I was as glad to find them as anyone."

Carter and Monk were more friendly now. Carter, in fact, had had his self-respect restored by the contribution he had made when he unquestionably saved all their lives in Four Hold by quickly discovering the case of Japanese Army gas masks in the cargo. The Japanese masks, they had surmised, were being shipped back to one of the Army centers where scientific inspections were made of enemy materials. This accounted for the masks being aboard the *Empress.*

"What," Monk asked Doc, "did the Jap have to say?"

Doc Savage went to the door, flung it open and searched the corridor. Satisfied, he wheeled and explained, "Johnny Littlejohn is aboard. He's hot on their trail, because they've given him a nickname. They call him the Screaming Man, probably because of the kind of words he uses."

"Where is Johnny?"

"The Jap didn't know. And that isn't the worst of it, either. Johnny may be a prisoner."

"Good God!" Monk said hoarsely. "If they've laid hands on him, he's dead. They'll kill him in a minute."

"Not," Doc said, "if they had a good use for him."

"Use? What do you mean?"

"I think finding Johnny on their trail would scare them badly. They would want to know how much danger they were actually in—whether Johnny was working alone. And Johnny is smart enough to take out life insurance by giving them the impression that he had plenty of outside help. And outside help, to those fellows, would mean you, Monk, Ham, myself and Carter here."

Monk nodded gloomily. "That would give them a motive for jumping us in Manila. They were scared. Thought we knew more than we did."

Carter had been listening, wide-eyed. Astonished, he said, "You seem to know plenty—more than anybody thought you did!"

He was ignored.

Ham Brooks asked, "What about this Jonas Sown?"

"The Jap—his name is Kusumura—seemed to think Jonas Sown was aboard."

"He know where we could lay a hand on Sown?"

"Not by a lot. He had never seen Jonas Sown. He was even a little vague, deep in his heart, I think, that Jonas Sown exists."

"What about the other?"

"What other?" Doc asked.

Ham chewed his lower lip, uneasiness gathering back in his eyes. "The whole thing," he said. "Is there anything to it? Or is it just a crazy dream?"

"It's no dream," Doc told him. "It's real enough that Kusumura, who is after all a typical Jap, is so sickened by it that he wants to kill himself. And probably he will, if they don't watch him continually."

"Then it's real?"

Doc nodded.

Carter was staring at them in horror. "For God's sake!" he

said hollowly. "I've been hoping all along that the thing couldn't be true. I don't think I've ever allowed myself to believe at any time that it could be as bad as—"

A rattle of the doorknob.

The door flung open.

"Ah, I beg your pardon," said the fat man named Van Zandt Basset, looking in at them. Then, in surprise: "Why, hello there! Quite a coincidence, what?"

Doc Savage watched the fat man with the intensity of a tiger about to spring.

"Some coincidence!" he agreed.

Van Zandt Basset entered, held the door wide for the man who was with him, and said, "I don't believe you have met Jack Thomas, my friend."

Jack Thomas examined Doc and the others with studious blankness. "I believe I saw this gentleman in a restaurant last night."

The fat man inspected the number on the cabin door. "Nine. Really, I thought for a moment there must be some mixup. Perhaps there is." He smiled at Doc, added, "This happens to be the cabin assigned to Jack and myself. Do you suppose there has been a mistake?"

"There may have been a mistake," Doc agreed coldly.

"Nothing, I trust, that can't be straightened out," the fat man said.

"I hope not."

"Do you gentlemen have your cabin assignment stubs?"

Monk Mayfair answered that. He fished in his coat pocket, but what he brought out was not a cabin slip, but a bulky and extremely nasty looking machine pistol. He did not point this at anyone, but held it in a rather inclusive fashion.

Van Zandt Basset seemed not to notice the weapon. "Won't you gentlemen join me in that drink I've been trying to get Mr. Savage to have?"

Doc started slightly in spite of his effort to remain composed.

"So you know my name?" he said.

"Oh, yes, naturally. Haven't we been meeting each other off and on for the last twelve or fourteen hours?"

"I never," Doc said, "gave you my name."

"You didn't!" Basset pretended surprise. "Then it must have come to me out of a clear sky. After all, you're not a man who is totally unknown."

This isn't, Doc thought grimly, a coincidence in meeting. It

157

isn't an accident at all, and probably Basset and Thomas are not the rightful occupants of the cabin any more than we are. Without turning his head, without taking his eyes off the fat man and the studious man, Doc told Ham Brooks, "The purser's office is on this deck. Mind dropping in on him right now and getting this matter of cabins straightened out?"

Ham nodded and went out.

The fat man smiled enigmatically.

The studious man, Jack Thomas—which Doc would have bet plenty wasn't his name—had remained completely sober and scholarly looking, which was another way of being completely expressionless. That one, Doc reflected, is probably the more dangerous of the two. Perhaps not the thinker, but the doer, when something violent and quick and deadly had to be done. He decided to give Jack Thomas first attention if violence began, and he didn't look forward to the possibility with any pleasure.

Then the fat man raised their hair.

He said, "It seems that the unusual is dogging my path today. For instance, I saw a very terrified young lady a few moments ago. Her name, I believe, was Miss Annie Flinders."

Doc Savage had the absurd feeling that astonishment had lifted him off the floor and was holding him suspended in space. His voice sounded far away, and as if it didn't belong to him at all, when he spoke.

"Where is she now?" he asked.

"In A Suite, this deck," the fat man said calmly.

Doc Savage caught Carter's eye. Carter seemed completely dumbfounded.

Monk Mayfair now made no pretense of not pointing his pistol at anyone. He pointed it at the fat man and his studious friend.

"Is she okay?" he demanded.

"I don't," said Van Zandt Basset, "imagine that her health will continue, although it seemed fair when we saw her."

Doc got hold of himself. "How many Japs with her?"

"No Japs."

"Don't tell me," Doc said grimly, "that there was no one with her."

"I said no such thing. There were two men. Two fellows who look totally unlike Nazis, but are."

"More in the suite?"

"Probably."

Ham Brooks now returned from the purser's office. He reported, "These two fellows are now registered in this cabin. But they weren't when the ship sailed. They made the change after sailing, about an hour ago, paying the purser two hundred dollars to make the change. The purser's a little worried about it."

"An hour ago," Doc said, "would be after we took over the cabin. What about the original occupants?"

"Oh, they gladly gave their okay to the swap, because they got a better cabin out of it."

Doc wheeled on the fat man. "All right, let's have the truth. You made the swap because you found out we were using the cabin as a hideaway, that right?"

"That is correct," said Van Zandt Basset blandly.

Doc frowned. "Why did you do it?"

"As a service."

"Eh?"

"A slight contribution," said the fat man, "to your success."

Doc shook his head. "I don't get it. But we'll go into the matter later." He wheeled to Ham, explained, "These fellows say Annie is in Suite A, on this deck. They say at least two men are guarding her, maybe more."

Jarred by surprise, Ham couldn't speak.

Doc leveled an arm at Carter. "Carter, you stay here. Watch these two fellows. You have a gun, haven't you?"

"Who the hell *are* they?" Carter demanded, producing a revolver and using it to point at Basset and Thomas.

"I have no idea," Doc said, and strode out into the corridor, beckoning Monk and Ham to follow.

A few yards down the corridor, Doc drew Monk and Ham into an unoccupied cabin, the door of which was open, for a conference. "I haven't the least notion who those two birds are. They just gave me about as complete a surprise as I ever had. I don't know what their game is. But it may not be good."

Monk expressed a definite opinion. "I don't like that one who looks like a professor and doesn't say anything. He doesn't look as if he had a soul in him."

"You think they're pulling something on us?" Ham demanded.

Doc nodded. "I'm sure they are. But I'm not sure whether it is going to be good or bad for us."

159

"It'd have to be bad."

"Not necessarily."

Monk had an inspiration. "Could it be that they know where Annie is, but don't want the job of rescuing her because it is going to be tough? So they walk in on us and hand us the job?"

"That," Doc agreed, "is a mighty good guess."

Ham said, "Suite A is forward. It's one of the best suites of cabins aboard, if I remember the layout of these ships correctly. I had a similar suite once. It probably consists of a parlor, bedroom, bath and private sun deck. What do we do, barge in?"

Doc was uneasily eyeing the cabin they had just left. "I hope Carter can handle those fellows with that bad arm of his."

"He'll handle them," said Monk, whose opinion of Carter had skyrocketed since Carter had dug up the gas masks that had conveniently saved their lives. "If they get careless with him, Carter's in the frame of mind to haul off and fill them full of lead."

"I hope he keeps that pair cornered. I want to ask them some questions."

Monk registered sudden excitement. "Blazes! Maybe one of them is Jonas Sown!"

"Carter himself could be Jonas Sown, and no one would know the difference," Doc said thoughtfully. "Come on. We've got something tough on our hands."

XI

Mr. Wilberforce, in A Suite, poured tea. He did this effeminately, as he did everything, for the sissified manner remained with him always, no matter whether he was butchering a man or pouring tea, as he was doing now. "For a knocking together of the knees, there is nothing like a spot of tea," he remarked.

The squat man who had turned the gas into Hold Four when he had thought Doc Savage was inside—or at least had supervised the job—was present. "I don't feel like funny conversation," he said unpleasantly. He poured half his tea in a vase and filled the cup up with a brand of rum suitable for removing hair from dogs. "Savage is not quite as dead as we thought he was, and Hans picks this time to get an attack of appendicitis."

There were three other men in the sitting room, and this group, a total of six, made the place seem somewhat crowded.

Hans, the fellow who had actually turned the valve on the gas cylinder during the episode at Hold Four, had been falsely accused of being squeamish when he fainted, they had since discovered. Han's trouble was, they believed, his appendix.

They had not called a doctor. Hans lay on a couch, sweating with pain, and eyed them anxiously. He asked them again to send for a doctor as quickly as possible.

"*Schicken Sie nach einem Arzt so schnell wie möglich,*" he said.

Mr. Wilberforce gave him a girlish glance of disapproval. "Really, you shouldn't speak German, my friend."

"I'm sick," Hans complained in English. "You've got to get a doctor for me."

"How," asked Mr. Wilberforce, "would you explain the presence of the girl?"

Hans was frightened and angry, and his rage seized on Annie as an object. He cursed her bitterly in German and English, then wished to know how long it would be before she was dead. Mr. Wilberforce assured him it would not be until they figured out a way of getting her body out without being observed.

"She's not going to talk, that's obvious," he said. "So we have no use for her. It was a mistake in the first place to bring her aboard."

The squat man said, "When we grabbed her, there at that restaurant, Savage yelled at her not to tell his plans. Hell, she doesn't know his plans."

"Savage outsharped us," Mr. Wilberforce agreed.

He went into the bedroom to gaze malevolently at Annie, who was being guarded by another man. Annie looked back at him out of one eye in which terror and rage glittered. Her other eye was swollen and discolored with an unladylike shiner, and she was also gagged and tied hand and foot.

An imperative knock on the cabin door made Mr. Wilberforce spring to the middle of the room and snatch out a revolver.

161

"Lifeboat drill!" said a voice outside. "Everyone out for lifeboat drill. Take your boat stations."

Mr. Wilberforce released a relieved breath. He had been badly startled.

Hans rolled his eyes, asked, "Hadn't somebody ought to go on drill from here?"

Mr. Wilberforce snorted.

But he looked considerably less contemptuous presently, when the door was tried, then an imperative fist hammered the panel.

"What is it now?" Mr. Wilberforce demanded angrily.

"Lifeboat drill!" a voice rapped. "All out for drill. No exceptions."

"We're skipping it," said Mr. Wilberforce. "So scram."

The voice outside became angry and said, "That's what you think, buddy. Wartime regulations are still in effect on this ship, and they say everybody out on drill. So it's everybody out."

Mr. Wilberforce, pale with rage, wheeled to the others and said, "Duck into the bedroom. I'll tell this goof Hans is sick and I've got to stay with him." The others hurriedly disappeared into the bedroom. Mr. Wilberforce then yanked open the door and began, "My friend is sick and I've got to stay—uh, ugh, awk!" The ending of the speech was due to the difficulty of speaking around the pistol barrel which had been jammed, with grim accuracy, into his mouth.

From behind the pistol, Monk Mayfair said, "How does it taste?"

Doc Savage came around Monk into the cabin, swept the place with his eyes, and went on to Hans, who was trying to get off the couch. He hit Hans a short uppercut and Hans lay back down. Ham Brooks entered the cabin, selected two chairs, carried them to the door and told Monk, "Get your friend out of the way." Monk crowded Mr. Wilberforce farther into the cabin. Ham laid the chairs across the door, where they would impede the footwork of anyone trying to leave in haste.

The bedroom door opened a crack. Doc kicked it as hard as he could, driving the door back and ruining the face that was behind it.

Monk Mayfair grinned at Mr. Wilberforce, then hit Mr. Wilberforce under the jaw while the gun nozzle was still in

Mr. Wilberforce's mouth. As a result, teeth broke and flew like gravel from Mr. Wilberforce's lips.

Several bullets came into the cabin from the bedroom, but they were fired at random and did not hit anyone.

Ham said, "I'll look in the other bedroom." He went toward the second bedroom door, stopped at a banging noise in the bedroom. With displeasure, he eyed the splinter-edged holes bullets had made in that door. "We seem to have a houseful," he said.

Doc Savage fished some smoke grenades out of his pockets, standard U.S. Signal Corps grenades of the type used for making colored smoke signals. He got them to functioning and tossed them on the floor. There followed a short silence while they waited for the smoke to get effective, and while the men in the bedrooms tried to get organized.

Monk had an inspiration.

He yelled, "Get your masks on, guys! Let the poison gas finish the job!"

This did not have exactly the effect he had anticipated, because men began coming out of the bedrooms like weasels out of a hollow log. They came fast, full of the idea there was poison gas in the cabin, hence anxious to get out into the corridor without pausing for any foolishness such as fighting. They seemed, in fact, to all come at once.

Ham yelled, collared someone, was knocked loose. A gun slammed deafeningly. It was the cue for everyone to start emptying his gun. The room became a pandemonium of shooting, howling and running. Ham's chairs across the door brought down the first ones, but they got up and went on, and the chairs were kicked out of the way.

In ten seconds, the noisy part of it was over.

The smoke from the grenades was green. It was the most infernally greenish green Doc believed he had ever seen, and dense. He tested its denseness with his fingers in front of his nose and barely distinguished the digits.

"Monk?" he ventured cautiously.

"I'm in one piece. We didn't do so good, did we?" Monk muttered.

"Ham?"

"Right."

"You and Monk see if the girl is here. I'm going to see if I can follow and collar some of those fellows."

The following operation did not turn out well. Doc went

out into the corridor, and suddenly there were too many bullets there. He got back into A Suite in haste.

Monk called, "Doc?"

"Yes?"

"We've got a girl here. In this smoke, you couldn't see a stroke of lightning on the end of your nose, but I imagine it's Annie."

Doc tried to remember whether the deluxe cabins had round portholes too small for a man to pass, or whether they were large window affairs. He asked Ham, "Are the portholes big enough to let us out?"

Ham reported, "One whole side of the sun porch is plate glass."

"Break it, and let's get out of here," Doc said. "Monk, help me look for some of the gang who may have been left behind."

Presently the plate glass shattered loudly. Doc crawled around on all fours, seeking the man who had been on the divan, and whom he was positive he had knocked senseless. He didn't find the fellow. Someone had been quick-witted and taken the unconscious man along.

Suddenly, in horror, Monk grunted, then said, "Jeepers!"

"What's wrong?"

"Here's one. But he stopped a bullet, and I think I've got him all over my hands."

Hastily, Doc said, "Let's go."

Ham was on deck, clear of the green smoke that was pouring through the shattered glass. Quite a number of passengers and crew, drawn by the shooting, uproar and smoke, were gathering.

Doc endeavored to sound loud and important and told them, "Better get the fire brigade to work. Something is wrong in there."

In the ensuing confusion, he helped Ham carry Annie—the girl was Annie—inside and to the cabin in which they had left Carter guarding Van Zandt Basset and Jack Thomas.

"Whew! It sounded like the war had broken out again!" Carter gasped. "Is she all right?"

Doc said they would see, and he untied Annie. Annie immediately earned their secret approval by announcing freely and in detail exactly what she thought of the world in general and particularly their method of rescuing her. It was not flattering. Annie felt they had shown scant consideration of her life, that they had behaved like idiots who didn't give

164

two cents for their own necks. It was not a speech of gratitude, but somehow it fitted the circumstances exactly. It showed Annie was human.

"An appropriate speech," said the fat man pleasantly.

The mild speech had the effect of fixing every eye on Van Zandt Basset, all with suspicion except for the fat man's companion, Jack Thomas, who smiled slightly in approval. It was the first sign of anything like a normal emotion that Jack Thomas had exhibited.

"You," Doc told the fat man, "are a nut that is about to be cracked. A can about to be opened. A mystery to be solved."

"I'm perfectly agreeable," Basset said.

Doc nodded.

"Talk," he directed.

"Why, I explained that I am a Dutch oil man," Basset stated. "I lost my holdings in Borneo—"

"You're not," Doc interrupted, "fooling with the oil business now. You may be an oil man; I wouldn't know. But that isn't the story I want to hear." Doc turned to Carter, asked, "Did you search him?"

"No. I was afraid to get that close to him," Carter confessed.

"Search him, Monk."

Monk mined various documents, assorted cigars, and an impressive roll of currency out of the fat man's clothing. After consulting the documents, he reported, "They say he's a Dutchman in the oil business."

Doc pointed at Jack Thomas. "Try him."

The scholarly young man had cigarettes instead of cigars and a roll of bills which would not choke quite as large a bull as his friend's would have.

Monk examined the loot. "Ex-college professor. Specialty is Social Sciences. War refugee. Last place he taught was Chungking. Has a lot of documents entitling him to enter the United States. The last all look genuine, but I wouldn't know whether they are or not."

"No guns?"

"Not a gun."

"I'm glad you're satisfied," said the fat man triumphantly.

"We're not," Doc told him. "Not any part satisfied."

Jack Thomas made his second speech since Doc had known him. He spoke with scholarly preciseness. "What do you think you are going to do about it?"

165

Doc looked at him coldly. "Plenty," he said. "And you won't like it."

Jack Thomas' face darkened. "You'd better make sure you know what you're doing, my friend."

Doc leaned forward tiredly. He was angry and worried. "I hope you know what *you're* doing," he said bitterly. "Because we're not going to fool around with you. This whole filthy, fantastic mess is beginning to blow up in somebody's face, and it's not going to be our face if we can help it. We have a friend named Johnny Littlejohn who—"

He stopped. The fat man had started slightly, and the sight made the words cramp in Doc's throat. He was gripped by all the fears he had been feeling for Johnny's safety for days, and these terrors held him speechless. He could say no word, and watched Monk step forward, and, his voice terrible with intensity, address Basset.

"What about Johnny?" Monk demanded. "You know something about him, don't you?"

Basset said with thin-lipped grimness, "I know he's in a mess."

"Where is Johnny?"

"I know something else, too," the fat man added. "I know this ship is going to become once choice corner of hell, and I don't see anything anybody can do to stop it."

A gentle knocking sounded on the door. A quiet voice called, "This is Captain Stromberg, commander of the vessel. Will you gentlemen kindly open up and avoid trouble for everyone concerned?"

Eyes fixed on the door, Doc tried to recall whether anyone had locked it from the inside. He didn't believe they had. Out of the corner of his eye, he saw Ham Brooks glide silently to the porthole, which was round and looked out on the deck. Ham looked, then turned a shocked face.

"There's half a dozen sailors out here with more guns than a Commando squad."

"Do they seem genuine crew members?"

"As far as I can tell."

Suddenly showing so much alarm that it startled all of them, Basset said, "For God's sake, don't take any chances!"

Doc moved to the door and called, "Who did you say this is?"

"The captain of the ship," the quiet voice replied.

"What do you want?"

"Open up, please."

"Not," Doc said, "unless you give us some proof you are the skipper. And you'd better not try to come in here until you're invited, either."

The voice added grim determination to its quietness and said, "There has been a lot of excitement and a murder in one of the deluxe cabins. Some men were seen leaving the suite through a broken window, carrying a young woman who was bound and gagged, and these gentlemen were seen to enter this cabin. If you have an explanation, admit us and we'll be glad to listen. If you want to get tough, we can get tough also. I'll give you thirty seconds."

Jack Thomas spoke thickly.

"That's the skipper of the ship," he said. "I know his voice."

It was not this statement which convinced Doc Savage. Instead, it was the unbounded relief which swept the fat man's face that led Doc to decide it was really the captain of the ship outside.

"Come in, Captain," Doc called. "The door is not locked."

XII

Twilight, the brief unreal twilight of the tropics, had laid its fleeting warm glow over the sea, and was generally giving a placid feeling to the liner that didn't belong at all. The *Empress Margaret* charged through the sea at better than twenty knots, throwing the sea aside with her bows in a sound like heavy, uneven breathing, as if she were suffering, which was appropriate, Doc Savage reflected.

Doc was on the bridge. So was Monk, Ham, Carter, Annie, Basset and Thomas, the steersman, the deck officer and Captain Stromberg, who had paused to listen to Major Stevens, who was in charge of the armed guard for the prisoners of war.

"Something queer," Major Stevens was telling the Captain anxiously, "is happening to the prisoners. I can't make it out, but it's beginning to frighten me. The prisoners, the Nazis as well as the Japs, are starting to boil over. That is, they've given symptoms. And I don't like it."

"What kind of symptoms?" Captain Stromberg demanded.

"You saw how terrified those Japs acted after that fellow Kusumura jumped overboard? Well, it's getting worse. There's no sense to it, and I don't see what they're afraid of, or what's upsetting them. It's fantastic. But something is getting them worked up to the point where they're going nuts, and may do anything."

"You had better increase the guard."

"I know my business," said Major Stevens briefly. "I have all my men alerted."

As yet, Captain Stromberg had had no time to question Doc's party. He faced them, but hesitated when a sailor came on to the bridge. "Yes? What is it?"

"That Jap who jumped overboard, sir. That Kusumura."

"What about him?"

"He just committed suicide, sir."

"What," demanded the Captain bitterly, "was the guard doing?"

"The Jap pulled the bed sheet over his head, sir. Then he tied his pajama coat around his throat and strangled himself, and the guard didn't notice him because he was under the sheet."

Captain Stromberg looked at Major Stevens blankly. "There was certainly something on that Jap's mind."

"There's something on all of their minds," the Major said uneasily.

Stromberg suddenly leveled an arm at Doc Savage. "Some stranger got into that Jap's cabin with a ruse and questioned him. The Jap said it was you, and the description the guard gave answers your looks."

Doc nodded grimly.

"We've got trouble on our hands," Doc said. "It isn't going to help us a bit if half of us don't know what we are doing. We had better get the whole story of this thing told right now."

Jack Thomas cleared his throat with scholarly dignity. "That's an eminent idea, undoubtedly."

"How would you like to start the story off?" Doc demanded.

Jack Thomas looked about the group with studious mildness. "I have no objections."

Before Thomas had spoken a dozen sentences, Doc Savage was convinced that the young man possessed a brain far from ordinary. Doc was inclined to judge men a great deal by their

168

speech, not basing opinion too much on any one thing, but weighing the man's pronunciation and grammatical delivery —these were usually a fair indication of background and education—and the clarity with which ideas were expressed and topics dealt with. This Jack Thomas was clever. He was, Doc felt, an intellectual giant.

Jack Thomas was giving his background—English by birth, public schools, Oxford, Heidelberg, then social sciences and travel. He had, he explained, finally settled in China because he was interested in some of the aspects of ancient Chinese philosophy—the Chinese the world over had a reputation of being versed in philosophical tenets which they had perfected coming down the centuries, and Thomas had believed that they had something to offer, in spite of the fact that in a material sense—automobiles, bathtubs and radios—the Chinese national economy was negative in position when compared to other nations such as America and England.

"You probably understand now that my special interest is the philosophy of mankind, the way men think," he remarked. "Now I'll take up the matter at hand, which I at first greeted with about the same degree of incredulity which you will be inclined to present to it."

From somewhere below decks, far away, there was a single report. A shot.

"Find out what that was," Captain Stromberg ordered. A sailor departed hurriedly.

Annie had paled at the shot. Since her pointed remarks about the way they had risked her life in rescuing her, she hadn't had much to say.

Now she spoke, asking, "Is this supposed to be secret?" and nodding at the helmsman.

"Too late for secrecy to do much good," Doc said, when it was evident no one else was going to speak. "Anyway, no one is going to really believe it, unless the proof is in front of their eyes—the way we're going to have it in front of our eyes before long."

"God forbid," said the fat man, Van Zandt Basset. He sounded horrified.

Jack Thomas resumed his recital.

"It was in Chungking," he continued, "that I first heard of there being an individual who had caused the current cycle of wars. The story was told me by Wo To Sei-gei, an elderly scholar, who had received it as a rumor. However, as it developed, Sei-gei's story was remarkably accurate in the primary details, which attributed great mental genius to the fellow, together with infinite psychological ability. The machine, too, was a part of old Sei-gei's story, together with a fairly reasonable theory of how it must work. I never was able to ascertain the source of the old Chinese's rumor, but it was amazingly accurate."

Captain Stromberg suddenly lost color, and in a moment perspiration beaded his face.

He demanded, "Am I to understand a *human mind* is responsible for these wars?"

"Exactly."

Major Stevens cleared his throat. "You mean Hitler, Mussolini and the Tojo crowd, don't you?"

"No. Although Jonas Sown unquestionably had prominent Nazis as underlings, perhaps Hitler himself."

"Who," demanded Major Stevens, "is Jonas Sown?"

"Jonas Sown," said Thomas, "is an example of how dangerous genius can be to humanity."

"You mean this Jonas Sown is—is—"

"He caused the last ten years of war, yes."

Major Stevens started to pull in a great breath of surprise, but when half-drawn, it exploded out of his lungs again in hysterical laughter. Not amused mirth. Disbelief, wild and incredulous and a little unhinged. The Major kept laughing, a silly expression on his face, for several moments, and toward the last he began to look as if he doubted his own sanity.

Jack Thomas said calmly, "That is what I meant—one's mind refuses to accept the thing."

"Go on with the story," Doc directed.

"I work for the Chinese government now," said Jack Thomas. "My commission is to find and destroy Jonas Sown, which in general terms means finding and destroying a creature no one believes exists. I have been three years on the assignment. I will not detail those three years, but they were heartbreaking. But in the end I found Jonas Sown does exist."

Doc Savage interrupted, "Sown was in Japan?"

Jack Thomas nodded. "When Germany fell, he went to Japan. From Japan he fled to China, to Japanese occupied China, and from there to inside the American lines, thence to Manila. This he managed very cleverly, for he became an Axis war prisoner deliberately, and contrived to get into a group which is being sent to America. He is—and this I think, but cannot prove—one of the war prisoners now on this liner."

Now Jack Thomas turned to the fat man, Van Zandt Basset.

"Mr. Basset," he said, "is a secret agent of the Dutch government. His assignment is also to find and destroy Jonas Sown."

Basset cleared his throat. "We teamed up, Thomas and I, in Manila, after we found we were both after the same fox."

"It's obvious, from what I've told you, why we're aboard," Thomas added.

"Just why," Doc asked thoughtfully, "were you in the Avion restaurant last night?"

"Some of the men we know to be Jonas Sown's agents were hanging around there."

"Why not grab one of those agents and force him to lead you to Sown?"

Thomas smiled grimly. "We've tried that. None of the agents apparently know just who he is."

Captain Stromberg eyed Doc Savage suspiciously. "I've heard of Doc Savage, so I'm inclined to trust you," he said. "But I'd like to know where you hitch into this, and whether you believe the whole goofy story."

Doc said readily, "I hook into it much the same as Mr. Thomas says he did. I first heard a rumor of such an individual as Jonas Sown. That was several months ago, and my reaction was what anyone's would be—disbelief. However, the thing stuck in my mind. The whole approach of Italy, Germany and Japan to this people has been so deliberately inhuman that it *could* be the work of an evil force personified by one man. So I assigned one of my friends, who is also my aide, to investigate. The man was Johnny Littlejohn, archaeologist and geologist. I picked Johnny because he happens to speak Japanese fluently, as well as a number of Chinese dialects, and he can impersonate an Oriental rather well."

Doc paused. The sailor who had gone to investigate the shot had come back. He said, "The guards had to shoot one of the war prisoners. A Nazi. The fellow attempted to make a break, although he should have seen he didn't stand a chance."

"How is the situation?" Major Stevens demanded.

"Not good, sir," the sailor said.

There was very little more to his story, Doc Savage explained. Johnny Littlejohn had not been heard from on the

171

assignment until recently, when he had despatched a hurried summons from Manila for Doc Savage.

"He had learned the identity of Jonas Sown," Doc said.

Everyone jumped at that. Jack Thomas particularly. "How do you know he found out?" Thomas demanded.

"From the wording of Johnny's summons," Doc explained. "We had previously agreed on a general code for communicating intelligence of a general sort. The words he used told me he had found Jonas Sown, although the text of his message contained no such information."

Doc indicated Carter.

"The United States Army, I learned on arriving in Manila, had been cooperating with Johnny in the investigation. Mr. Carter, here, is one of the Army men assigned to assist me in finding John Littlejohn, who had disappeared after communicating with me."

"What happened to Littlejohn?" Captain Stromberg demanded.

"He had the misfortune to be caught by Jonas Sown's men, I imagine," Doc said. "At any rate, the Jap who jumped overboard, Kusumura, said Johnny was on the ship, and I'm inclined to believe that correct."

Captain Stromberg scowled. "I'm half inclined not to believe a damned word of this witch's tale!"

Annie spoke an explosive word.

"Dope!" she said.

The skipper wheeled on her to demand skeptically, "Where do *you* come into this affair?"

"I rode into it," Annie told him, "on my bump of curiosity. I had an attack of a disease called inquisitiveness, of which, incidentally, I'm cured. I started following Mr. Savage around to pass the time. I thought I might see some excitement. That made the U.S. Army suspicious, and they threw me in jail, investigated me, then turned me loose. That called Jonas Sown's attention to me, and he had me grabbed and sneaked aboard this ship."

"Sounds thin to me," Captain Stromberg said briefly. "Why should they smuggle you aboard?"

"To ask me questions," Annie said. "And, believe me, they asked plenty. They had more than they could ask before the boat sailed, so they brought me aboard to continue asking them."

"What kind of questions?"

"What did Doc Savage know? Who was I? What was Doc

Savage going to do? He had more questions than snakes have holes." Annie looked bitterly at Doc and added, "You certainly got me into a fine mess."

Captain Stromberg remarked that everything was in a mess, if anyone asked. He demanded, "Savage, what is this Jonas Sown going to do?"

"Escape, if he can," Doc said. "That means he'll be rough on anyone in his way. However, he's not going to get away with it. He's not going to get away with it because we have him in the bag."

The effect on those in the room was what Hollywood would call a double take, with the full import of Doc's last few words being missed; then the statement landed like a thunderbolt.

Jack Thomas sprang to his feet. He looked wildly eager. "My God, I've gone through three years of hell for a chance at Jonas Sown!" he cried. "I hope you know what you're talking about."

Monk and Ham reacted almost as strongly, as did Stromberg. Carter and the fat Van Zandt Basset, however, didn't take it as big, and Doc thought they exchanged brief glances.

Doc turned to Captain Stromberg. "Suppose," he said, "you get these people in a cabin where they are safe, while you and I have a talk."

"Why can't you talk here?"

"This talk had better be private."

"Just you and I?"

"Exactly."

"What about Major Stevens?"

"This talk," Doc said, "has to be between you and me. And I want everyone else—and I mean everyone—to go to a cabin and wait."

The skipper wheeled. "All right, I don't know what Savage has up his sleeve, but I'm going to play ball with him. My cabin is large enough to hold everyone comfortably, so you'll wait there."

Doc Savage and Stromberg withdrew to the first mate's cabin, which was not particularly commodious, where Stromberg voiced his suspicions.

"I don't know what you are trying to pull, but it had better be good," the Captain muttered. "I don't like the way the war prisoners are acting." He scowled suddenly. "By the way, what are the prisoners actually trying to do?"

173

"Create a diversion, probably," Doc said. "In other words, get us involved in suppressing a mutiny and so busy at the job that Jonas Sown can cover his tracks—which he can only do by killing, or having killed, those who know enough about him to be dangerous."

"Tell me this: how are the prisoners being stirred up?"

"I can't imagine," Doc said. "But to a man who has stirred up whole nations until they actually became inhuman, a little matter of arousing some war prisoners should be simple."

Stromberg pondered.

"Hell, do you believe that Jonas Sown yarn?"

"I certainly do."

"You mean the guy has some kind of a magical gadget that can make people think the way he wants them to think?"

Doc Savage smiled grimly.

"Let's be sane about this," he said. "The way to be sane is not to attribute too much to Jonas Sown, but also not to underrate him. The fellow may be a genius."

"You said you had him trapped. Did you mean that?"

Doc corrected quietly, "I did not say trapped. I said he was in the bag. What we've got to do now is tie the mouth of the bag shut before he gets out."

Captain Stromberg frowned. "How?"

"Listen," Doc said. "I want you to pick six men you can trust, and get them here quick."

"Will two of your friends do as part—"

"I want six of the crew," Doc said. "Six men who've been with you a long time, and have some sense, and can follow orders."

"You'd better explain what you want them to do, so I'll know what kind of men to pick."

"I want one of your men put on the trail of each one of the group to whom we were just talking," Doc explained. "I want Monk trailed, and Ham, Carter, Thomas, Basset and the girl, Annie."

"Good God, you don't think this arch-fiend could be the girl?"

"Could be. How soon can you get six sailors you can trust?"

"Mighty quick," Captain Stromberg said. "You wait here."

"Hold it," Doc said. "I want a small bottle of perfume, and six pistols or revolvers, one of them loaded with blanks."

"What kind of perfume?" Stromberg was puzzled.

"Any kind, just so it's strong."

"I have blank cartridges for signalling—"

"Won't do," Doc interrupted. "These must have lead in them and look natural. Useless cartridges, I should have said. They don't need to make a noise."

"Okay to just pull the lead out of the bullets, empty the powder and put the lead back?"

"That will be fine."

"All right, you wait here," Captain Stromberg said.

Later Captain Stromberg watched with interest, but without comprehension, while Doc Savage placed a small quantity of the perfume, a very small quantity, on the handgrip of each gun, and filled one of the guns with the useless cartridges.

"These the six sailors who are to follow the different people?" Doc demanded.

Stromberg introduced the sailors. He knew them by name, and it was evident that they had sailed with him on many voyages. "They're good men," he said.

Doc began assigning the sailors the persons they were to trail, not too easy a task because he had to do the allocating by description alone. To be sure they had their respective quarry clearly in mind, he questioned them about the descriptions until satisfied.

"You're not to show yourselves," he warned. "A great deal depends on this, and if you muff it, there'll be the devil to pay. So be careful."

"When do we report?" a sailor asked.

"I was coming to that," Doc said. "You let me, or Captain Stromberg, know the minute one of the persons you are following enters a cabin or a hold or a storeroom."

"You mean *any* cabin?"

"Exactly."

"Okay."

"And let us know quick," Doc said. "Now we're ready to go. You fellows hang around the Captain's cabin and keep your eyes open. As soon as you see your man or woman come out of the skipper's quarters, get on his trail."

Doc beckoned to Captain Stromberg. "Come on. We'll set up the rest of the machinery for this scheme."

They moved toward the skipper's cabin. "I don't see the object," Stromberg said. "Do you think one of your gang is in with the crooks?"

"Possibly."

Stromberg snorted. "If one of them is, he—or she—won't be fool enough to lead the way to Jonas Sown. They won't be that dumb."

"Did you ever raise chickens?" Doc asked.

"Huh? Chickens? Not since I was a kid on the farm—"

"You'll recall that normally any old hen had sense enough not to run or fly into a chicken-wire fence, but the same old hen at the sight of a hawk would lose all judgment about fences, and plunge headlong into it."

"Well—"

"We are going to make like a hawk," Doc said.

Doc Savage confronted the group in the Captain's Cabin, held his metallic face in an expression of grim concern, and made a speech which Captain Stromberg, who was expecting the earth to shake, did not consider alarming.

Doc said, "The increase of uneasiness among the war prisoners looks bad. We don't know who is working with Jonas Sown, which means we are hardly in a position to trust anyone but ourselves. Therefore we've got to handle this ourselves, and the thing we want first is information about the initial move the war prisoners are going to make."

Doc paused and eyed the group thoughtfully.

"I want a full report of the situation on the ship as of right now," he added. "So I'm going to assign each of you a section of the ship to survey."

He spoke rapidly to each in succession, giving decks and hold sections which he wished reconnoitered.

"Report back here at once," he said. "Then we'll make our first move."

The fat man, Basset, blinked at Doc. "Mind telling me your first move? I mean, all this seems a bit aimless to me."

"We're going to rescue Johnny Littlejohn," Doc said. "That comes first. And before I do it, I want to know the distribution of the enemy, anything suspicious going on. Because after we get Johnny, he is going to be able to tell us enough to pop this thing wide open. Things are going to hum."

Basset grinned. "You know where Littlejohn is?"

"I can lay hands on him when the time comes," Doc said.

"Where is he?"

"That," Doc said, "comes under the heading of restricted information."

Basset's face darkened. "If you don't trust—"

176

Doc said, "If you knew where Johnny is, and something inconvenient happened to him as a result of a tip-off, I wouldn't trust you as much as I do now."

Basset wet his lips. "I see."

Doc extended the weapons.

"Here," he said. "Take these guns. You may need them."

Basset hefted the revolver he had been handed. "I like my own gun better."

Captain Stromberg made the speech Doc had told him to make. He said, "An officer took the guns we removed from you after we arrested you, and I can't find him now and don't know where he put the weapons. These will have to do."

"Get on the job," Doc urged. "We haven't any time to lose."

XIII

The sailor, Caleb Edwards by name, was a long young man with a deep south way of saying you-uns and you-all, and he was quite certain the hatch he was pointing out was the right one.

"The party you-uns told me to follow went in hyar," he insisted.

"How long ago?" Doc asked.

"Shucks, tain't been long. Didn't let no grass grow under my feet."

"Captain, where does the hatch lead?" Doc asked.

"Cargo hold." Captain Stromberg rubbed his jaw briskly, and added, "You know, down there wouldn't be a bad place to hide a man."

Doc laid hold of the hatch fastening. "Try to block the other exits and inlets," he ordered. "And make it quick. I'm going in." He turned and called back, "Jerk the lights."

In a moment, the lights—it was quite dark night outside now—were extinguished. Doc wrenched open the hatch, made sure there was no glow behind him to frame him in silhouette, and went inside. He pulled the hatch shut behind him and waited and listened.

"Carter!" he called softly. "Oh, Carter!"

He kept his voice low, and changed it as much as he could, enough that no one would recognize it, he hoped.

After silence had gripped the place for a while, he added,

"Carter! They're getting close to us! Let's have some light!"

A voice, not the voice of Carter, demanded, "Who're you?"

"Turn a light on," Doc said, then moved swiftly, ducking down and going to the right. It was intensely black and he bumped into something, some case of merchandise that upset noisily, although he got his hands on it.

The voice said, "All right, take him!"

Instead of taking his hands off the small packing case that he had upset, Doc lifted the thing and threw it toward the breath-noise of a man coming toward him. A light came on while the case was still in the air, a light that showed one of the men who had staged the seizure at the Avion restaurant in Manila. The box hit the man, then box and man bounced apart, and the man's place had changed.

Doc followed the box, got to the man, got behind him, hooked an arm around the fellow. The man held a revolver, and this landed on the floor. Doc sank, using the man for a support, reaching for the gun. He got his fingers on the weapon as another gun began making ear-splitting noises and red spurts of light behind the flashlight. Bullets one and two, then three went into the man's body, but not through it. The shock upset Doc and the man, then Doc fired from the floor.

The flashlight moved, lazily at first, turning its long funnel of light over and over—there must have been dust on the lens to give the illusion of turning—and swinging it around to hold. The light passed over boxes, bales, casks. It was still moving when the man who had done the shooting made a loud surprised sound as if he had just discovered there was a bullet hole in him.

The light toppled off the box on which it was resting, and its beam did crazy gymnastics as the light bounced from box to bale to floor.

Doc was in darkness now. He moved fast. The man he had shot was still standing, holding both hands over his right shoulder as if the splayed fingers might stop the crimson leakage. Doc hit him above the left ear with his gun, using the cylinder rather than the barrel as a bludgeon. The man sat down foolishly and the boxes and bales supported him.

There was silence.

"Johnny!" Doc called.

A violent beating of heels against wood came from somewhere near.

Johnny Littlejohn—William Harper Littlejohn, archaeologist and geologist—had always been a remarkably thin man as well as a tall one. His skinny build was always a subject of conversation, and it was frequently stated, in humorous reference, that undertakers seemed to become cheerful when they saw him. As a matter of fact, he was remarkably healthy. But now Doc Savage stared at him in amazement.

"You look like a concentration camp guest," Doc said.

"How many," Johnny demanded, "did you pot-shoot?"

"Two," Doc said. "That is, two got shot."

"That's all of them," Johnny said.

Doc began untying the ropes which held Johnny, and obviously had held him for a long time. There was a crashing at the bow end of the hold, noise of a hatch being forced. To allay Johnny's alarm, Doc explained it must be Captain Stromberg and his men, which it proved to be.

Reaching them, Stromberg stared at Johnny in horror. "They've starved him to death!" he said hoarsely.

Johnny Littlejohn seemed surprised.

"A presbyopic incognitance," he remarked.

Freed of the ropes, Johnny calmly stood up and stretched, although there seemed to be no visible reason whatever for his not falling down and becoming a pile of bones and not much else.

"How long," Doc demanded, "since they fed you?"

"Ten days, approximately," Johnny stated. "Although the interregnumical metaphoricality was a bit bemused."

Monk and Ham now arrived, and Monk yelled, "Johnny! My God, we've found Johnny!" He rushed forward and seized Johnny and bellowed, "How do you feel? You okay? And don't use any of them words on me!"

"I feel fine," Johnny declared. "The diet seemed to agree with me."

"Diet of what?"

"It was composed," Johnny admitted, "mostly of threats."

Basset came lumbering up, trailed by Jack Thomas, and Annie. Thomas snarled, "Where's Carter?" Thomas had his gun in his hand.

Johnny was looking strangely at Thomas.

"You'll find him over there," Johnny said, and pointed.

Jack Thomas cocked his revolver. "You know who Carter's got to be?" he asked them hoarsely. "He's got to be Jonas Sown."

179

Then, suddenly and fiercely, he rushed the spot where Johnny had pointed. He fired as he went, shot twice; then suddenly he stopped, aimed deliberately, and fired three times more, emptying his gun.

Doc Savage, suddenly very pale, leaned against a packing case. He had, he was thinking, just received one of the great shocks of his lifetime.

Jack Thomas lowered his gun. His face looked yellowish, slick with perspiration, and his voice was queer as he said, "He's dead."

Johnny Littlejohn was looking fixedly, and even more strangely, at Thomas.

"He was," Johnny said, "already dead."

No one spoke.

Johnny added, finally, "That fellow, Carter, came in here a few minutes ago. They were laying for him, knew he was coming. They had been tipped off. It was a trap. Someone had told Carter he would find someone here who would tell him where I was."

Johnny eyed Thomas intently.

"He was already dead," he repeated. "They killed him."

Thomas said hoarsely, "I didn't—I—I'm sure he was going to shoot me."

There was silence again, and it became almost weird.

Doc Savage said at last, "Johnny."

"Yes?"

"You know this fellow?" He pointed at Thomas.

"Yes, I know him."

Jack Thomas moved wildly, going back and to the side, trying to find cover. At the same time he tried wildly to get a hand into his coat pocket, bring out cartridges and reload his gun.

Fat Van Zandt Basset croaked, "Damn! He's Jonas Sown!" Then his gun began hurting their ears with its noise.

Jack Thomas stopped going backward, stood up very straight, aimed his empty gun at Basset, and began pulling the trigger. He was still snapping the empty gun when he leaned forward and fell, and they could see the empty gun snapping underneath his body for several moments after he was on the floor. It was the last sound he made.

Doc said, "Have Major Stevens watch the war prisoners closely for the next few hours, and I think our troubles will be over."

They had breakfast in the morning sunshine, eating at a table which a steward set up on the deck. All of them, Monk and Ham and Basset and Captain Stromberg and Major Stevens, neglected their ham and eggs and listened to Johnny Littlejohn tell Doc his story. Annie looked particularly lovely this morning, and for her Johnny was using small words.

"The weird part of it is that I never really got a look at Jonas Sown, and never was absolutely positive that he was one individual," Johnny explained. "But I think he was. I picked up his trail in Japan, where he fled after Germany fell, and I think he soon learned that I was on his trail. At any rate, I had a lot of trouble, and finally—I'm skipping a lot—trailed him down through China and Burma to the Philippines, to Manila. The only time I ever saw the man you know as Jack Thomas was in Japan, and I saw him under circumstances which led me to believe he was Jonas Sown."

Basset growled, "He told me he'd never been in Japan. Which proves he was lying."

"He was Jonas Sown for my money," Johnny said. "I'm satisfied."

Johnny helped himself to a fourth portion of ham and eggs, added two flapjacks, a pair of sausages, and poured maple syrup over the pile.

Alarmed, Annie said, "Isn't it dangerous to eat so much after going without food as long as you have?"

Johnny grinned. "So I've heard."

Captain Stromberg asked Major Stevens how the war prisoners were behaving.

"Quieting down," the Major said with relief. "I can't understand what happened to them, what stirred them up that way."

"That's easy," Stromberg said. "It was Jonas Sown's gang. There were nine of them aboard. Anyway, we've caught nine. And some of the war prisoners, like that fellow Kusumura who committed suicide, were Jonas Sown's henchmen, too."

Annie asked, "Why were they among the war prisoners, if they were Jonas Sown's employees?"

"Taking that way of getting to America," Stromberg explained. "We've got that much out of them."

Ham Brooks said, "Johnny."

"Yes?"

"How did this Jonas Sown do his dirty work? Did he have some kind of a machine to work on people's minds, or what?"

The question struck Johnny unpleasantly, and he put down his knife and fork. "I wish to God I knew for sure," he said. "There could have been a machine, because I know they dumped some stuff overboard as soon as they found Doc and the rest of you were alive. It was something in cases. I don't know what it was, but if it was a gadget, it's where we'll never find it."

Stromberg nodded with pleasure. "That's good." He turned to Doc Savage. "Say, what did you put that perfume on the guns for?"

"What?" Doc came out of deep thought. "Oh, the perfume. It was an idea that I didn't have time to use, one that might not have worked anyway. I intended to pretend to find traces of the perfume at the first spot we located where we were certain Jonas Sown had been, then give the idea each of you had a different perfume on his gun, on the chance it would trick Thomas into giving himself away."

Stromberg jumped visibly. "You suspected Thomas?"

Doc nodded.

"It was Thomas to whom I gave the gun with the useless cartridges in it," he said.

"How'd you happen to suspect him?"

"I hate to admit playing hunches, but that is about all I did," Doc admitted. "Thomas was obviously possessed of an amazing mentality. I think I caught glimpses of an almost frightening cleverness in the man. It was that, more than anything else."

"Didn't you have any direct evidence?"

"Well, yes. He looked sick as the dickens when I made that remark about our having Jonas Sown in the bag, which was a slight exaggeration."

Monk was frowning at Doc.

"That wasn't any empty gun he had," Monk said.

Doc shuddered. "So I noticed. He must have found the useless cartridges and substituted real ones. And that, I want to tell you, gave me one of the worst shocks of my life. I was planning to walk up and collar him, thinking his gun was harmless."

Annie picked up the percolator and asked gaily, "Does anyone want coffee? And I wish you fellows would find something pleasant to talk about. Personally, I've had enough trouble and excitement to do me."

Doc smiled at her. "Just why did you mix yourself in it in

182

the first place?" he asked. "It was for the excitement, wasn't it?"

Annie came back with a look that gave his ears a crisp burn.

"That," she said, "was what I thought."

Doc decided he shouldn't have brought up the subject.

"But sometimes," Annie added, "a girl doesn't know her own mind—at first."

"Uh—nice morning, isn't it?" Doc remarked.

Annie examined him thoughtfully. "I am," she said, "known as a forthright baggage. I always give warning."

Doc had trouble with a piece of toast. "I—you do?"

"Brother, have you ever been pursued by an amorous female?" Annie demanded.

"Well, I—"

"You can," said Annie, "consider yourself warned."

To the world at large, Doc Savage is a strange, mysterious figure of glistening bronze skin and golden eyes. To his fans he is the greatest adventure hero of all time, whose fantastic exploits are unequaled for hair-raising thrills, breathtaking escapes, blood-curdling excitement!

☐ 13421	**DOC SAVAGE #97 and CARGO UNKNOWN #98**	**$1.95**
☐ 14348	**HELL BELOW #99 and THE LOST GIANT #100**	**$1.95**
☐ 14615	**PHAROAH'S GHOST #101 and TIME TERROR #102**	**$1.95**
☐ 14616	**THE WHISKER OF HERCULES #103 and THE MAN WHO WAS SCARED #104**	**$1.95**

Buy them at your local bookstore or use this handy coupon for ordering:

FANTASY AND SCIENCE FICTION FAVORITES

Bantam brings you the recognized classics as well as the current favorites in fantasy and science fiction. Here you will find the beloved Conan books along with recent titles by the most respected authors in the genre.

☐	01166	URSHURAK	
		Bros. Hildebrandt & Nichols	$8.95
☐	14844	NOVA Samuel R. Delany	$2.50
☐	13534	TRITON Samuel R. Delany	$2.50
☐	14861	DHALGREN Samuel R. Delany	$3.95
☐	13127	TALES FROM GAVAGAN'S BAR	$1.95
		de Camp & Pratt	
☐	13837	CONAN & THE SPIDER GOD #5	$2.25
		de Camp & Pratt	
☐	13831	CONAN THE REBEL #6 Paul Anderson	$2.25
☐	14532	HIGH COUCH OF SILISTRA	$2.50
		Janet Morris	
☐	13670	FUNDAMENTAL DISCH Disch	$2.50
☐	13189	DRAGONDRUMS Anne McCaffrey	$2.25
☐	14127	DRAGONSINGER Anne McCaffrey	$2.50
☐	14204	DRAGONSONG Anne McCaffrey	$2.50
☐	14031	MAN PLUS Frederik Pohl	$2.25
☐	11736	FATA MORGANA William Kotzwinkle	$2.95
☐	11042	BEFORE THE UNIVERSE	$1.95
		Pohl & Kornbluth	
☐	13860	TIME STORM Gordon R. Dickson	$2.50
☐	13400	SPACE ON MY HANDS Frederic Brown	$1.95
☐	13996	THE PLANET OF TEARS Trish Reinius	$1.95

Buy them at your local bookstore or use this handy coupon for ordering:

Bantam Books, Inc., Dept. SF2, 414 East Golf Road, Des Plaines, Ill. 60016

Please send me the books I have checked above. I am enclosing $_____
(please add $1.00 to cover postage and handling). Send check or money order
—no cash or C.O.D.'s please.

Mr/Mrs/Miss_____

Address_____

City_____State/Zip_____

SF2—7/81

Please allow four to six weeks for delivery. This offer expires 1/82.

Bantam Book Catalog

Here's your up-to-the-minute listing of over 1,400 titles by your favorite authors.

This illustrated, large format catalog gives a description of each title. For your convenience, it is divided into categories in fiction and non-fiction—gothics, science fiction, westerns, mysteries, cookbooks, mysticism and occult, biographies, history, family living, health, psychology, art.

So don't delay—take advantage of this special opportunity to increase your reading pleasure.

Just send us your name and address and 50¢ (to help defray postage and handling costs).